HIDE AND SEEK

HIDE AND SEEK

BARRY BERG

ST. MARTIN'S PRESS   NEW YORK

Design by Jaye Zimet

Library of Congress Cataloging-in-Publication Data

Berg, Barry.
   Hide and seek.
      p.   cm.
   "A Thomas Dunne book."
   ISBN 0-312-02976-4
   I. Title.
PS3552.E699H53   1989   813'.54—dc19   89-30146

First Edition
10 9 8 7 6 5 4 3 2 1

For My Mother and Father

ACKNOWLEDGMENTS

I would like to express my deepest gratitude to family and friends who supported me through the years it took to write this book. Special thanks must go to Anne Edelstein for her skill in helping shape the book, and to Al Zuckerman for the faith and persistence that brought this book to publication.

HIDE AND SEEK

1

T H E important thing was to not attract attention. Every movement had to look natural. Richard tried to imitate his normal walk. He shuffled his legs and swung his arms stiffly against the padding of the nylon jacket.

It wasn't working. His balance was off. He felt like a robot and almost laughed, but when he looked ahead he became terrified. A man, dark as a storm and pounding an umbrella against his leg, was heading right for him. The man cursed and nearly knocked him over. Somehow Richard managed to keep his balance.

"Crazy," he told himself. "A nut case. Nothing personal. He doesn't even know me. Have to relax."

He got his feet moving at a slow, casual pace. Better, he thought, and came upon a woman standing against a mailbox.

"Oh, my god . . ."

She was wearing just a top—no skirt or pants. Just a top and lavender panties. She stood there, half-naked, and stuck out her tongue at him as he passed by. Another New York nut. At least *he* wasn't crazy, he thought with some comfort. He might be a little panicked right now, but he wasn't crazy.

Suddenly the noise of the city seemed to pause. It was weird—as if some alien hand had turned down the volume. Richard found himself weaving silently through the sidewalk traffic. The soles of his running shoes seemed barely to touch the ground. A moment ago he was a spastic; now he glided like a ghost. Maybe he was a ghost! Maybe he had been shot and killed at the airport, or had crashed the car on the expressway! He tripped over a man kneeling on the sidewalk, beating on the pavement with two drumsticks. The man yelled at him and Richard's knee twinged from the collision, but he kept going. He wasn't any ghost.

"Oh Christ!"

A cop car was cruising down the block. Richard abruptly stopped and turned away, facing a window of a bookstore. In the glass, the reflection of the police car rolled by.

He took a deep breath. They didn't see him. But thinking about it now, why should he be so scared? They would be looking for a boy his age, and maybe they had his height and a general description of how he looked, but there were a million kids who looked like him. All he had to do was be cool. He examined his face in the window. No bruises. No guilty look. Nothing to give him away . . .

Nothing except his passport!

"Shit!" They had his passport. With his picture inside it.

He resisted an impulse to run. Instead he walked slowly, inconspicuously, he hoped, timing each step to two heartbeats, and turned a corner away from the crowded avenue. Above him was a sign: "Bo-Mond Hotel—Newly Decorated Rooms—Reasonable Rates—$12 and Up." He walked through glass doors, finding himself in a narrow, dark hallway that ended in a flight of stairs.

He went back outside and checked the sign again. No, no mistake, this *was* a hotel. He went back in and quietly climbed the stairs. At the top he peeked around a corner and into a cramped lobby. A haze of pot filled the room. He saw a man sitting behind a desk, looking at a magazine. A lit joint glowed in his hand. Richard walked in.

"I'd like a room, please," he heard himself say.

2

The man looked up from the magazine and put the joint into an ashtray. Then he picked up a toothpick and stuck it in his mouth. He didn't say a word, but made kissing sounds as he sucked at the pick.

"I said I'd like a room, please," Richard repeated, a little more loudly.

The man's mouth opened into a wide grin, showing sharp, fishlike teeth. "How old are you, Ace?" he asked.

"Eighteen," Richard lied. "My dad is flying in from California on business. He and my mom split up last year and he can't stay at the house, so he asked me to get a hotel room for him."

He stopped. He had no idea where the story had come from and was amazed that it hung together so well.

The clerk sucked and kissed and narrowed his eyes. Richard shifted uneasily under the stare. It felt like two lasers were piercing his skull. He put his hands in his jacket pockets and pressed the coat against his body for comfort.

"Okay, Ace, let me tell you how it is," the man said, finally. He spoke in a low, tired voice, and kept the toothpick in his mouth the whole time. Richard had to strain to hear.

"You're fifteen years old, maybe, and you ran away from home this morning, and you just discovered the cops'll pick you up if you try to spend the night on the street. Am I right or am I right?"

The toothpick jumped up and down, then slid over to the other side of the mouth. The man practically had no lips.

"So you come dancing in here thinking you can rent a room from me like I was some kind of mental retard who didn't know his own ass from a hole in the ground. Have I got the general picture?"

The face was as narrow as a hatchet; deep pockmarks made little moonlike craters in each cheek.

"You see, Ace, the problem for me is—if I sign you in all legal and everything, and the cops pick you up here, it'll be *my* ass in a sling, you follow?"

Richard didn't, exactly, but the answer sounded like no. He turned to leave.

"Hey, where you going?" The clerk came out from behind his desk. "What are you, sensitive or something?" He seemed almost hurt.

"You said you weren't going to rent me a room."

"No, Ace, I didn't say that at all. What I said was if I *did* rent you a room, all legallike, my asshole would be winking at the world."

Richard still didn't understand.

"How much money you got?" the clerk breathed.

He didn't know. He took out his wallet and opened it. The laser eyes peered in.

"Well, it ain't the U.S. Mint, but we might work something out."

Richard had no idea how much a hotel room cost, but he didn't think he was in any position to negotiate. Two thin fingers dipped into his wallet, and he felt the man's bony arm around his shoulder, turning him back into the lobby.

"As I said, I can't sign you in legal, but why can't I do us both a favor and let you stay for the night on a sort of informal basis? That wouldn't hurt anyone, right?"

Richard sighed with relief. It looked like he was going to get a room, and the bony arm lifted off his shoulder. The clerk even seemed friendly now.

"What's your name, Ace?" he asked.

"Richard."

"Nice name, Richard." He took a key from a row of pegs on a wooden cabinet. "Had a brother once named Richard. Drowned off Coney Island summer of sixty-three." He held out the key. "Here you go, Ace. Room two-oh-eight." He pointed to a flight of stairs. "Just remember, anyone finds you here, we never met. I don't know how you got that key. I don't know nothing."

Richard nodded. He looked around the lobby and saw a threadbare couch and two ripped-up easy chairs. A musty red carpet led him to the stairs. He put his hand on the bannister and nearly pushed it over.

"One more thing, Ace," the clerk called after him. "You got to be out by seven. The day manager ain't so understanding."

Richard started climbing the stairs. Halfway up he saw a blonde girl heading down toward him. He turned sideways as she passed, keeping his eyes straight ahead. He took the rest of the steps two at a time.

The light in the corridor was dim, and he had trouble reading the numbers on the doors. Finally he found 208. He fumbled with the key. The lock squeaked as it turned.

Inside, he switched on an overhead light, locked the door behind him, and took off his jacket. Then he took out a penknife and sat on the bed. His heart was beating as though he was in the last lap of a mile race and he dried his palms on his jeans. Carefully now, starting with the collar, he began cutting through the stitches in the jacket lining.

Christ, he's just a kid! Lisa thought. Coming down the stairs she'd only had a brief look, but there was no doubt about it. He was barely in his teens. What the hell was Francie doing? Coming out of the closet, maybe? Maybe trying to work some boys himself? She wouldn't put anything past that sleazy piece of shit.

She didn't even bother to curl her lip at him as she walked through the lobby. She stepped onto Forty-seventh Street, still puzzled. Maybe it wasn't Francie. Maybe the kid belonged to Leo! The idea disturbed her.

She didn't mind that Leo had three girls working for him. That was okay, somehow. But a teenage boy? It left a bad taste in her mouth, and she made a mental note to talk to Leo about it.

She turned onto Eighth Avenue and felt better. The street was exciting. It was open, filled with light and sound. It didn't suffocate her the way the Bo-Mond did. Most of the people who worked it, of course, were the infected pimples of God's creation—take Francie for instance—but still, it was *her* street.

She winked an invitation at a man in a business suit. Lisa liked men in business suits. They were clean and they carried thick wallets. All she needed was one and she could make the hundred Leo demanded, and then go to the arcade for the rest of the evening.

The businessman smiled back but shook his head no and hurried on. Lisa didn't mind. They were like buses. Another would come along. Eventually one would stop. She didn't really care. She slipped a Chiclet into her mouth and enjoyed the first crunchy bites. Idle thoughts flitted through her mind.

Miss Piggy was awesome. Miss Piggy had balls. Leo could scream all he wanted about her missing commuter traffic, but the "Muppet Show" came first. She thought about her dolls and stuffed animals back home. . . .

Fuck Leo, anyway! she thought angrily. He said he was going to set her up on dates this week so she wouldn't have to work the street, and not one had come through! He was filled with so much bullshit flowers should be growing out of his ears. Maybe she would go back and dance at the Frolick for a few weeks. But then she would have to deal with Sid, and all those horny old men trying to grab her, and teenage boys laughing and shouting out stupid things. Teenage boys were the pits, that was for sure. And what the hell was that one doing at the Bo-Mond anyway . . . ?

Lieutenant Michael O'Hare tried to stretch. His chair was too small. There wasn't enough room under his desk for his legs. The desk itself was too low, and as he hunched over it again his back was starting to hurt. In his seventeen years with the Department he had yet to find furniture that would comfortably fit his six-foot-four frame.

In the dismal yellow light he flipped through the case folder in front of him. In it were statements from a Kennedy Airport customs agent, a customs guard, a man who had reported a car theft, and the man's girlfriend. Also, a thick pad of notes from more than a dozen phone calls. And finally a passport with a picture of a fifteen-year-old boy, the face staring at the camera with a wide-eyed expression that was half-defiance and half-fear. O'Hare studied the boy's face once more. He didn't put it down until every feature was etched in his memory.

"Richard Knowles," he said aloud. He shook his head sadly and lit a cigarette.

It wasn't really a case at all, he thought. At the moment it was only an incident, a brush at Kennedy between a teenage boy and a customs agent that had to be followed up. Nothing important enough for Narcotics. Certainly nothing to worry the Bureau about. Just a scrape that could be easily bandaged at precinct level. The Department would have been just as pleased to pretend it had never happened.

The call he had received from headquarters had been casual. O'Hare's interest in narcotics was well known, and since no one downtown was particularly keen on following up this incident, they wondered if the Lieutenant might want it.

Well, yes he might. O'Hare had masked his excitement. His current inquiry was in a holding pattern, he had told headquarters, so he had a few days free. He would be happy to go to Kennedy, take some statements, make a few phone calls, and put together a team to try to find this fifteen-year-old boy. . . .

His eyes drifted to the framed photograph that sat on his desk. A teenage boy and his mother taken on a sailboat not two years before. The sun was strong and both had their hands raised to shield their eyes. O'Hare let a few memories filter in. That summer had been special. The three of them had spent a lot of time together. Patrick had learned how to sail. O'Hare had promised that the following summer they would buy their own boat.

He sealed off the memories, but his eyes stayed on the photo. The boy had broad shoulders with a thick neck and a wide, Irish face. Mother and son had the same complexions, the same features, really. Anne's strong nose and chin worked well on Pat. Their hair had the same fine, silky texture. The picture was only two years old, but it might as well have been from a previous century.

There was a knock on the squad-room door and Sergeant Wilhite looked in.

"How's it going, Mike?"

O'Hare took a final puff on his cigarette, his third and last of the day, and waved Wilhite in.

"Not bad, Ernie. And you?"

"Normal shit."

They shook hands warmly. O'Hare liked Wilhite. He thought they made a good team. Wilhite was thin and angular, almost as tall as O'Hare but with half the bulk. Wilhite was smart, O'Hare thought, and more important, he cared.

He motioned to a chair and Wilhite folded himself into it, legs crossed like a pair of scissors. "Let me tell you what this is all about, Ernie," he began, and outlined what had happened earlier that afternoon at the airport. The sergeant listened attentively.

"The kid's father!" Wilhite exclaimed at the first mention of cocaine. The outrage showed plainly in his face. O'Hare nodded, pleased that he didn't have to fill in the gaps. "Either as part of a mob or with some mob backing."

"Steve Knowles." O'Hare read the name from his pad. "Thirty-nine, lives up in Rye, works for Lexington Aeronautics, sells planes to foreign governments. No known mob connections. Was working in Bogota, Colombia where Richard joined him for Easter vacation . . ."

Wilhite interrupted. "Where is Knowles now?"

"Home." O'Hare smiled. "I called to sell him a subscription to the *New York Times*. He picked up on the first ring."

"Waiting for the kid to call! You think he will?" Wilhite's mouth was tight.

O'Hare shrugged. "Don't know. The boy's in a panic. There's no telling what he'll do."

Wilhite unfolded himself and stood up—six feet plus full of nervous energy. "Well, let's go find him!"

O'Hare appreciated Wilhite's energy, but continued at his own methodical pace. "There won't be eight-hour shifts on this one, Ernie," he warned. "We're going to stay with it until the boy is safe."

"Fine with me."

"We'll get word out on the street, circulate the passport picture, knock on a lot of doors. But until the car shows all we have is the father."

"So let's pay him a visit!" Wilhite was at the door. "His son ran away from a customs agent and we have to ask a few questions. Purely routine."

He looked like a young thoroughbred at the starting gate. "We're waiting for Leverton," O'Hare said. Wilhite's head snapped back in surprise.

"Mike . . ." the sergeant began in a pained voice.

"We need a team of three for round-the-clock cov-

erage, Ernie. And Leverton's perfect for this assignment."
Wilhite didn't look convinced. "Don't worry," O'Hare
assured him. "It'll be fine."

"But why do you want to do this to yourself, Mike?"

O'Hare didn't reply. Wilhite was out of line and knew
it. The sergeant went to the window and looked unhappily
into the street below. But it was a good question. O'Hare
just didn't have an answer.

Instead he outlined their plan of attack. They would
drive out to Westchester in separate cars. They would dou-
ble-team Steve Knowles—O'Hare up front, and Wilhite
and Leverton undercover. They would try to find out who
Knowles had bought from and who he was selling to. They
would spin a case as straight and strong as piano wire, then
loop it around the son-of-a-bitch's neck and pull.

2 **RICHARD** had cut through the top few stitches of the jacket lining when the first bag fell out. It was a clear plastic tube as long as the jacket, and it was filled with white powder. It weighed maybe half a pound. He cut carefully through the stitches of the collar and took out a second tube. One by one he removed them all until there was a total of eight narrow plastic tubes on the bed, one pierced by a pin. He touched the pin prick and a trickle of powder fell on his finger.

He put it to his tongue. Bitter. Like aspirin. The tip of his tongue turned numb.

He examined the tiny pearl flakes with interest. Cocaine. Though he knew some juniors and seniors at school used it, he had never seen cocaine up close before. He scraped his tongue against the roof of his mouth until some feeling came back.

"Big deal!" he said aloud.

Actually, it *was* a big deal. Four pounds of coke was an awesome deal. His tongue tingled. He was thirsty but there was no sink in the room. He crawled onto the bed, next to the plastic bags, and closed his eyes. His body was exhausted. He tried to remember what had happened at the airport, but his mind had gone as numb as his tongue.

The customs area . . . a stewardess passing through and remembering him from the plane . . . the silver pin she attached to his jacket, two wings in flight, shining against the blue nylon . . . the spill of powder . . . bushy hairs growing out of the knuckles of the guard whose fingers clamped his arm . . . running . . . up stairs . . . down stairs . . . into a crowd . . . then his father's face, wide with surprise . . .

Pressure grew in his chest. He struggled for breath and swallowed enough air to fill his lungs. He held it as long as he could. When he thought he would burst he let it out, and as he did he began to shake. Tears welled in his eyes and his chest heaved with sobs.

Goddamn!

He was crying. He felt like a little kid with tears running down his cheeks and with his stupid lower lip trembling.

"Will you goddamn stop it!" he yelled at himself.

The last time he cried was his first night at Pierce, and that was four years ago when he was eleven. He hadn't wanted to go to boarding school but his father said they had no choice.

"It's because of my new job," Steve had told him. "I'll be traveling all over the world now and I won't be able to take care of you. It won't be so bad. You'll make new friends and we'll take vacations together."

Vacations. Sure.

On vacations Steve was either busy with work or flying off somewhere with some moronic girlfriend. And Pierce wasn't the way his father had billed it either. It wasn't really a school as much as a prison where rich parents could send their asshole sons. The seniors, who ran the place, had names for everyone. The teachers were old farts, and everyone else was a shithead or a scumbag or a faggot. Richard managed to survive mostly because he could run. The seniors didn't like him much, but he was the fastest kid in the school so he won a grudging respect. But mostly they bullied each other and bulldozed the teachers—except, of course, for Mario.

Mario.

He wondered what Mario would be doing now. Probably watching TV with Jo and Paul and the younger kids. Probably getting ready for school tomorrow. Mario would be worried that he hadn't shown up. Maybe Mario was even trying to reach him. He would have to call and tell Mario he was all right.

He *was* all right! He just had to stop crying.

He dried his eyes on a flap of pillowcase and looked around the room for the first time. It was a cell, the same size as the singles at Pierce, but infinitely more depressing. The only furniture was the lumpy bed and a small night table next to it. But it was a hotel room! He had actually rented a hotel room!

"I must be out of my mind."

Then he wondered if he actually was. For one thing he was talking to himself. For another, he had just had this idiotic crying jag. And for a third thing, he had entered the hotel only minutes before but couldn't remember anything about it. He had an image of a hatchet-faced man with no lips, but had no idea of what he had said to the man or even how much he had paid for the room.

His stomach sank as he took out his wallet.

Empty.

"Great!"

He couldn't recall how much money he had started with, but the clerk had taken it all. He found seventy cents in his jeans pocket.

"Fucking great!"

He had to move. The room was closing in and it was getting hard to breathe again. He slid the plastic bags back into the compartments of the jacket lining and put it on.

Leaving his room, everything began to register at once: the dank smell of decay in the corridor, the oppressive gloom of the lobby, the hatchet-faced clerk smoking a joint and thumbing through a dirty magazine. He looked up as Richard went by, but Richard kept on walking, eyes straight ahead.

Eighth Avenue was like a scene from *Star Wars*. Mutant life-forms filled the street. Taxis that looked like huge metal fish darted to the curb to swallow up people and spit them out. Hookers in stiletto heels and stretch pants—half-women, half-birds of paradise—strutted and flapped. One caught his eye and cooed at him. Richard felt the blood rush to his head and he quickly walked on. Store windows were liquid crystal displays. A sex shop was lit like a Christmas tree with two drunks sprawled out in front, their clothing rumpled like tissue paper. A police car rounded the corner. Richard slipped into a side street and watched it pass.

Grasping fingers clutched at his shoulder. He twisted and jerked away.

"Got some change, young fella?"

It was an old drunk with sandpaper for a beard and a cut the color of raw beef over his eye.

"No, I don't." Richard sidestepped the man and jogged away. "Sorry." He looked to all sides now as he walked. He almost had to laugh. All he *did* have was a little change.

He saw a pay phone. He took out a quarter and dialed the operator. "Holton, Connecticut," he said. "Could you reverse the charges, please?"

A black kid carrying a ghetto blaster passed by and the rock music pounded Richard's brain. He had to use all his concentration to hear the ringing phone.

Paul Federici answered and quickly said yes, he would accept a collect call from Richard Knowles.

"Hey, Rabbit, how're ya doing?" Paul sounded excited.

"Just great," Richard answered.

"How was your trip?"

"Terrific."

"Hey, your father called a couple of hours ago."

"Oh?" Richard tried to sound unconcerned. "What did he say?"

"Just wanted to know if we had heard from you. Where are you, anyway?"

"In the City. Listen, is Mario there?"

"Yeah, sure. Hold on. See you tomorrow, right?"

"Yeah, right." Richard could hear Paul call to his father. The black kid with the ghetto blaster rounded the corner. The music finally faded. Mario's voice came on the line.

"Richard?"

"Hi." Mario sounded so close. Richard could almost smell the sweat and chlorine of the gym.

"How was your trip?"

"Terrific."

"You run every day?"

"Yeah. I did twelve miles on Saturday."

"No kidding. That's great." Mario paused and Richard could hear the unspoken questions. "Did Paul tell you your father called?"

"Yeah."

"He expected you home. He sounded worried."

Richard felt his throat closing up. He forced out his words. "Yeah, well there was a little trouble."

"What kind of trouble?"

"Listen, can you come see me?"

"Where are you?" Mario asked.

"Here, in the City. Manhattan."

"Why don't you come here? Grab the first train out of Grand Central and I'll pick you up at the station. You can stay overnight and tell me about it."

"I can't, Mario, please." Richard swallowed hard, holding back the quiver in his throat. There was a pause at the other end of the line.

"Where are you now?" Mario finally said. "I mean what street?"

Richard looked up at the corner sign. "Eighth Avenue and Forty-fifth."

"Is there a restaurant or someplace we can meet?"

"Well, I'm standing in front of a Beef and Brew."

"Okay, Beef and Brew. Corner of Eighth and Forty-fifth. Give me an hour and a half."

Mario hung up before Richard could even say thanks.

3 **O'HARE** rang the doorbell and put on the official look of a civil servant doing his duty. He didn't think it would fool Knowles—he did it for himself, to prevent his own excitement from showing. He pushed the buzzer again, wondering what Knowles would look like. He pictured a composite of every anemic, sallow-faced, hollow-chested junkie he had ever seen.

The door opened. Steve Knowles exuded health. His face was tan, his body slim with muscles toned like those of a cat. He was a head shorter than O'Hare, but his brown eyes were clear and direct. O'Hare felt them measuring his own strength even before introductions were made.

"Yes?" Knowles said.

"Mr. Knowles, I'm Lieutenant Michael O'Hare of the New York City Police. I'm here to ask a few questions about your son, Richard."

"Oh? Is something wrong?" Knowles replied, and the game began—the slow cat-and-mouse charade that both players knew, knew the other knew, yet found in their own best interest to play. O'Hare unfolded the story with an air of straightforwardness.

"It's nothing serious, Mr. Knowles. I don't mean to alarm you. It's just that, as you know, Richard arrived at Kennedy Airport at three-thirty this afternoon from Bogota . . ." he consulted his pad, "on TW flight number three-seventeen."

"I know he was supposed to be on that flight, Lieutenant," Steve Knowles interrupted, "but I was beginning to think he might have missed it because he was supposed to call me when he landed."

Just the right amount of parental concern. Knowles was good at the game.

"He was on that plane, Mr. Knowles, I assure you. Because after deplaning, it seems that your son ran away from the customs agent who was examining him. Do you have any idea why he might have done that, Mr. Knowles?"

Knowles's attitude shifted from concern to disbelief. "Are you sure you have the right boy, Lieutenant?"

O'Hare took out the passport and handed it to him.

Knowles nodded, now showing bewilderment. "Yes, that's Richard all right."

"The agent and a guard tried to catch him, but he got away."

"And the agent has no idea why my son ran?"

O'Hare avoided answering with a shrug. "Frankly, Mr. Knowles, we're as much concerned with his safety now as we are with why he took off."

"I assure you I am too, Lieutenant!" Knowles shook his head and gestured O'Hare into the livingroom. "I just can't imagine Richard doing something like that."

O'Hare looked around. Although it was twilight the drapes were drawn. Behind them, O'Hare knew, the windows were locked. There was an alarm box by the door with a light that glowed red. All systems were functioning. The air was close and stale in the house of a drug dealer.

He sat on a couch. Knowles took a seat in an easy chair, across. "You weren't at the airport to meet him, then?" O'Hare inquired.

Knowles shook his head. "We arranged that when he arrived he would call here. Then he would take a train and I would meet him at the station."

O'Hare screwed up his face to show puzzlement and leafed through his pad. His blunt fingers made it difficult to do something as precise as turn an individual page. "The customs guard who chased the boy heard him call to someone. He called the name Steve. That's your name, isn't it?"

Knowles shrugged. "I don't know who Richard saw or thought he saw, Lieutenant. I wasn't there."

O'Hare nodded and made a note. He consulted his pad as he spoke. "Okay, let's see if I've got this straight. Please correct me if I'm wrong."

"My pleasure," Knowles said, smiling.

"Richard flew to Bogota to stay with you for a week during his Easter vacation from school. You were in Colombia concluding a deal between Lexington Aeronautics, the company you work for, and the Colombian government. On your return home, however, you decided to separate. You flew to the Bahamas last night and landed at Kennedy at noon today, while Richard flew directly from Bogota, landing in New York at three-thirty."

Knowles held his look of parental concern, but a slight edge to his voice moved the game to a new level. "That's a lot of work over a fifteen-year-old boy who's been missing only a few hours, Lieutenant."

O'Hare shrugged off his effort. "Just a few phone calls, Mr. Knowles. Standard procedure." Knowles didn't blink. O'Hare cleared his throat. "Of course, there are some aspects to this situation that are unusual. Your flight to the Bahamas, for instance."

"An emergency meeting. Financial backing for the deal. I had to go but decided it would be easier for Richard to stay with his original reservation."

"I see." O'Hare tried to look as though he actually did understand. "I suppose Richard often travels alone?"

"He's an independent boy, Lieutenant. He's been on his own most of his life. It's no big deal for him to travel alone. And as for his running away from the customs agent, maybe he had something in his suitcase he wanted to hide. Some pornographic pictures, or maybe a joint or two. You know teenage boys."

O'Hare managed a half-smile. Pornographic pictures! A joint or two! Knowles had balls.

"Surely, Lieutenant, you're not suggesting you think Richard is guilty of some serious crime."

O'Hare held up the palms of his hands. "Not at all, Mr. Knowles. All I am saying is that we'd like to talk to your boy about it." He started to smile, then put on a look of concern. "Of course, there *is* the problem of his stealing a car."

He tossed the information in casually and was pleased to see the confused look on Knowles's face.

"A stolen car?"

O'Hare nodded. "It appears that after Richard escaped from the terminal he ran into the airport parking lot . . ."

"You're crazy! He's just a kid!"

Knowles's disbelief was genuine. O'Hare leaned back in his seat. He could almost enjoy this part of the story. "A young man and his girlfriend were at the airport making out. The man in question is married to someone else and had no place to take the girl, but that's another story. Anyway, your boy comes along, opens the front door, and yanks the poor guy out. The girl runs off screaming and Richard gets in. The key is in the ignition . . ."

Knowles was speechless.

"It's the truth, Mr. Knowles. The man is awfully embarrassed. He says he could have handled Richard but his pants were around his ankles and he kept tripping when he tried to stand up. By the time he got himself squared away, Richard was gone." O'Hare couldn't hold back a grin. Knowles had no quick answer this time.

"But of course," Knowles finally spoke, "you can't be sure that boy was Richard."

"Huh?" O'Hare didn't follow.

"You seem reasonably certain that the boy you chased out of the terminal, for no apparent reason, was Richard."

"We have his passport, Mr. Knowles."

"But how do you know that the boy who commandeered that car was Richard too? It could have been someone else altogether."

"The man and woman identified your son from his passport photo."

"Please, Lieutenant, the incident couldn't have taken more than a few seconds. That couple in the car was surprised and embarrassed. I doubt they really got a good look at the intruder. Did you show them a lineup of passport photos of teenage boys? Did they pick out my son's picture?"

O'Hare took a deliberate breath and forced a smile. "You're absolutely right, Mr. Knowles. They could have been mistaken. And that's another reason why we want to find Richard. We want to clear his good name if he's innocent." He noticed his fist was clenched and decided he had better bring this interview to an end.

"Do you have any idea where your boy is now?" he asked.

Knowles shook his head no.

"Did you make any calls to reach him?"

"I tried his school—Pierce Academy. It's in Holton, Connecticut."

O'Hare made a note. "And they haven't heard from him either?"

"No," Knowles replied.

"What about relatives and friends?"

"If he has any close friends outside school, I don't know about them. Richard keeps to himself a lot. And we aren't close to anyone in my family."

O'Hare cleared his throat. "The boy's mother . . . ?" he inquired tactfully.

"She walked out on us when Richie was six months old. I don't know if she's dead or alive."

Of course. What else was new? O'Hare felt a tightness in his chest. The phone rang.

Knowles jerked his head, then rose to answer it. But O'Hare acted faster. Instinctively, he reached for the receiver and put it to his ear. Knowles cursed loudly, but through the shout O'Hare was able to make out a coarse, gravelly voice on the other end.

"Steven?"

Knowles was on his feet now, his face red, a vein pulsing visibly at the base of his neck. He grabbed the phone from O'Hare.

"Thought it might be Richard," O'Hare murmured, honestly enough. Knowles turned away and listened into the phone without replying. Then he placed the receiver back on the hook and stood perfectly still for a moment. By the time he turned around to face O'Hare he was his old, unruffled self.

"Do you have any more questions, Lieutenant?" he asked.

"Not for now," O'Hare replied. "You do intend to stay here in case Richard calls."

"Of course."

Knowles was politely ushering him to the door. "I'll probably want to talk to you again," O'Hare said.

"I'm sure you will, Lieutenant."

O'Hare left without offering his hand.

From the driver's seat of a rust-eaten Plymouth, Sergeant Leverton watched O'Hare emerge from the house. She could have picked the lieutenant out of a crowd a quarter of a mile away. His outline was extraordinary, his walk a heavy, bearlike shuffle. He climbed into his car without a glance at the Plymouth and drove away.

Leverton probed for a feeling but found nothing. It was like trying to feel a tooth through a shot of Novocaine.

She came upon an inner surface, smooth and impenetrable, but with no sensation.

Amazing, she sighed, but just as well. There was no way for them to work together without some anesthetic. And Anne Leverton did want to work on this case. O'Hare had judged that correctly. The desire to save this boy burned equally in both of them.

There was a movement, a curtain had parted in an upstairs room of Steve Knowles's house. She strained but could not make out his form. But he was there. Looking. Watching O'Hare drive away. He would be sure to see the Plymouth parked not quite out of sight with a figure behind the wheel. And he would know it was another cop. Leverton wondered what he would be thinking. What did go on in the mind of a man who used his own child to smuggle drugs?

4 **"AND** just what the hell are you doing here?" Mario Federici growled as he came up to Richard standing on the corner.

"Waiting for you. Just like I said."

"I mean why aren't you at school? What the hell are you doing here in the middle of Manhattan?"

Richard looked at the fake scowl on Mario's lips and the put-on exasperation in his eyes and wanted to hug the man, but that was impossible. So he just shrugged his shoulders.

"At least you could have waited inside!"

"I was fine here," he answered matter-of-factly. "I was enjoying the show on the street."

"What? All these perverts and degenerates?" Mario shook his head disgustedly. "You look terrible," he grumbled. "I hate that tan. Hungry?"

"Starved."

"Come on."

He put his arm around Richard's shoulder and led him into the restaurant. Richard felt a glow spreading inside him. They slid into a booth. A waitress came over with menus.

"So, how was your trip?" Mario asked again. He was looking hard at Richard, studying him.

"Fine." Richard bent his head to the menu. The trip *was* fine. It was just the last part. . . .

"You liked Colombia?"

"Yeah. I ran every day."

"You told me on the phone."

A cheeseburger sounded good. He decided on that with french fries and onion rings, and a vanilla shake. He could feel Mario's eyes on him. He didn't dare look up.

"Your father called. Did I tell you that?"

"Yeah, you told me."

The waitress reappeared. She stood there, snapping her gum. Richard gave her his order.

"Forget it!" Mario broke in. "We'll have two steaks, medium-rare, baked potatoes, and green salads. I'll have a draft. He can have his vanilla shake."

"You know what that greasy shit does to your gut?" he said, after the waitress had left.

"Bill Rodgers lives on Twinkies," Richard countered.

"When you run like Bill Rodgers, you can live on Twinkies, too!"

Richard went back to the safety of the menu. He looked at all the foods listed and began to feel nauseous. The whole business of eating was pretty disgusting, when he stopped to think about it. First slaughtering some innocent animal. Then wrapping it in cellophane. Then cooking it, grinding it with your teeth, swallowing it into your stomach where acids turned it into mush. Then squeezing it through your intestines . . . He felt as though he might gag, and swallowed until the feeling went away.

Mario's hand came over the menu and gently pushed it away. "You want to tell me about it?" His voice was softer now.

Richard shrugged again. "I had a fight with Steve."

"About what?"

"It's personal."

Mario's eyebrows furrowed and Richard shifted in his seat—the plastic of the booth was sticking to his jeans.

"You mean you call me in the middle of the night to

ask me to drive an hour and a half to see you because you've got some problem, and then you tell me it's personal?"

"I'm not going back to school. Mario," Richard said quietly.

"What are you talking about?"

"I can't." He traced a marbled line on the Formica tabletop with a finger. "Don't ask me to explain."

"I'll damn well ask you . . . !" Mario stopped himself. He took a breath to control his anger. "Richard, what could have happened that was so bad?"

He didn't want to cry in front of Mario, and he knew Mario wouldn't want that either. He bit the inside of his mouth. The pain kept away the tears.

"Richard, what I mean is, if you drop out of school, what will you do?"

"I don't know." He played with the saltshaker. "I don't know," he said again, miserably.

Mario reached out and took his wrist. "Look, why don't we drive back. You can stay with me and Jo for a few days. You don't have to go to classes, you don't even have to tell your father where you are if you don't want."

Richard shook his head. "I have to be by myself for a while, Mario."

"By yourself?"

He lifted his face and met Mario's eyes.

"Alone?"

He nodded.

"Richard, you're fifteen years old!"

"I'll be sixteen in three months."

Mario was working hard to keep his control. "You can't be on your own at sixteen in three months!"

"Why not?"

"Because you can't!" The anger grew in his face. "What do you mean, why not? You're just a kid! That's why not!"

"I'll manage."

"How? What will you do for money?"

"I thought maybe I could borrow some from you."

Richard was surprised that Mario seemed startled. He opened his mouth to say something, but then stopped.

The waitress arrived with their order. "Anyone want ketchup?" she whined.

"No!" Mario barked.

"I was just asking!" She snapped her gum and began to walk away.

"I'll have some," Richard called after her. She turned around and glared angrily.

"This is good steak!" Mario hissed. "You don't put ketchup on good steak!"

The waitress returned, slamming a bottle of Heinz in front of them, and then stalked off. Richard shook a healthy glob of the stuff onto his plate and began to eat. He couldn't taste his food. He could hardly even swallow. The Federicis were his only friends in the world. Mario was the only person he really loved.

"How much do you need?" Mario said, suddenly.

"Huh?"

"Money. You were saying you needed some money. How much?"

"Oh." Richard had practically forgot what had caused the argument. "I don't know." He kept his eyes on his plate. "Some. I don't have any."

"Of course you don't!" Mario kept his voice low but spoke intensely. "You're a kid. That's one of the differences between kids and adults. Kids don't have money. Adults are supposed to work for a living and kids are supposed to go to school. So why the hell don't you come back to where you have a room to sleep in and three meals a day and friends . . ."

Tears welled up in Richard's eyes and there was nothing he could do to stop them now. He rested his elbows

27

on the table and pushed his palms into the sockets, hoping the pressure would force them back. He felt Mario's hand on his arm.

"It's okay, Richard. Whatever it is, you don't have to tell me. And of course I can't make you come back."

Richard dried his eyes with his hands.

"But where are you going to stay?"

"I have a place. I'll be okay."

Mario looked to the ceiling in silent prayer. He forced a smile as he took out his wallet. Richard could see three twenties and a ten.

"You mind if I keep twenty for myself?"

"No, that's okay," Richard sniffed.

"Thanks."

Mario slid three bills across the table. The waitress came with the check and slapped it on the only wet spot she could find. Mario showed her his teeth as he picked it up from the puddle.

"Thanks, too," Richard said softly, carefully folding the money into his wallet. There was pain in Mario's face. Not awful pain, Richard thought. More like the discomfort of the man in the TV commercial who complained about acid indigestion.

When they got outside Richard didn't know what to say. "Thanks again," he blurted out. "For everything."

"Yeah, sure."

He wanted to say more. He wanted to tell Mario about the cocaine in the jacket, and driving a car to Manhattan, and getting a hotel room—but he couldn't. He wasn't even sure why.

"One promise, Richard. Call me tomorrow afternoon. I'll be home."

"Okay, I can do that." That was all. The hug was still impossible. A handshake was stupid. "I'll talk to you tomorrow," he assured Mario, and then he turned and walked away. He walked fast, crossing to the east side of the avenue and then around the corner.

In a store window a mask of E.T. watched him pass. Frankenstein's monster grinned. Richard knew Mario was worried. He didn't want to upset Mario, but he couldn't help it. He needed a few days to think things out. He stopped for a moment, confused. What was he trying to think out, anyway? He couldn't decide. He would have to figure that out, too.

He passed the Flying Saucer News and Nutrition Center and peeked in. The proprietor, looking extremely human, was reading a Spiderman comic. Richard turned onto Broadway. The street looked like a carnival. Under a neon sign he passed a tall, shiny black man hawking gold chains. Another man, fat and bearded, stood in a doorway filled with photos of naked girls and called to him to check out the action. He passed movie marquees, one after another. *Flash Pants. Dallas School Girls. Fist of the Dragon* together with *Bruce Lee's Revenge*.

"Why not?" he said to himself. He had no curfew. He wasn't at school anymore where it was worth three demerits to leave the grounds. Why the hell not? He walked up to the lady in the ticket booth, gave her a ten-dollar bill, counted his change, and entered the theater.

Except it wasn't like any movie theater he had ever seen before. This was a huge, magical cave—hooded lanterns lit up patches of the wall, red coals of incense dotted the orchestra, crystal stalactites hung from the ceiling where a white beam caught the dust and swirling smoke.

And the smell! He sniffed, trying to identify it—a combination of moldy velvet and stale cigarettes and sweat, mixed with caramel. There was litter, everywhere—candy wrappers, paper cups, newspapers, cigarette butts. As he walked down the aisle his running shoes stuck to the carpet. He turned into an empty row and popcorn crunched under his feet.

He sat down in the middle of the orchestra and looked around. The theater was almost empty! There were maybe thirty people in the whole place, and most weren't even watching the movie. A group of older boys, across the aisle, were laughing and passing around a joint. He looked more closely and noticed there was a girl in there, making out with one of them. He didn't get a really good view until she switched seats and began necking with the boy on the aisle. He had his hand under her sweater, and her hand was down low, out of sight. Their mouths looked like they were glued together. Richard was embarrassed and excited at the same time. He didn't want to be caught watching, but couldn't take his eyes off them. He scrunched down in his seat to get a safer view when an old man and woman banged into seats in the same row, blocking his line of sight. Reluctantly, he returned his attention to the screen where a gang of bad guys, dressed in black pajamas and carrying long poles, had surrounded Bruce Lee, who was holding only a small piece of chain.

"Come on, ya little yella motha'! Break his ass! Break his face!"

He turned to see who was shouting. It was the old woman a few seats over. She was watching the screen with a glazed look in her eye.

"Get him in the t'roat!" she screamed. "Break his ass! Chop! Chop!" Her husband sat completely still beside her. His face looked like it was made out of wax. "Kick him," she shouted, "kick him in the grapenuts!" Richard thought of moving away but he didn't want to hurt her feelings. Instead he just scrunched down a little more and tried to ignore her.

The seat was comfortable; the theater felt warm. The movie wasn't very interesting, so he hung his legs over the seat in front of him and drifted off. He thought of Paul Federici and the boys at school. He would have stories to tell when he got back. Stories of women who looked like tropical birds, and desk clerks with no lips, and crazy ladies in movie theaters, and the Flying Saucer News and Nutrition Center . . . Paul was laughing excitedly, putting an arm around his shoulder, down his back . . .

He woke up with a start. The hands were for real!

He sat up straight and instinctively flailed his arms, smashing his elbow into hard flesh. He heard a groan and bolted to his feet. A short, thin man in a dungaree jacket was running quickly up the aisle. Richard stood there, paralyzed. He thought about chasing the man, but couldn't. He seemed stuck to the floor. In seconds the man had run out of the theater and there was nothing he could do. His heart was thumping as he sat back down and stared at the screen. No one in the theater seemed to have noticed. Suddenly, the obvious thought occurred to him and he jerked his hand into his back pocket. Empty! His wallet was gone! He pressed his arms against the jacket and felt a little better. The heavy bulk of the lining was still there.

He took a few breaths as he registered this new assault. It was only fifty dollars. Actually, he was lucky. He could have been killed, for God's sake! He sat, rigid, waiting to regain his breath. Finally the trembling inside him stopped and he got up and left the theater.

He kept on the bright, busy avenue as he walked back to the hotel, his eyes wary of every stranger, his mind churning with thoughts of what he could do for money. He couldn't call Mario again. There was Paul at school, but it wasn't safe to go back there. He saw two cops standing on a corner and quickly crossed the street. He wasn't safe anywhere.

In the hotel lobby the clerk grinned and waved him over. "How's it going, Ace?" He was holding a joint and a thin stream of smoke drifted from his nostrils.

"Fine." The smoke, together with the dank lobby smell, made him feel nauseous again.

"Hey, you want some good grass? I got some joints.

Just a buck a piece for guests of the hotel." The clerk fished out two hand-rolled cigarettes and held them up.

"No, no thanks." Richard just wanted to get to his room. He headed toward the stairs and was at the first step when the idea came to him. He stopped to consider it. It wasn't really right, but what choice did he have? At least it was worth a try.

"Listen," he turned back to the clerk, "maybe you'd like to buy something from me."

"Yeah? What?" The clerk sucked deeply on the joint, then put the ember under his nose and sniffed some more.

"Cocaine," Richard heard himself say.

The clerk looked confused. "You got cocaine?"

"Yeah."

The eyes narrowed into thin, steel slits. It took all Richard's strength to withstand the scrutiny.

"Bullshit!" the clerk finally said. "How the fuck do you got cocaine?"

"I have it. Don't worry how."

"Shit!" The clerk was getting angry. "After I been so good to you? Letting you stay in one of my rooms? Offering a toke on my joint? You trying to set me up or something? I should call the fucking cops!" He moved to the phone.

"My father's a doctor," Richard said without even thinking. The clerk stopped. He seemed interested.

"Say what?"

"I said my father's a doctor. He had some cocaine in his office. I don't know if it was for a patient, or what, but before I left I ripped it off." The clerk still looked suspicious, but it was a good story. It could be true.

"Tell you what, Ace, why don't you get me a sample? How about that?"

"Sure," Richard said. "I can get you a sample. No problem. You wait right here."

No problem . . .

He could feel the clerk's eyes on his back as he walked up the stairs, casually, as though he really had no problems at all.

"Unbelievable," he said softly to himself. "Unbefuckinglievable."

Up in his room, he slipped off the jacket. He took out the plastic tube that was already damaged and carefully undid a corner of the zip-lock top.

"Damn!"

He had nothing to put the sample in. He opened the table drawer and found a Bible and a plastic ashtray. The ashtray would have to do. He poured out enough powder to cover the circular bottom, then a bit more for good measure. It would be enough of a sample for the clerk.

He reclosed the plastic bag, carefully slipped it back into the jacket lining, and put the jacket on. Holding the ashtray cupped in his hands, he started back down to the lobby.

At the top of the stairs he saw a man and his daughter coming up, straight toward him. He stopped and turned sideways, nervously waiting for them to pass. The man looked fat and buttery and stepped delicately on the stairs, his eyes studiously examining the carpet. He seemed almost embarrassed taking his daughter to their room . . .

Holy shit! Richard said to himself. It wasn't a man and his daughter at all! She was a prostitute, and she was taking him to *her* room. His pulse quickened as he looked at the woman more closely. In the dim light her short platinum hair glowed with a sheen of its own. Her lips were bright pink and encouraging as they whispered in the man's ear, and showed white, even teeth. She had emerald eyes and her eyelids were sky-blue. Her face was a painting made with the most beautiful pastel colors Richard had ever seen.

He stood there, frozen, his hands cupping the ashtray. She looked straight at him and now he had no choice but to go on down. The fat man kept his eyes on the carpet, but the woman flashed a radiant smile, then seemed puzzled.

"Hey, what have you got there?" She sounded just like a teenage girl. "A dead mouse?"

Richard was too embarrassed to answer. As she passed she wrinkled her nose and giggled. She giggled like a teenage girl, too! He turned to look at her from behind—a girlish waist, jeans glued to a terrific ass and disappearing into knee-high boots. She *was* a kid, he thought! Probably not much older than he was! She must have known he was watching her because she looked back and winked at him before disappearing with the fat man into the corridor.

Richard took a breath. Right now he should be in his dorm room at Pierce getting ready for school tomorrow. Instead, he was in a Times Square hotel with a couple of ounces of cocaine in his hands being winked at by a gorgeous hooker . . .

Unbefuckinglievable.

He continued slowly down the stairs, to the desk.

"Here," he said with surprising confidence, and placed the ashtray on the counter, in front of the clerk.

The clerk seemed startled and leaned forward to examine the powder. His small eyes jumped nervously as he put a bit on his finger and tasted it.

For a moment he looked as though he had turned to stone. Then he cleared his throat and spoke in a hoarse voice. "I'll just take a small snort of this, if you don't mind."

Richard shrugged casually as the clerk looked around. There was no one else in the lobby. He took a razor blade and a small straw from below the counter and etched some of the powder into a thick line. Then, with a quick look toward the front stairs, he lowered his head, put the straw to his nose, and vacuumed up the line in one swift snort. Now he straightened up again, holding his breath, standing absolutely still with his head back and eyes closed.

Minutes passed. The man just stood there like a statue. Richard was about to reach out and shake his arm when he opened his eyes.

"Not bad, Ace. Not great, but not bad." His pupils sparkled. Beads of sweat dotted his brow. "How much do you want for what's in the tray?"

Richard couldn't believe his luck. Not only did the clerk like the stuff, but he hadn't realized it was intended as a free sample! "I don't know. What do you think it's worth?"

The clerk narrowed his eyes, then sucked on his tooth-pick. "Nah, it's your stuff. You put a price on it."

There wasn't much in the tray, Richard thought. Maybe three or four teaspoons. He hadn't even made a dent in the first bag so he couldn't ask for too much. But he didn't want to ask for too little either. "I don't know. How about twenty bucks?" He held his breath.

The clerk turned to stone again. Richard felt his hands start to sweat. He had asked for too much!

"Okay," the clerk finally said. "You need the bread and it's decent enough stuff." He took out his wallet and gave Richard two tens, and in a second smooth motion slipped the ashtray under the counter. Richard didn't dare breathe. "I assume we can do business again, in the near future?" the man said.

"I think it's possible." He felt his confidence return-ing.

"In other words, you got some more of this stuff?"

"Yeah. Some." Just enough information to keep him interested.

"The reason I'm asking, see, is I got this friend who's in town just for tonight and I'm sure he'll want to buy some. You think you can swing that?"

"Yeah, I think so."

"But you see, the problem is he's gonna be leaving soon so he'd want to do the deal in the next hour or so."

"No problem." Richard felt good. His money troubles, for the moment, were over. He started to leave the hotel.

"Hey, where you going?" The clerk seemed anxious, suddenly. Almost protective.

"I thought I'd buy a few baggies. For the stuff."

"No problem, pal. My friend'll have his own bags. And a good scale. We want to do this all fair and square. Here, have a free joint." The clerk held out a marijuana cigarette and Richard, after a slight hesitation, took it. "Why don't you go up to your room and have a smoke. You got a TV up there?"

"No," Richard said.

"Shit! Well, here's something to look at." The clerk reached down to his private shelf and pulled out a stack of magazines. "You go and relax. I'll be up with my friend in a few minutes and we'll do some business."

Richard took the magazines. On the cover of the top one was a blonde girl who looked a little like the hooker he had seen on the stairs. She was staring at him, beckoning to him, one rosebud of a nipple poking through a lacy negligee, her legs up and slightly parted. He felt a flush of excitement and then a strange satisfaction. He had been in Manhattan for just a few hours and aside from sideswiping a garbage can when he tried to park that damn car, and having his pocket picked in the movie theater, he felt he was doing very well. Very well indeed.

5 **LEVERTON** turned up the volume on her Walkman and put a stick of gum into her mouth. She chewed in time to the music. How anyone had ever sat through a stake-out before they invented the Walkman, she didn't know.

She looked at her watch. Nearly midnight. There had been no movement from Knowles's house for hours. She would probably be there all night, just watching.

She got out of the car to stretch. The night air chased away her drowsiness and she began singing along with the song. Then she found herself dancing. The movement felt good. God, she hadn't danced in years. That's what she should be doing tonight, she thought. She should be getting drunk on a bottle of good champagne, and picking up some gorgeous twenty-five-year-old boy, and dancing her brains out. . . .

She stopped suddenly. A shadow had moved on the crest of the hill in front of Knowles's house. She took off the earphones and squinted hard. Knowles's blue BMW was slowly rolling away.

"Son-of-a-bitch!" she said under her breath.

She jumped back into the Plymouth and reached for the ignition key. How the hell did he get into his car without her seeing him? The Plymouth roared to life and she pressed the pedal to the floor. He must have come out through the backyard and crawled into the BMW from the passenger side.

"Damn!"

She couldn't move fast enough. By the time she slammed into gear, Knowles had his ignition and lights on and was screeching around a corner.

Fast, she thought. Something had gotten him excited. The boy must have called. She skidded around a corner, but Knowles was already turning into the next block. She wanted to give him the chase of his life, but it wasn't part of the plan. The Plymouth wasn't that well balanced, anyway; she'd probably just end up killing herself. After two more corners the BMW was gone.

Leverton pulled over to a curb and reached for the radio mike. On the slim chance that Knowles had a unit of his own, she signaled Wilhite in code.

"Ernie, you on? Over."

Wilhite's voice crackled through the speaker. "Right here, lady. Come back."

"I thought I'd take a drive your way. Over."

"Good enough. See you soon, I hope. Over and out."

"Yeah," she replied and hung up the microphone. "See you soon." Leverton wouldn't be seeing anyone soon. Her assignment, now, was to stay with the house in Rye. If Wilhite picked up Knowles, and if Knowles *was* meeting his son, Wilhite and O'Hare would make the arrest. So much for the women's movement, she thought.

She felt a flush in her face and chest as she waited for Wilhite's return call. She had to admit that Knowles's escape had been impressive. She also had to admit that it had stirred up an excitement in her—something she hadn't felt in a long time.

Wilhite's voice brought her back to her job. "You there, lady? Come back."

She pressed the mike button. "Go ahead. Over."

"Something just came up and I'm heading into town. Catch you later. Over and out."

She switched off the radio. Wilhite had picked up Knowles. Now to report in. She started the car and turned around, heading for the center of town. Her mouth felt dry as she pulled up under a neon sign in front of a bar. There had to be a phone in the place, somewhere.

O'Hare was emerging from a youth shelter on Forty-second Street when his beeper sounded. He fought through his exhaustion and found a pay phone a block away. For two hours he had been crisscrossing the streets of Times Square, leaving a copy of Richard's passport photo with every patrol car and shop owner he passed, looking into every young, male face. The number of propositions he had turned down was depressing. He wanted nothing more than to go back to his room and sleep, but he couldn't. Richard would be at his most vulnerable now. Every hour's work tonight would be worth five tomorrow.

He dialed the precinct operator.

"O'Hare here. What's up?"

"Sergeant Leverton's on the line for you, Lieutenant. If you wait a minute I'll patch you in."

O'Hare waited. After seventeen years on the force O'Hare was good at waiting. And walking. And asking questions. And filling out forms. His feet were killing him as he scanned the street.

Richard was here somewhere, O'Hare was certain of it. The car had been found crosstown at Thirty-eighth and First. Where would a fifteen-year-old boy go from there? Where everyone else goes—toward the heat and light—to Times Square.

A girl wobbled up to him wearing a miniskirt and five-inch spikes. She looked like she went to junior high school during the day. She certainly hadn't learned how to manage the heels.

"Wanna go out?" she asked.

O'Hare thought if he'd had any heart left a piece of

it would have died. He shook his head sadly and the girl wobbled off. Three teenage boys, shaking with laughter, stumbled out of a taxi. Each held a beer and one—the one laughing hardest—was smoking a joint. He doubled over, then tripped and fell, tearing his jacket at the elbow. O'Hare could see a slick of blood, but the boy didn't seem to feel a thing. Still laughing, he climbed to his feet and weaved his way back to his friends.

How *do* you bring up a child today? O'Hare wondered. What do you do? Wrap them in Saran? All you can really do is give them love and support, and a few rules. You can try to get them going in the right direction, but then you let go. It's like separating yourself from your own flesh, but you have to let go. But at what age? Certainly not at fifteen. They don't even *want* independence then, not really. Even if, like Pat, they say they do.

Leverton's voice came on the line and O'Hare could barely speak. He was grateful that she kept her report short and impersonal.

"Something came up and he left a little after twelve," she said. "He spotted me. I let him get away."

"Good," O'Hare murmured.

"Whilhite picked him up at the turnpike entrance."

"They're heading toward the City?"

"Yeah."

"Thanks," he said. "Good job."

"Yeah."

"You'll stay with the house, just in case."

"I know." There was an edge to her voice. Then she hung up. O'Hare felt nauseous. He had nearly an hour before Wilhite would be within radio distance. Enough time to walk over to Port Authority and pass out some more photos. Enough time to stop off at Stanley's for one quick, stomach-settling drink.

6 **H E E L - T O - T O E**, heel-to-toe, Richard measured the room. It was sixteen shoe-lengths long by twelve shoe-lengths wide. He went to the window, which was encrusted with grime, and tried to force it open. No luck. It didn't matter. It just faced the dirty, brick wall of a building a few feet away.

He felt depressed, but couldn't understand why. Just half an hour ago he was feeling terrific. He threw himself on the bed; it wouldn't bounce. No fun there. The mattress smelled awful, even worse than Mickey Federici's mattress, and Mickey was only two and still wetting his bed. He decided to sleep with his clothes on tonight, on top of the blanket.

He took a *Penthouse* from the stack of magazines the desk clerk had given him and leafed through it.

Boring.

He put it down.

What was wrong with him? he wondered. He had always loved dirty magazines. Most of the kids at school used the centerfolds as wallpaper, but for Richard, alone in his room, the glossy photos were movie frames that would unfreeze, and the girls would move, and breathe, and call his name, and perform for him. Now he couldn't get even a little aroused. Of course it had been a pretty tough day, and the clerk would be knocking on his door any minute, but still . . .

He wished there was a phone in the room. Not that

he had anyone to call, except for maybe Paul. It would be nice to talk to Paul again for a few minutes.

The joint the clerk had given him was sitting on the night table. Well, why not? he said to himself. The idea of putting any kind of smoke into his lungs had always seemed stupid, though he and Paul did sometimes go behind the bleachers at night to drink a couple of beers, or try a joint when they could get hold of one. But he had never really gotten high. Paul said it was because he couldn't keep the smoke in his lungs long enough.

He lit the marijuana cigarette, tightened his lips, and took a deep drag. He tried to hold it in for a count of ten.

He started coughing, and at the same moment heard a loud crash coming from the room next door. Then a girl shrieked. He couldn't make out the words, but there was definitely a violent fight going on. He opened the door and looked into the hall.

"Get away from me, you prick," he heard the girl's voice scream. "You touch me again, I'll rip your eyes out!"

There was a brief pause, then more crashes and screams. Richard was wondering whether he should get the clerk when the door to the room opened and the blonde girl he had seen on the stairs came out. She was wearing nothing but a T-shirt and panties, now; her boots and jeans and leather jacket and purse were gathered in her arms. She looked quickly up and down the hallway. When she saw Richard she ran toward him.

"Can I come in?" she panted. "This guy's gonna kill me!"

Without waiting for an answer she pushed her way past him, then pulled him in after her and slammed the door shut. Her chest was heaving; the outline of her erect nipples showed through the thin cotton of her shirt.

"Fucking asshole!" she glowered.

He felt his face burn and embarrassedly shifted his eyes from her chest to an abstract point on the wall.

42

"Fat pervert!" she went on, and Richard breathed a sigh of relief. She was talking about the fat man next door.

"Now I don't mind a little controlled S and M," she explained. "I mean if some guy wants to get off on a few minutes of light spanking, what the hell? It can even be fun, right?"

"Yeah, sure," Richard replied.

"But this fucking creep, you know what he took out of his pants?"

Richard didn't want to guess.

"A prick!" she said with enormous indignation. Richard didn't see why that was so unusual so he said nothing. "A fucking rubber prick! Maybe a foot long!" She held her hands apart to show the full length.

"Now I've seen dildos before," the girl quickly added, "and if some guy wants to pay to see me make it with Mr. Goodyear, well, it's his money. But this prick's prick is not just twelve inches of rubber, it's twelve inches of rubber loaded with little steel balls! Can you believe that?" She stood there angrily with her hands on her hips.

Richard didn't know what to say. It was hard to picture what she was describing. "Wow!" he exclaimed.

She leaned forward and whispered. "It was a blackjack! He had made his dildo into a blackjack!"

Now he understood. At least he thought he understood.

" 'Not on your life, fatso,' I told him. That's when he got crazy and came after me with the thing. So I started throwing stuff around. But he wouldn't stop! I thought I'd never get out of there alive!" She seemed to be calming down as she told the story. Her panting had stopped. "Thanks for taking me in."

"Don't mention it."

Richard felt a little flushed himself. Partly he was excited from the story, but mostly it was from the sight of her standing there, half-naked. She put her leg up on the

43

mattress and began to inspect it. Two red welts showed on her thigh.

"Fucking creep . . ."

"Does it hurt?"

"I've been worse." She examined her other leg and, finding no further damage, sat wearily on the bed. Her eyes caught sight of the half-smoked joint on the night table and her face brightened. "Hey, do you mind?"

"Not at all. Go ahead."

Richard watched as she lit it. She took a deep drag, and made herself comfortable, leaning back against the headboard and stretching out her legs. Her thighs fell open. She didn't seem to mind the view it gave him. She looked at him and smiled.

"How's your dead mouse?"

Richard went blank for a moment, but then he remembered the ashtray. "Oh! I buried it," he replied.

She nodded as though his answer made perfect sense, then motioned with her head at the jacket he was wearing. "You about to go out or something?"

"Oh no. I was just chilly. I have a low metabolism."

She seemed to accept that, too, and passed him the joint. He put it to his lips, sucked in as much air and as little smoke as possible, and gave it back.

"My name is Lisa," she announced.

"I'm Richard."

She held out a stiff arm and Richard extended his. He was surprised at the firmness of her grip.

"I saw you on the stairs, before," she told him. "When you first came in." Her eyes found the stack of sex magazines on the bed. "You come to hotels to jerk off?"

"No, no," Richard blushed. "They were given to me. By the clerk downstairs."

"Franciefuck?"

"Huh?"

"Francie. The night clerk. He has a real fuckface so we call him Franciefuck. Has he been after you?"

"What do you mean?"

"You know what I mean! Has he tried anything funny?"

Richard knew what she meant. His cheeks felt hot. "No! Of course not!"

"You watch out for him, Richard. He's no good."

"Why? He seems okay to me."

"He's got no lips."

Richard couldn't help a laugh. "Yeah, I noticed."

She took another toke at the joint and passed it over. "Sit down," she said, patting the blanket next to her. Richard took the joint and sat. His leg brushed against hers and she didn't move away. He inhaled the smoke deeply and this time didn't cough. He was beginning to feel very relaxed.

"So what are you doing in this place anyway?" Lisa asked, taking back the joint.

"I'm meeting my father." Her nipples were no longer erect but he could see the roundness of her breasts through her shirt. "He's flying in from the West Coast. From Los Angeles. He's meeting me here." A few curls of blonde hair had escaped the elastic of her panties.

"At *this* hotel?"

"Yeah."

She looked at him with some doubt in her eyes.

"It's true!" he insisted.

"How old are you, anyway?" she asked.

"Eighteen." Even with her lipstick smeared pink over the side of her mouth she was the most beautiful thing he had ever seen. "I'm graduating high school this year. That's why my dad's flying in. From Los Angeles. I'm graduating high school, you know."

Richard had the uncomfortable feeling he might be

repeating himself. He looked at her face to see if he was making sense, but couldn't tell. She certainly was looking at him strangely.

"Well, how old are *you*?" he challenged back.

"Nineteen," she answered smoothly.

"Oh, sure! You're nineteen!" he snorted.

"Well, you're no eighteen either! What *are* you doing here? Hustling?"

"What do you mean, hustling?"

"I mean turning tricks. Are you turning tricks out of this hotel?"

"You mean am I a hooker? How could I be a hooker?" Richard giggled at the thought. "I'm a boy, if you haven't noticed."

"So? What does that have to do with anything? There are more boys out on the street than girls. They do better business, too!"

Richard's head was swimming. "You mean there are boys who get girls to pay them for it?"

"No, dummy! I mean boys who get men to pay for it!"

Richard was surprised. "You mean queers?"

"Yeah, queers. Not the boys, the men."

He tried to make sense out of what Lisa was saying. "You mean there are boys who aren't queer who do it with men who are queer, for money?"

"Christ, you really don't know anything, do you? How old are you really, fifteen?"

Richard became angry at the guess. "I don't have to tell you how old I am! And for your information, just because you're a cheap hooker you don't have to think everyone else is. I happen to be a student, if you really want to know."

Lisa sat upright. "Who the hell are you calling a cheap hooker? I happen to be a professional dancer! And when I do turn a trick I am anything but cheap! I get fifty bucks a shot! And that's for a quickie. Anything special and I get

46

plenty more. I got one guy who's a vice-president at Exxon, and he pays me a hundred!"

"Congratulations!" Richard said. "I'm sorry I called you cheap." He regretted his words the moment he said them. Lisa stormed off the bed and began putting on her jeans.

"Boy, you *are* an asshole! I prefer fatso next door to you!"

He didn't know what to do. He didn't want her to go but didn't know how to stop her. He was trying to think of what to say when there was a rap on the door. It opened, and in leaned Francie, sucking on a fresh toothpick.

"Hi, Ace. I'm here." In his hand was a small, chrome-plated revolver. "And here's my friend." He pointed the gun directly at Richard's forehead. "Can we come in?"

Lisa had no idea what was going on, but she knew enough to stand perfectly still when someone was holding a gun, particularly when the someone was Francie.

The clerk saw her and bared his teeth. "What are you doing here?"

"Baby-sitting!" she snapped back. "What are *you* doing?"

"It's none of your business, cunt. Just get out!" He waved the gun in the air. Lisa felt a stubborn anger. He was just like every other goddamn man, barging in like that, waving a piece, threatening her. Fuck him! She didn't move.

"Lisa, I'm warning you!" The gun shook. Lisa was surprised she felt so little fear.

"He owes me money, Francie," she said matter-of-factly. "A little half-and-half." She grinned and ran her tongue under her front lip. Francie always squirmed when she talked about her work. "I'm not leaving till I get paid."

"Pay her!" Francie hissed at Richard, but he might as well have been talking to a statue. The boy just stared with glazed eyes. Francie furiously pulled three ten-dollar bills out of his own pocket and threw them on the floor. "There! You're paid. Now get out!"

Lisa shook her head. Francie was a gold-plated shit and this kid was in trouble. "No good, Francie. I have to get it from him. Leo has his rules."

She could almost hear him grinding his teeth. A drop of spittle formed at the corner of his mouth. He turned his attention to the boy. "Okay Richard, where is it?"

Richard tried to speak but no sound emerged. His second try was more successful. "You said you were going to buy some . . ."

'Yeah, well I'm a little short of cash just now. I'll owe you." Francie's eyes jerked around the room. "Where is it!"

"I'm not going to tell you," Richard said.

Francie reached for the closet door and pulled it open. Two hangers rattled to the floor. There was nothing else inside. He ripped the drawer out of the end table. A Gideon Bible flew across the room.

"What's the problem, Francie?" Lisa asked in a soothing voice.

He didn't hear. With his left hand he tore the mattress off the bed. The spring beneath was bare save for a limp rubber that hung forlornly over a wire. He turned back to Richard with such a fierce look that for the first time Lisa felt fear.

"I'll give you ten seconds, Ace," he said softly. Then his eyes fastened on the boy's jacket. Lisa heard him gasp. "Okay, sport, take it off."

Richard was trembling. "No," he whispered.

Lisa tried to keep her voice light. Francie looked capable of anything just now. "Richard, whatever it is, give it to him. He's not fooling around."

"In five seconds I'm gonna take it off your dead body, Ace."

"It isn't mine," Richard said. "I can't give it to you."

Francie's chest heaved. His voice squeaked with indignation. "What the fuck do I care whose it is? Just give it to me or I'll blow your head off!"

Richard didn't move. Lisa felt a tightness in her throat. "Francie," she began, but the shot stopped her. The gun made the sound of a snapping stick, and the windowsill behind Richard splintered.

"Richard!" she screamed, "for God's sake!" She leaped over to him and pulled at the jacket. He stood inert, not helping her and not resisting. She finally tore it off him and threw it at Francie. "Here. Now get out!"

Francie squeezed the jacket. Beads of sweat lined his forehead. He slipped his free hand into the lining and half-pulled out a long, plastic tube filled with white powder. Lisa took a sharp breath. This boy had somehow got hold of a godawful amount of . . . something! Heroin? Cocaine? Francie moved to the door. He tried to sound menacing but the excitement made his voice squeal.

"Now the two of you go back to what you was doing before I came in! You forget about this, Ace, you hear me? I see your face again, I'm gonna put a hole in it!"

The door clicked silently behind him.

"Goddamn!" Lisa said. She stuffed the three ten-dollar bills into her pocket and sat on the bed frame to pull on her boots. Francie was an asshole, but not a *stupid* asshole. Whatever was in that jacket was worth a bundle. Richard was shaking. He had slid down onto the floor, limply holding himself with his arms.

"Come on, let's go!" she urged, as she slipped on her jacket and pulled him to his feet.

"What are you doing?"

"Just follow me!" She looked out into the empty corridor, then grabbed his hand and started running down the hall.

"Lisa, if he sees us again he'll kill us!"

"You just leave that to me, huh?"

At the stairwell, she directed him up to the third floor. They took the stairs two at a time. "What did you have in there?" she asked. "Cocaine?"

He nodded his head dumbly.

"Jesus!"

There were pounds of the stuff in the jacket! Lisa had no idea where this kid could have gotten it from, but one thing was for sure—that fuckface wasn't going to end up with it. No way!

She ran down the third-floor corridor and knocked on Leo's door. No answer. So far so good. She found Leo's key on her keychain and let them in, switching on the light. A red glow lit the room.

She moved quickly. Past the TV sets stacked floor-to-ceiling. Past the uncountable radios, tape decks, video recorders, and stereo components. Past the narrow, unmade bed to a dresser. Richard followed close behind.

"Whose room is this?" he asked.

"Leo's." She rummaged through the top two drawers.

"Who's Leo?"

"Ah!" She found what she was looking for. A revolver with a mother-of-pearl handle and steel-blue barrel that could have belonged to Dirty Harry.

"Does Leo sell electronic appliances?"

She looked into his blank face. No question about it, the kid was a space shot. "Come on," she said again.

They ran down the flight of stairs to the top of the staircase that led to the lobby. Lisa stopped there and peered down. The lobby was empty. Richard had sunk down behind her. He was sitting on the floor with his back against the wall.

"Come on," she whispered.

"He's got a gun," Richard said miserably.

"So do we!"

"Lisa, someone's going to get killed!"

Maybe it would be better to leave him here, Lisa thought. He was so scared he'd probably screw things up and maybe someone *would* get killed.

"Okay, you stay here. I'll be back in a minute." She left him sitting with his knees supporting his chin, his palms pressed together as though he was praying.

She walked quietly down the stairs, praying for a little luck. If Francie had stopped in his room, behind the lobby desk . . . He had a cot there, and some clothing. Twice she'd seen him go in with a twelve-year-old boy . . . if he was stupid enough to hang around now, or take the time to pack a bag . . .

Her heart jumped. There were muffled sounds from the room. She tiptoed to the door, and then she tensed. There were footsteps from below. Someone was coming up from the street!

"Fuck!"

She stuck the gun in her pants and just had time to zip up her jacket when a man entered the lobby. He looked at her sharply. She took on a casual air.

"Can I help you?" she asked.

"You work here?" the man inquired.

"No, I'm a guest."

He wasn't tall, maybe five-eight or so, but Lisa didn't want to tangle with him. He had a quick, nervous energy that made her uneasy. His eyes were all over the place. He wanted something. Maybe he was a narc!

"Is the manager here?" he asked.

"No. No one's here right now. If you'd like to come back in half an hour . . ."

The door behind the desk opened and Francie stepped

out. He was wearing a sports coat and held a small suitcase. For an instant he glared furiously at Lisa, then he saw the stranger and forced a smile.

"Sorry, we're filled up for the night . . ." His eyes shot a warning at Lisa to keep quiet.

"I don't want a room," the man said. "I'm looking for someone. A boy." Francie's head turned back to the man. "He's fifteen. His name is Richard Knowles."

Lisa had to give Francie credit. The fish face didn't flinch. "Never heard of him," Francie said. "Now if you'll excuse me, I got an appointment."

He tried to leave but the man blocked the way. "Excuse me, but I know he's here. He was seen coming in about an hour ago."

Francie tried to brazen it out. "I told ya, Ace, I don't know nothing about it." He made another effort to get by and the man exploded. He grabbed Francie's shoulder, whirled him around, and slammed him against a wall. Francie yelped and crumbled to the carpet. The suitcase flew open and everything tumbled out—a pair of alligator shoes, a bunch of tropical, satiny shirts, two plastic vibrators, and a blue nylon flight jacket.

Lisa didn't have time to think. Francie's fingers were in his coat pocket. Instinctively she lunged toward him, kicking his hand as it came free, and sending the shiny revolver flying across the room. His shriek rang in her ears as she struggled to get her own gun out. But before she could manage it, the man had her wrist and was twisting her arm behind her back. She screamed in pain. The gun dropped to the floor.

And then, suddenly, all the action stopped.

Richard was there, his face perfectly white. He had picked up Leo's long-barreled revolver and was pointing it at the stranger. In his free arm he clutched the nylon jacket. Curiously, the stranger seemed to be at ease.

"Hello, son," he said.

52

Lisa looked from man to boy. Now she saw it; the resemblance was clear. "Jesus Christ!" she murmured.

"I'm glad to see you, son," Richard's father said.

"I'm not," Richard breathed in a voice just above a whisper.

"Richie, I'd like to explain . . ." but Richard was shaking his head and backing away. "I'm proud of you, son," the man went on, his voice a low caress that Lisa had to strain to hear. "I'm proud of the way you handled the situation at the airport, and then getting a car and driving all the way to the City."

Lisa watched as Richard took another step back, and the man stepped forward. Francie was half-sitting, flexing his sore hand, peering out of narrow eyes. Richard pressed the jacket under his arm and held the gun with both hands.

"Richie, if we can talk alone for a few minutes . . ."

"No!" he shouted. "I have nothing to say to you. Just get out of here!"

The man nodded thoughtfully. "All right, Richie. I can see you're too upset to talk now. You give me the jacket and I'll go."

He shook his head. "Sorry, it's mine now. You gave it to me, remember?"

The man's voice stiffened. "Richie, I need that jacket. I have no time to play games." He took another step and Richard raised the revolver so it pointed directly at his father's face.

"You wouldn't do that," the man said.

"Try me," Richard whispered.

"I'll have to, son. I have no choice."

The man took another step and Richard's hand shook. His knuckles were as white as the pearl handle. Lisa saw him move the line of fire to just above his father's head and pull the trigger.

A sharp click filled the room.

The man looked astonished. Richard was swaying

slightly as though he might faint. The man reached out and caught him. "Come on, Richie, we're going home." He put the nylon jacket under his own arm.

"No!" Lisa shouted. It wasn't right! Richard should not be going with this man, he should not be giving up the jacket! She moved a step closer, ready to fight, and felt a rush from behind.

"You ain't gonna get it, mothafucker!" Francie screamed.

He knocked her out of the way and jumped on the man's back. "Mothafucker!" he screamed again.

For the moment Richard's father was helpless. Francie had a stranglehold around his neck and was pounding fierce little jabs into his ribs. He dropped the jacket in an effort to wrestle with the clerk's strangling arm.

Lisa quickly grabbed it, and as she straightened up she put her arm around Richard, trying to pull him away. His body was dead weight.

"Richard! Come on!"

The two men were rolling on the floor. Francie screamed in pain as Richard's father kneed him in the groin.

She pulled harder. It was like moving a standing corpse. "Richard, for God's sake!"

Richard's father let out a short, low howl. Francie had the man's hand in his teeth. Blood dripped from his mouth like he was in a Dracula movie.

Finally Richard moved. She pushed him in front of her, scrambling with him down the flight of stairs and onto the street. Once outside, she grabbed his hand and broke into a run toward Broadway. When they got to the corner she noticed the gun still in his other hand.

"Jesus!"

She took it from him and stuck it back in her pants, under her leather jacket. Then she looked him over quickly. His face was the color of chalk, but he seemed to be all right. She looked back. No one from the hotel was following. She led him at a jog, north, up Broadway.

Richard kept up easily. "Where are we going?" he asked.

She was almost out of breath. "To the place where I dance."

They would be safe there for the night, Lisa thought. She looked back again. No Francie and no Richard's father. She slowed to a fast walk, and squeezed the nylon jacket. There were pounds of the stuff in it! Pounds! If it *was* cocaine it was worth a fortune. It *had* to be worth something. First Francie had gone crazy over it, and then that man . . .

"Was he really your father?" she asked in wonder.

"Who?" Richard replied.

"That man just now." Richard didn't seem to understand. She repeated herself, slowly. "The one who came in and jumped Francie. The one who said 'hello, son.' "

Richard remembered. "Oh yeah! That's my father."

"And you tried to shoot him?"

Now he didn't seem to hear. Maybe he wasn't all right, Lisa thought. Maybe he was crazy. Lisa knew a lot of crazy people. Some of her clients—that fat fuck an hour ago, for example. Her father was a flake. Her stepfather Jack wasn't really crazy, he was just a prick, but Leo was bananas. Richard fit right in.

She shifted the jacket to her other hand. It seemed three, maybe four pounds heavier than it should have weighed. Good coke went for a hundred bucks a *gram*. She couldn't begin to do the arithmetic. What did her horoscope say for today? Something about making new friends. Yeah. "A new friend will bring opportunity."

"Huh!" she said to herself. There really was something to that stuff!

They reached the Frolick Burlesk and she headed Richard up the stairs.

7 **O'HARE** tried to make himself comfortable in Knowles's car. He had moved the driver's seat back and swung the door open, allowing himself all the room he could to stretch out his large body. It was a relief to be off his feet. He drew deeply on his cigarette, filling his lungs with smoke. It tasted good. When he exhaled it made a soft haze over the harsh white light of the garage. This was not going to be a one-pack week.

The car was parked just inside the garage, facing the entrance. From where he sat O'Hare had a full view of Wilhite, sitting in his own double-parked car across the street.

He stared hard at Wilhite's angular profile. He couldn't blame the sergeant for Knowles's getting away. Wilhite had performed expertly, following his man down the turnpike, then radioing O'Hare as he trailed Knowles into Times Square. Wilhite couldn't have known *which* garage Knowles would park at, so it was impossible for O'Hare to have been on the scene to help out when Knowles dropped off the BMW and took off around the corner. Wilhite had rounded the corner in time to see Knowles hopping into a cab, but by the time he found a cab of his own, Knowles was gone.

But O'Hare had hope. If Knowles had been contacted by his son, and if he thought he had lost his tail up in Rye and was just taking normal precautions here in the city, and if he was now successful in retrieving the cocaine, and if he then felt safe enough to bring it back to the car . . .

Those were a lot of ifs.

He stretched back and lit another cigarette, then turned the ignition key. He switched on the radio and fiddled with the dial until he found some soft rock music. Soothing, he thought. He never could get into that heavy metal stuff that Pat liked so much . . .

He sat up abruptly. He had caught a movement from across the street—Wilhite's head jerking forward—and now turning in his direction, nodding quickly. O'Hare put out the cigarette and switched off the radio. The next moment Knowles turned into the garage entrance.

"My, my," O'Hare said to himself, pleasantly surprised.

Knowles was a mess. He had obviously been in a fight. His clothes were ripped, his face scratched and bleeding. He looked like he had spent ten minutes in a sack with a dozen cats. But his principal wound seemed to be on his hand, which was wrapped in a blood-soaked handkerchief.

He stepped out of the car. Knowles casually walked toward him, showing no surprise.

"Hello, Lieutenant," Knowles said.

O'Hare matched the even tone. "Good evening, Mr. Knowles. You've had some trouble, I see."

"The streets of this city, Lieutenant . . ." Knowles shook his head unhappily. "Two kids jumped me. Punks. I managed to fight them off. You know, you can never find a cop when you need one."

O'Hare was not amused. "But what are you doing here? I thought you'd be at home, waiting for your son to call."

"I ran out of cigarettes."

O'Hare kept a stony face. The cat-and-mouse game was wearing thin. Knowles had no energy for it, now, and neither did he. He returned Knowles's stare with open hostility.

"But imagine my surprise seeing *you* here!" Knowles pressed.

"We found the car," O'Hare replied. "The one your boy stole. It was parked crosstown. He must have come through the tunnel, then abandoned it."

"If Richie *was* the one who commandeered that car."

"Yes, well we're checking it for fingerprints, which we'll compare with prints taken from his room at school."

"Very thorough, Lieutenant," Knowles sighed. "Is there anything else?" He held his bloodied hand and winced. O'Hare was happy to keep him in pain a little longer.

"As a matter of fact, there is." He paused for a brief second, intentionally marking his words. "It seems that the customs agent who was examining your boy, before he ran away, found some cocaine."

"Cocaine?" Steve Knowles repeated with a slight inflection of surprise.

"You've heard of the stuff, Mr. Knowles? A white powder? Derivative of the coca plant grown in South America? It seems that a stewardess who had become friendly with Richard on the flight saw him at customs and gave him a souvenir pin. A set of wings. She was pinning it to his jacket when—lo and behold—cocaine trickled out. That would explain the boy's running away, don't you think?"

Steve Knowles's face was void of expression. "That's quite an accusation, Lieutenant," he said.

"I'm not making an accusation, Mr. Knowles. I'm just giving you some facts."

"Facts?" Knowles couldn't keep a note of irritation out of his voice. "You call those facts?"

"I have the agent's statement."

"But do you have any proof? Do you have a sample of the substance?"

O'Hare breathed deeply. He would have loved finishing the job on Steve Knowles's face that some well-intentioned citizen had begun. "No, I guess we don't, Mr. Knowles. But I'm sure you can understand why I'm more interested than ever in finding your boy, and clearing up this mystery."

"Mystery?" Knowles affected surprise. He spoke with the serenity of a monk. "Surely, Lieutenant, you don't suspect me of using my own child to smuggle drugs."

O'Hare wanted to hit something. The violent impulse within him was becoming irresistible. "Of course not, Mr. Knowles," he replied evenly. "Why, a man who did that would hardly be human at all. He would be beneath contempt."

A flush of anger spread across Steve Knowles's face and a vein pulsed in his neck. O'Hare prayed the man would take a swing. Just one. Instead Knowles took a breath and regained his composure.

"Nice running into you, Lieutenant. You can tell your friend outside that he doesn't have to bother following me anymore. I'm going home now. He can meet me there if he wants."

He moved to the BMW. Making an elaborate show of his displeasure, he opened the windows and readjusted the seat.

"And if you're going to use my car, Lieutenant, please don't smoke."

O'Hare stood in the garage and watched Knowles ease into the street, giving Wilhite a friendly wave before driving off. There was nothing O'Hare could do but swallow his rage. And light another cigarette.

There was nothing more boring than watching an empty house, Leverton decided. With Knowles inside at least she'd had a role as a decoy. But her job now was insurance work. She would only be useful if Knowles hadn't picked up the coke and returned home, or if, miraculously, the boy showed up here with the jacket, or if Wilhite lost Knowles and Knowles did get the stuff and was stupid enough to come back here. . . .

This time she had made an effort to conceal the car. She was parked on a dark side street, a hundred feet in, diagonally across from the house. If Knowles did show up, there was a good chance he would miss her.

She slipped a new tape into her Walkman and turned up the sound. The explosion of music in her head filled the empty spaces, driving out all conscious thought. She didn't even want to listen to the words anymore. All her life she had tried to understand the words and look where that had got her! Better to just relax and enjoy the beat.

A white Lincoln Continental drove by on the main street. It slowed down in front of Knowles's house, then continued on. Three minutes later it drove by again.

Leverton slipped off the earphones and watched more closely.

The Lincoln pulled into the side street directly across from Knowles's house and parked. A moment later two men got out, one huge man carrying a suitcase, the other short and square. They didn't bother with the front door of the house, but went directly into the backyard.

Leverton got out of her car and quickly crossed the intersection, her hand instinctively checking for the gun at her hip. Cautiously, she made her way around the house until she could see into the backyard. A flashlight was gleaming by the side of the house. The big man was bending over a suitcase. Then he straightened up and she heard the soft whir of a motor, followed by the whine of saw teeth biting wood.

She watched in amazement. They were sawing into the house!

They finished in a few minutes and vanished. She waited a full five minutes, then crept up to where they were working and found a three-foot-square hole cut in the wall. There was neither light nor sound within. Leverton crouched beside the new entrance. A battery pack and circular saw rested at her feet.

Some friends Steve Knowles has, she thought. The doors are locked and the windows are wired—so they come in through the walls! Life was simple for the bad guys.

She thought she heard a car pull up in front of the house. She focused her attention and heard the unmistakable slam of a car door. Then—through the hole—sounds from within. The turning of a lock . . . the opening of the front door . . . a rustle of footsteps.

To hear better she leaned into the hole and found herself with her head in Steve Knowles's kitchen. It was dark, but she could make out the sink and refrigerator. Across the room was a half-open door that led, she supposed, to the livingroom. Through it she saw a sudden glow of light. Then a gravelly voice spoke.

"Hello, Steven."

Her own heart was pounding. She waited for what seemed like minutes, half in the house, half out.

"Hello," a second, hesitant voice replied. "I wasn't expecting you until tomorrow." Leverton strained a little, wishing she could turn up the sound another notch.

"The idea is, Steven," the gravelly voice said, "that you don't expect us at all."

Silence. Leverton tried to picture the scene. The intruders were probably sitting, comfortably, with guns drawn. Knowles would be standing in front of them, defenseless, his pulse racing, his mind churning furiously, examining the possibilities of escape.

"Sorry, I was out. I was trying to track down the stuff. As you can see, I had a bit of trouble."

No answer.

"I'm sure I'll have it by tomorrow."

More silence. Leverton could feel the fear in Knowles.

"Can I offer you gentlemen a drink?"

Despite the fear he sounded cool, almost casual. It was obvious he couldn't fight them—he was trying to talk his way out. Leverton felt an annoying stab of admiration.

"We didn't come for a drink, Steven," the gravelly voice rasped.

"Mr. Casper, you know what happened at the airport . . ."

The voice cut him off. "I know what happened, Steven, that's not my concern. My concern is that you pay your debt."

"If you hurt me, Mr. Casper, it won't help get your stuff back. We're on the same side—"

"You're not on any side, asshole!" Casper interrupted, furiously. "You're playing some kind of stupid middle! You think I'm a moron?"

Knowles didn't have time to answer. There were quick steps. A loud grunt. Leverton leaned in further and heard the dull thud of metal against flesh. She found her hand gripping the rough edge of the hole in excitement. Knowles was getting exactly what he deserved. But she also felt a touch of pity. He had stood against them well. He had shown courage.

There was a flurry of noise and movement in the livingroom now, and Leverton had to move fast. She quickly crawled out of the hole and ran through the backyard to behind a hedge, where she could watch safely. After a few minutes the visitors emerged. The large, hulking man repacked the saw and battery pack into the suitcase, and then, like two businessmen checking out of a motel early, they left.

She took the number of the Lincoln as it drove off, then went back to the hole to listen. There was no sound from within. With her gun in one hand, she crawled in through the hole. Casper and his friend had left the lights on, and she could easily see her way. It was a dull, suburban house filled with dull, suburban things. A microwave oven.

An open box of chocolate-chip cookies. Magnets on the refrigerator shaped like little slices of fruit.

She walked cautiously into the livingroom.

Thick, beige carpet. A glass-and-chrome coffee table. A couch and two easy chairs covered in crushed, red velvet.

It was all wrong, she thought. This was a house made for dull, ordinary traumas—delinquincy, adultery, divorce. This was not a house in which drug dealers waged war.

She found Knowles lying by the side of the couch, on his back, unconscious. She knelt next to him and put a hand to his throat. His breath was shallow but his pulse firm. Beneath the scratches on his face she could see he was good-looking—dark and slender with fine, chiseled features. His lips formed a half-smile as though he was dreaming a pleasant dream. His body was bent in a way that indicated broken bones on the left side.

She moved to the phone to call the hospital and heard the sound of a motor outside. She darted to the window. An ambulance had pulled up. For a moment, she didn't understand, and then she did. Knowles's guests must have called the hospital before they left.

"Nice people," she murmured, and noticed the front door had been left slightly open to allow the medics in. "Real thoughtful." She quickly retraced her steps—into the kitchen and through the hole, into the backyard.

This certainly changed things, she said to herself as she took a wide detour back to her car. Knowles would be in the hospital for a few days. She could join O'Hare and Wilhite, looking for the boy. She could zero in on Mr. Nice Guy—Casper. But they were the sideshow, really. Steve Knowles was at the center of this case. Steve Knowles was the one they wanted to get.

She sat in her car and watched the ambulance take Knowles away. There had to be some useful angle here, she decided. She just had to be clever enough to find it.

8

F R O L I C K BURLESK.

The lightbulb letters blinked at Richard.

INGA! the marquee said, YOU SAW HER IN HUSTLER! NOW SEE HER IN THE FLESH!

He followed Lisa up a flight of stairs that led to a desk. A sign said "Be 18 or Be Gone." Another read "$10—No Refunds." Behind the desk sat a sour old man copying figures into a ledger. Frank Perdue, Richard thought. When he saw Lisa, the man's hangdog eyes brightened happily, but then, seeming to catch himself, he changed them into a harsh, critical stare.

"Well, hallelujah!" Frank Perdue cried. "If it isn't Princess Di favorin' us with a royal visit. To what do I owe the honor, your highness?"

"Okay, Sid, I'm sorry," Lisa began.

"She's sorry!" the chicken salesman wailed to the ceiling. "The whole world is bustin' my chops! My rent is goin' up five hunnert next month. The cops want a hunnert-fifty a week. The cash-register broad pockets half the take like she was my partner! And now Princess Di waltzes in after disappearin' for a month and says she's sorry!"

"Don't pay any attention," Lisa murmured to Richard, during the harangue. "He's really very sweet."

"Listen, Sid," she said, after he ran out of breath, "I need a favor. I need a place to stay tonight."

"Oh!" Sid nodded his head vigorously. "She needs a favor. *She* walks in and out of this joint like I had a revolvin' door and *I* got to do *her* a favor!"

"Sid, please . . ."

"I thought you was with the dwarf."

"Leo and I haven't been doing well lately. He's getting rough." She touched a black-and-blue mark on her arm.

This time the chicken man exploded. "You see? What did I tell you? You lose that scum, Lisa! You stay a whore and one of these days you're gonna wake up dead!"

"Shit for brains," he complained to Richard. "She starts off here like she was God's gift to man. She burnt down the joint! She did better on tips than I did runnin' the place. And then what happens?" He turned to Lisa with both arms outstretched. "You tell me! You start dancin' like a fuckin' ballerina. You stop workin' for tips. You go back to that scumbag dwarf!"

"Okay, Sid, I made a mistake."

"Terrific! She made a mistake!" Richard watched the man melt. It was easy to see that he really liked Lisa, that the anger was just for show. "And now she wants a favor from me. How come I'm so lucky?"

"Because you're cute, Sid," Lisa answered. "You know I always thought you were cute." She wore a smile Richard hadn't seen before—pouty little-girl lips. She leaned across the counter and trailed a finger up Sid's bare arm. Sid pretended annoyance and brushed her hand away, but he couldn't help an embarrassed laugh.

"Then you ain't going back to Leo?" he asked with as much brusqueness as he could muster.

"No way, Sid. That's why I need a place tonight."

Sid considered this for a moment, then looked at Richard. "Who's he?"

"My cousin," Lisa confided. "His father and my mother are brother and sister. He just ran away from home. Tuscaloosa. He came to New York to see me. I can't take him to the Bo-Mond . . ."

"Jesus!" the chicken man moaned, but Richard was impressed. He had to work hard at his stories. Lisa lied as

65

naturally as she breathed. She leaned over the counter and spoke in a loud whisper.

"I'm trying to talk him into going back, Sid. If I can be alone with him tonight I think I can do it. Can we stay here? Please?"

He gave her an icy stare. "You gonna work tomorrow?"

"Seven shifts," Lisa promised.

"All week?"

"All month, Sid. Cross my heart and hope to die."

"An' no tap dancin' up there like you was fuckin' Ginger Rogers? You gonna put some pussy in your work?"

"You just watch me." She pouted at him again, and trailed her tongue across her upper lip.

"Jesus," Sid sighed once more, and fumbled with a keychain that he wore on his belt.

"Fuckin' broads!" Richard heard him mutter as he unlocked the theater door. "I swear I'm gonna turn this place into a gay joint. I'll make twice the money and I won't have to deal with broads."

Richard walked slowly through the dark. Ahead, somewhere, Lisa was looking for a light.

"Just a sec!" she called out, and then a light came on—a naked pink bulb shining in a corner of the stage, and he looked around. The theater was nothing more than a large room with maybe a hundred seats and a wide stage shaped like a "T", dividing the audience into two sections. In the center of the stage was a couch. He watched Lisa put his jacket down on it, then remove her own jacket and take Leo's gun out of her pants.

She thumbed open the chamber. "Stupid thing isn't even loaded!" she grumbled, and disappeared into the wings.

Richard climbed up onto the stage after her. He passed several small dressingrooms, then found Lisa in a large, walk-in closet. It was a small room, really, filled with rows of chiffon gowns, bikini tops, panties, two long whips, a Wonder Woman cape, a five-foot velvet snake, and a rubber mask of a woman's face that looked familiar, though he couldn't recall from where.

In the back of the closet Lisa was struggling with a double mattress. He helped her with one end, and together they walked it over to the stage. Then they went back for sheets, blankets, and pillows.

"There!" Lisa said as they dumped the bedding on the mattress. "How's that?"

"Great!" Richard sat on the couch. A bone-crunching weariness came over him and his eyes began to close. Lisa fitted a sheet to the mattress.

"We'll be safe here for tonight," she said.

From under heavy lids he studied the shape of her shoulders, the way her rib cage narrowed into her waist, the curve of her buttocks. . . . "Listen, I'm sorry about what I called you before," he offered.

"What was that?"

"Back in the hotel. I called you a cheap hooker."

"Oh yeah. Thanks for reminding me."

"I just want you to know I'm sorry."

"Forget it."

"And thanks for helping me get the stuff back." His hand rested on the jacket. Now that he knew what was inside he could easily make out the thick, sausage-shaped bags.

"No sweat." She finished with the bottom sheet and stood up. "You hungry?"

"No, I had a big dinner."

She disappeared again, offstage. Richard closed his eyes and a sense of how unreal his life had become overwhelmed him. He thought of the events of the last eight hours and wondered if maybe he was being used by an alien intelligence in some sort of test. Or for entertainment. Maybe visitors from Andromeda took Earthlings out of their normal lives and put them into bizarre situations that served as movies, or plays, or TV shows. For all he knew, all life on this world might be nothing more than a TV show for some superhuman race. . . .

He felt the couch move. Lisa was back, with a jar of peanut butter, and had plunked herself down beside him. "You want to tell me about it?" she asked, poking a finger into the jar.

"Tell you about what?"

"That." She pointed a peanut-buttery finger at the jacket.

"There's nothing to tell."

Richard closed his eyes again. The smell of the peanut butter brought back lunches with his father when they lived in New York, happy afternoons at Yankee Stadium, Sundays fishing off Sheepshead Bay. He heard Lisa's voice in the distance.

"I know what you need."

The couch moved again and the next thing he felt was her hand shaking his shoulder.

"Come on, this will wake you up."

He opened his eyes. She had moved a small table in front of them, and on the table was a mirror. And on the mirror were several lines of cocaine.

"Lisa!"

One of the plastic bags was out of the jacket lining, its top carefully opened. He was fully awake now.

"I just thought we should taste the stuff," she said. "Just to see how good it is." She held a cutdown straw.

"We shouldn't," Richard insisted. "It's not mine."

"Then whose is it?"

His mind was fuzzy. He couldn't focus on the question. He decided he must be overtired. "Okay," he finally said, "but just a little."

Lisa lowered her face and put the straw to one nostril. She breathed in and one line of the powder was gone. Then she put the straw to the other nostril and repeated the process. When she raised her head, her eyes looked like emerald saucers.

"Where did you get this stuff!" she gasped, and without waiting for an answer, held out the straw. "It's pure rock! You've got to do some!"

Richard fought down his panic. At school, all he had ever tried was booze and a little pot. And that was with Paul. Since he didn't even like the other boys he had never been offered anything harder, though he did think, under the right circumstances, he wouldn't mind trying just a little coke, just once.

Lisa was waiting expectantly. As she leaned forward with the straw, her breast pressed against his arm. Circumstances would never be more right. With a quickening pulse he took the straw, mimicked the ritual she had just performed, and quickly snorted two lines.

The effect was instantaneous—not at all like pot, which, if he could keep the smoke down long enough, made him a little silly—and definitely not like alcohol, which did make him high, and then sick. The cocaine thumped down with the force of a piledriver! A thousand small explosions went off in his head! His heart pounded as though he were kicking for the tape in a hundred-yard dash, and he began perspiring freely. Then a sinus behind his eyes started to swell, and he felt an uncomfortable postnasal drip.

"Like it?" Lisa asked.

He wanted to shake his head no, but was afraid it might fall off and bounce against every wall in the room.

"You sure don't look tired anymore," she grinned.

Richard tried to swallow and a bitter alkaloid taste slid down the back of his throat.

"Are you okay?" She sounded a little worried.

"Fine." He held his head very still. The photons in his brain began to fade.

"Richard, this stuff is dynamite! Where did you get it?"

"It was in my jacket. I flew up from South America this afternoon. They found it when I got to customs." He wasn't sure why he was telling the story, but the sound of his voice, recounting the day's events, felt reassuring.

"You smuggled it in?" Lisa was incredulous—also impressed, Richard could see.

"Not exactly." She looked at him oddly. "I mean, yes, I guess I did, but I didn't know it was there." She didn't understand. "Someone gave me the jacket."

"Who?"

"Nancy Reagan!"

He had just remembered the face on the rubber mask in the closet. But what, he wondered, was a mask of Nancy Reagan doing in a burlesque house?

"Richard . . . !"

"You should have seen me get out of that terminal! I must have done the hundred in ten seconds flat!" He wanted to see that impressed look again, but this time there was no response.

"Then I stole a car!" That got a reaction. Her eyes opened into wide circles.

"You stole a car?"

"It would have been easier if I knew how to drive. I went out a few times with my friend Paul in his car, on the back roads near school, but I never drove in traffic before. It was sort of like bumper cars."

Her voice came from far away and he couldn't quite make out what she was saying because he was hypnotized by the pink light bulb. It lit the theater like a red giant star, expanding into its solar system, casting a brilliant glow as it devoured its planets. . . .

"Richard!"

"Huh?"

"I asked who gave you the jacket?"

"Oh, my father," he said easily. "He gave it to me as a present. We were in Bogota for a week. I was on my spring break."

"Jesus!" She seemed angry for some reason. "Then he's the one who put the coke in it!"

He laughed at the thought. "Oh, no. I'm sure he didn't even know it was there."

"Richard, in the hotel just now you tried to shoot him because he wanted to take the jacket. He must have known about the cocaine."

He was laughing and then, suddenly, he was trembling with anger. "You shut the fuck up!" he yelled.

Lisa recoiled on the couch, frightened.

"What do you know about it? You weren't in Colombia! You don't even know my father! You don't know anything!" For a moment he thought he was going to hit her. He had never hit a girl in his life and the impulse left him shaking.

"Okay, okay, if you say so." Her palms were up in mock surrender.

"Well, I say so!"

He had to move. He had to do something to hold down the anxiety building in his chest. He jumped off the stage and nervously paced around the theater. From a window he could see the street below. A man was walking along the curb, trying the handle of every parked car. Lisa came over, not too close, but near enough to talk.

"Fathers can be real pricks," she said. He knew she was just trying to be nice, but for some reason that only made him angrier. "Mine split from me and my mom last year . . ."

"Is that why you became a hooker?" He knew the words would hurt her, and then felt miserable when they did.

"I'm not a hooker," she answered evenly. "I'm a dancer. I told you that."

"Sure. That's what you were doing with that fat guy in the hotel room. Dancing!" He didn't even mean to say that. It just came out.

Lisa trembled with hurt. "Why don't you just fucking go? You don't have to stay here! Why don't you just get out!"

Her voice was quivering and her hands were clenched into little white fists. She looked about to cry, but instead climbed onto the stage and vanished into the wings. The sound of a slamming door echoed through the theater.

Richard was numb again. It was uncomfortable, but better than the anxiety he'd just felt. He carefully closed the plastic bag of cocaine, replaced it in the lining, and put on the jacket.

His steps felt leaden as he walked down the stairs. The theater lights were off now. The sidewalk was dark and deserted. He looked uptown and then downtown, wondering which way to go. The cops were after him, and his father, and that hotel clerk. Lisa hated him. He practically didn't have a friend in the world. . . .

He sat down in a doorway next to the theater, too depressed to even cry.

"Hey, what are you doing?"

It was Lisa, shouting from a window above.

"It's two o'clock in the goddamn morning!"

He looked up at her and shrugged. He had no idea what he was doing.

"Well, come on back!" she said. "Come on!"

He reclimbed the stairs thinking that if an alien spaceship landed in Times Square tonight he would happily go aboard. Life on another planet couldn't be any more difficult than this.

"I didn't mean you should go right now!" Lisa said with exasperation, but also with relief. "What were you going to do? Walk the streets all night? You can leave tomorrow, if you want."

Richard stared at her. She looked different, somehow. She had washed off her makeup. Her cheeks were rounder, her lips softer. Her eyes looked a hundred years younger.

"You want to get some sleep?"

He nodded. Sleep was a good idea. He would be able to think things out more clearly in the morning. They didn't speak as Lisa finished making up the mattress.

"You take this side," she said, "so I don't have to climb over you if I have to pee in the middle of the night."

Richard gulped as he understood the sleeping arrangement. "Oh sure. That's fine." He edged toward the couch. "Or I could sleep here," he suggested. "If you want, that is. I mean, if you don't mind."

She was looking at him curiously.

"What I mean is, I thrash around a lot, you know? I'm not used to sleeping next to another person, or anything."

"I don't have AIDS, you know." She was very serious, suddenly. "I make all my dates wear a rubber, and besides, Sid won't let us work here if we don't get checked out regularly."

He forced a laugh. "Oh, it's not that!" The laugh seemed convincing, so he did it again. "It's just that you'd be more comfortable if I slept here. We'd both sleep better. God, I'm exhausted!" He opened his mouth in a wide yawn and avoided meeting her eyes. She had to think he was some sort of weirdo.

She shrugged. "Well, suit yourself. Here, take a blanket and sheet."

As Richard made up the couch, he tried to reason it out. Under normal circumstances he would have run a marathon for a chance to crawl into bed with this girl. But these weren't normal circumstances. How could he be expected to think about sex when he was wanted by the police, and was carrying around a few pounds of cocaine, and had been shot at in a hotel room . . . ?

She was pulling off her jeans. Her thighs looked like hard rubber. He felt a warm stirring inside and tried for some casual conversation.

"So you dance here, huh?" His voice cracked as he spoke.

"Yeah."

"What sort of dancing do you do?"

"It's a little-girl number, you know? Mary janes, pigtails, a pink party dress. When I bend over to pick up my lollypop, and they see I'm not wearing any panties, I can hear them practically coming in their pants."

Richard cleared his throat and nodded. This conversation wasn't exactly what he'd had in mind.

"What is it with men?" Lisa asked, angrily fluffing up her pillow. "I mean, I'm fifteen fucking years old and they want me to be ten!"

"You're fifteen?" Richard was shocked. He'd thought she was at least sixteen, or seventeen.

"Shit!" She pummeled the pillow with her little fist. "Well, how old are you?" she demanded.

"I'm fifteen too!"

"Oh yeah? When will you be sixteen?"

"In July."

"Well I'll be sixteen in June! I'm older!"

Richard didn't want to get into another argument. "So who cares?" he said. "It's no big deal."

"I never said it was." She smiled sweetly and straightened her blanket. "The mattress is really more comfortable, you know."

"It's okay," Richard murmured.

She got into the roughly made bed. Richard quickly took off his pants and crawled under his blanket, on the couch. It was weird, her being just a few feet away.

"I hope you don't mind the light," she called out. "I like having some light in the room when I sleep."

"It's okay," he said again.

They were both awake. He watched her hug her pillow. He could almost hear her breathe.

"How did you meet Leo?" he asked.

"He picked me up. I had this waitress job when I first got to the City. Leo came in as a customer." She sounded like a little girl now. "He was good to me. He took care of me."

"And you went to work for him?"

Her response was quick and sharp. "Are you starting again?"

"No," he assured her. "I just don't understand."

"What?" She was angry.

"Never mind." He was on dangerous ground, and they had had enough fights already.

"No, go on," she insisted. "What were you going to say?"

"Well . . ." He tried to choose his words carefully this time, "I just don't understand how someone can do it for money with total strangers." He cringed. That wasn't much better. Somehow, he had managed to call her a cheap hooker again.

"Because 'someone' might like it! Okay?" Lisa's voice was raised and tight. "Sex is fun, or don't you think so?"

Richard didn't know what to say.

"What's the matter, don't you like sex?"

"Sure I like it!"

"Hey, are you queer or something?"

Richard was shocked at the question. "No!"

"I was just wondering why you're sleeping over there . . ." Lisa suddenly sat up as though a revelation had come upon her. "You're a virgin!"

"I am not!" Richard shot back.

"Yes you are! You're a fucking virgin!"

He could feel his heart beating. "There's no such thing. It's a contradiction in terms!"

"Don't be a smart-ass. Just answer—are you or aren't you?"

"I'm not!" he shouted. "I've done it lots of time. Sort of."

"Sort of?" Lisa mocked. "What did you do? Put it halfway in?"

He tried to explain. "I go to this boy's school and we don't have much of a chance to meet girls . . ."

Lisa was enjoying herself now. "Shit! You're a virgin and you're hassling me about *my* sex life?"

"I'm not hassling you."

Her eyes shone and a half-smile formed on her lips. "Have you ever seen a girl naked, Richard?"

"Sure," he replied.

"Where? In this boy's school of yours?"

"I've seen tons of girls naked. In *Playboy*, and *Penthouse*."

"Oh, I'm not talking about pictures, Richard. I'm talking about a real, live girl." She stood up on the mattress and basked in the pink light. "You ever see a girl like me naked?" Her voice was suddenly lower, sultry. "Well let me give you a treat, and I won't charge you ten dollars, either."

She stood there, before him, wearing only a T-shirt and panties. She looked directly into his eyes and with one movement jutted out her pelvis and stiffened her arms, straight down. Slowly, she brought her fingers up along the insides of her thighs, drawing a sharp breath at the delicious teasing. She continued the self-caress along the edge of her panties, over her rib cage, and then to her breasts, cupping them through her shirt, holding them out to him.

"Usually I have music for this," she breathed.

Richard watched with fascination. In a matter of seconds he was hard. So much for *that* worry, he thought.

"You like me, Richard?" she murmured. "You like my tits?" With thumb and forefinger of each hand she rubbed her nipples until they poked through the shirt. "They like you!" She moaned as she inched the shirt up her waist, exposing one breast and then the other. "How about coming into my bed, Richard? Just for a few minutes. It's okay if you thrash around."

He couldn't have answered if he had wanted to. His mouth was dry and blood pounded in his ears. Lisa let one hand drift back down her thigh, and then slid a finger under the elastic of her panties. "Oh Richard, I feel so slippery."

He didn't dare move. The slightest friction would end in a flood. His mouth went dry as she turned and bent to give him a rear view. Slowly, she slid down her panties.

"Would you like to try it this way, Richard? I really like it this way." Her panties were off. She turned and came closer. He could have reached out and touched her.

"Do you like me naked?" she whispered. "Would you like to touch me? Would you like to touch me down there?" Her thighs were inches from his face and her hand traced over her belly, through the silky blond hairs, until she was touching herself.

"Oh Richard!" she cried. Her body trembled with small shudders and her other hand reached out to his crotch and grasped him.

He started to cry out but stopped, his body convulsing. One arm flew across his eyes to block the light and her face. The spasms lasted forever. Then the pressure eased; he removed his arm to see a glow of victory in her face.

"Good night, Richard," she said, and with her lips pursed in a satisfied smile, she quickly slipped under the covers of her bed.

He felt cold, the sort of cold that generated from within, as though a powerful refrigerator had been planted in his chest. He wrapped himself tightly in his blanket, trying to stop the shivering.

So many feelings had passed through him—fascination, annoyance, arousal, and now an awful sadness. What was wrong? She was a *Penthouse* letter come to life. How could it be so exhilarating and so depressing at the same time? He usually felt so relaxed after coming. It usually put him right to sleep. Now he just felt cold and unhappy.

His teeth were chattering. He curled his legs to his chest for greater warmth. And then, suddenly, he was crying. He couldn't stop his tears—he couldn't even muffle the sound.

"Richard, are you all right?"

He couldn't answer, but turned to the back of the couch and made himself into a tight ball. He was startled to feel her hand on his shoulder.

"I'm sorry," she said softly.

His chest heaved, but he managed to quiet the sobs. "Go away!"

"You're freezing!"

She lay next to him and molded herself to the curve of his back. She was warm. Slowly, his shaking stopped.

"I didn't mean to upset you," she whispered.

For a moment they just lay there—silent. Then he felt her gently pull at the blanket. She crawled underneath, and adjusted the pillow to make a place for her head as she snuggled against him.

"This is nice," she whispered happily. "Feel better?"

Richard didn't know how he felt. He had never slept with anyone before. He couldn't even remember being held. His mother was gone before he was a year old, and

Steve never held him. He remembered a story in a magazine about a boy who was born with no natural immunities in his system. He couldn't fight germs. If he caught a cold he would die. So they put him in a plastic bubble where he lived his life. Richard thought of that boy often after reading the story. Sometimes he wished he could be in a bubble, and not have to deal with people.

But now he just felt sorry for that boy. It was nice having Lisa's arms around him, hearing her rhythmic breathing in his ear, feeling her warmth. . . .

9

O'HARE awoke abruptly in a cold sweat. He had just had another nightmare, but couldn't remember anything about it—another one of those blank, anxious dreams that had plagued him for the past year.

He stripped off his soaked undershirt and used the blanket to rub himself dry. His head was throbbing. What had he done last night to earn this hangover? he wondered, and dug his thumbs into his temples to relieve the pressure. Slowly, the memories came back. Steve Knowles in the garage—his own fury as he returned home—and finally downing two red sleeping pills with a tumbler of bourbon in order to get to sleep.

Yeah, he had earned the hangover all right.

It was eight o'clock. He put a cigarette in his mouth and stood up in the small room that some slumlord had the nerve to call an efficiency apartment. Cell was more like it, he thought. A bed at one end and a kitchen table at the other, with a chair and TV in the middle to give the illusion of a livingroom.

He stumbled around, looking for matches, finally discovering a book on the kitchen table next to a plate encrusted with food from dinner two nights ago. He lit the cigarette and inhaled deeply. It eased the pain in his head, but his mouth tasted like garbage.

"Another damn crutch," he muttered aloud, and plodded to the kitchen sink where he turned on the tap.

"Fucking crutches!"

He remembered the weeks following Pat's death—the Valium, the alcohol, and those little red beauties that put him to sleep. Pretty soon he couldn't feel the pain. Finally he threw them all away. The pain was better.

"Fucking cigarettes!"

He took it out of his mouth and doused the ember.

"Fucking brown water . . ."

He began brushing his teeth over a pile of dirty plastic dishes and stained cups, careful to rinse only and not swallow, and felt a wave of revulsion.

"No more!" he cried angrily. He reached into the cabinet above the sink and grabbed the plastic container of pills. They rattled as they disappeared down the drain. The bottle of bourbon was already empty; all he could do was slam it into the garbage bag. Back at the nightstand, he emptied the pack of cigarettes into his hand and crumpled the tobacco and paper into a tight ball.

His chest was heaving and he sat heavily on the bed. Directly in front of him was the pad by the phone. On it, to his surprise, were four scribbled words: "Casper— Westchester Genl Hosp." He read them again.

A phone call . . . he dimly remembered. From Anne. The ringing had woken him from his drugged sleep. He closed his eyes to concentrate. She had reported that Steve Knowles was in the hospital. Two of his business associates had beaten him senseless.

He sat for a moment, digesting the information. Then, feeling a surge of anger he didn't understand, he grabbed a towel and stomped down the hall to the bathroom. Why should he be angry that that slimy bastard Knowles had been put into the hospital by his colleagues? Not only was the news personally satisfying, but with Knowles out of the way it gave them a better chance of finding Richard first. No, it was something else that was bothering him, something Anne had said. . . .

He winced as the memory surfaced. She wanted to go

undercover. She wanted to infiltrate Knowles's life—just in case he found the boy first. O'Hare groaned out loud when he remembered that in his drugged state he had given his okay.

He stepped into the bathroom and turned on the light. A three-inch cockroach was sitting in the tub. It froze for a second and then tried to scurry away, but O'Hare was too fast. His fist smashed down, twice, crushing its shell into a pulp. Then, his heart pounding with rage and disgust, he turned on the rusty water and washed the mess down the drain.

Westchester General was a modern building with airy, sun-lit rooms. Nothing like the dismal, overcrowded city hospitals O'Hare was used to. It felt rich—a place where people paid a few hundred bucks a day and actually expected to get better—the same people who then turned around and told you that money couldn't buy health.

"Steve Knowles," he inquired flatly at the information desk, and then stalked through the corridors, looking for the room.

The door was open. Knowles was lying in bed with an intravenous tube attached to one arm and a plastic cast on the other. His face was taut with pain. O'Hare's anger faded. The man had received a dose of raw justice, and justice made O'Hare feel good.

"Lieutenant!" Steve Knowles exclaimed in a strained voice. "So nice to see you again."

"Nice to see you," O'Hare replied politely. "I guess yesterday just wasn't your day."

"You won't believe it, Lieutenant." Knowles was trying to keep his tone light. "I know you'd like to hear some melodramatic story about a couple of Mafia goons busting me up because I lost their cocaine . . ."

O'Hare had to contain his surprise. Even beaten and hooked up to a hospital bed, the son-of-a-bitch hadn't lost his nerve.

". . . but the truth is, I missed a step on the stairs of my house, took a fall, and cracked my arm. I guess I was still dizzy from being attacked by those two punks."

"You're right," O'Hare admitted, shaking his head. "I would never have believed it."

Knowles almost smiled. "Any word of Richard?"

"Nothing yet. I'm counting on your getting back on your feet so you can help us find him."

"I know you are, Lieutenant," Knowles answered in a voice filled with sincerity. "And I'll be out of here and on the job as soon as possible."

O'Hare sighed. It was all so polite, while somewhere in that midtown snake pit a fifteen-year-old kid was on the run.

O'Hare started.

Leverton entered the room with a breakfast tray. She wore white stockings and a thin white dress, and moved with the brisk efficiency of an experienced nurse.

"And how are we this morning?" she chirped, flashing a bright smile at her patient. She barely glanced at O'Hare.

He got to his feet—too abruptly, he thought—then, feeling slightly dizzy, he tried to move casually toward the door. "You be careful on those stairs," he called back to Knowles. "More accidents take place in the home than anywhere else."

Outside, he rested against the wall of the corridor. It was a stupid thing to say, but it had got him out of the room. He reached for a pack of cigarettes that wasn't there. The dizziness passed and he wondered, for the first time, if maybe it was also a stupid thing to do—getting himself and Anne involved in this case.

She poured some water into a paper cup and presented two pills to her patient. "Here, these will help you sleep."

"But I don't want to sleep, Nurse Mary." Knowles read her name off the tag on her breast pocket.

"It's the best thing for you, Mr. Knowles. You didn't get much rest last night." She smiled warmly; Knowles patted the side of his bed.

"Sit down for a minute, Mary. Please."

Leverton considered the offer, then sat in the chair next to the bed and crossed her legs. She tried to appear unaware of the length of thigh that showed above her stockings. Knowles took it in immediately and she caught a hint of a smile. Without any preamble, he made his pitch.

"I have to get out of here, Mary, and I want your help."

She shook her head. "Mr. Knowles, you have a broken arm."

"And the doctors have done everything they can. All I need now is rest."

"And professional attention," she added.

Knowles had his answer ready. "I can rest better at home than here, Mary. And as for professional attention," he looked her straight in the eyes, "I can always hire a nurse for a couple of days."

"I suppose you could, Mr. Knowles." She held his stare. The ball was back in his court.

"Do you take private patients?"

"Sometimes." Her heart was beating rapidly. This crazy scheme was actually working!

"Mary, I have an important business deal in the works and it requires my constant attention. It's worth quite a few thousand dollars to me, and if I stay in the hospital I may blow it. If you help me, I'll make it worth your while."

She kept her face expressionless, but rose to close the door. When she returned she sat on the bed, by his side. "And just how will you do that, Mr. Knowles?"

Triumph was written on his face. The only thing left was negotiating the price. "We'll think of something," he said. "Can you take a few sick days?"

"I have a whole week's vacation coming, if I want it."

His look changed and her heart stopped. There was something in his eyes now besides excitement. Suspicion, she decided. It was all too easy. Why was she being so accommodating? What exactly did she want from him? He was shrewd, all right. She had underestimated him.

"Okay, Mary," he said, smiling cautiously, "why don't we start by taking this needle out of my arm."

She began laughing softly.

"What's so funny?"

"Oh . . ." she made her face bright with amusement, "I just find it ironic that you want me to take a needle *out* of your arm."

She went on laughing, biting her lip provocatively. Then she traced a finger along a vein in the crook of his arm that showed a ridge of pinprick scars.

It worked. Knowles burst into laughter. She had given him his missing piece. What she wanted from him now was perfectly clear. Leverton was excited and pleased with herself.

"Careful," she said as she removed the intravenous needle from Steve Knowles's vein. She was speaking to herself as much as to him. She had better be careful if she wanted to gain the trust of this man. She had better be careful, also, for her own safety. It would be dangerous to underestimate Steve Knowles again.

10

"RICHARD, we have to come up with some sort of plan!"

Lisa was getting annoyed. She had said the same thing twice already that morning, and both times he had ignored her. Now they were sitting on a bench in Central Park and again he didn't answer. He just sat in his own world. He was always in his own world.

"Everyone's looking for us," she persisted. "Francie, Leo, now that we took his gun, your old man . . . We can't go back to the Frolick again, and we certainly can't sit here for the rest of our lives."

He just sat there, scrunched down on his spine, with his legs sprawled out and his hands in the pockets of his open jacket. His eyes stared straight ahead, unfocused. The picture on his T-shirt showed a swirl of stars—the universe, it looked like—with an arrow pointing to one dot almost lost among the others. Above the arrow were the words "you are here."

"Earth to Richard," she murmured.

At least it was a nice spring day. She lifted her face to catch the warming rays and wanted to open her own jacket but didn't dare—not with Leo's gun wedged in her pants.

"Huh!" he exclaimed. A man walking a dog was passing their bench.

"What?" Lisa was relieved. At least he was saying *something*.

"You see that dog?" He pointed in front of him. "It knows."

"Knows what?"

"That it's alive. The grass is also alive but doesn't know it."

"Yeah," she said numbly. The boy was looney tunes.

"I'm talking about levels of consciousness, Lisa. The grass is alive but doesn't know it. The dog is alive and does know it!"

"So?"

"So humans are alive, and we know it, but we also *know* we know it. Do you understand?"

"No."

He lapsed into thought and Lisa wondered what they were talking about.

"I wouldn't mind being that dog right now," Richard said softly. "Or maybe even a tree. It would be nice to be a tree. Then I wouldn't even know. I'd just be."

"I'd think your arms would get tired," she offered.

He didn't even smile. He just gave her a funny look and went back to his own world. This was ridiculous, Lisa thought. If he was going to trance-out all the time, and then, when he did come back to life, say he wanted to be a dog or a tree . . .

"Richard, I was saying we have to come up with some plan."

"I heard you!" he snapped angrily. "I'm not deaf!"

"Well, fuck you!" She stood up. "If you want to handle this all by yourself—"

"Lisa, I didn't mean—"

"I'm sorry for intruding into your room last night. I'm sorry for getting your stuff back from Francie, and then hiding you out. I'm sorry for bothering you at all. You can just take care of yourself from now on!" She turned and briskly walked away. A second later he was at her side.

"Lisa, it's not you," he explained unhappily, trotting

to keep up. "I'm just upset about everything. Can't you understand?"

"Sure I can understand." She didn't lose a step. He ran in front of her now, jogging backward.

"I really appreciate your help."

"Sure."

"And I do want to hear your plan."

She stopped, finally, and cried out in frustration. "I don't have a plan! I haven't had a plan since coming to this fucking city! What I said was we *need* a plan!"

"Okay," he agreed quickly, "we need a plan."

Shit! He was looking at her with those large brown eyes that made her think of Bambi. It wasn't easy to be angry with him when he looked like Bambi. "I'm hungry," she finally said. "I say our first plan is we go to the zoo and have a hot dog."

"A natural leader," he replied, and walked next to her just like a little kid, bouncing as he went along.

She didn't talk to him the whole way to the zoo.

Moody bastard, she thought. First he spaces out. Then he wants to be a dog or a tree. Then he's insulting. Then he wants to make up. Well, maybe it was understandable. Last night had been pretty scary, and he was just a kid, and this really was his first day on his own in New York. Lisa could remember her own first days in New York, how scared she was and what she had done. Sleeping on a bench in Central Park the first night—God that was dumb! Waitressing in that coffee shop with the fat Greek's greasy hands under her skirt. Meeting Leo who made her laugh, and then seemed to be the only person in the world who cared. And then starting to work for him . . .

The memories made her uneasy and she pushed them out of her mind. But what she couldn't help thinking about, as they walked through the daffodils and magnolia blossoms, was why she felt so protective of this kid. It was stupid! He certainly wasn't boyfriend material—no chance of that! It had to be because of the cocaine. With all that stuff on him he *needed* protection—for his own good, and for hers too, really. In the plan she was forming—the only idea that made sense—they would sell the stuff and split the take. He had the coke and she had the clients. They were a perfect team. They could make each other rich. That was it! He was half her business partner and half a kid brother. She felt much better now.

At the entrance to the zoo they passed a couple kissing under a tree. The girl was lying on top of the boy and Lisa found herself staring as they walked by.

"Jesus, they're practically doing it!" she whispered. "Right out in public!"

"Yeah. Imagine that!" Richard was pretending to be shocked. "Some people have no shame!"

"Richard!"

He was teasing her. She could tell by that shit-eating grin on his face. She gave him an angry look but couldn't say anything because he was right. Here she was, turning tricks for a living, and shocked to see two kids making out in the park.

But it wasn't the same! She could never make anyone understand. What she did with her clients was nothing to her, nothing personal, anyway. None of them were *boyfriends*. Her major sorrow in the fifteen years and ten months of her life was that she had never had that one special boy that all the songs talked about, that her girlfriends used to giggle over in hushed conversations. Before her father left she hadn't been allowed to date. Until last year she had never even let a boy kiss her, for fear she'd be visited by agents of the devil and carried off to hell. Then, when Jack moved in . . .

Jack!

She shut her eyes and erased all thoughts of him. But she could still see the house in Lancaster, the front porch with the swing and the floorboards half-rotted through, and that damn woodpile next to the porch—that was the most embarrassing thing! All her friends had oil or electric heat and they had that stupid wood stove and lived like hillbillies, practically. Except for some lights, her dad wouldn't allow anything electrical in the house. Conveniences of Satan, he called them. And those statuettes and paintings of Jesus in every room . . . God!

She tried to remember what she had been like then. Her virginity was the big thing, she remembered. Her father used to call it her treasure. Thinking about it now she had to laugh. When she got to New York her treasure lasted about as long as the fifty dollars she had brought with her, and when the Greek took it in the kitchen of the coffee shop that second morning, she didn't feel anything except worry that the potatoes were burning.

Then, of course, came Leo . . .

Sex was work. Lisa understood that now. She had a list of twenty men who would take her to a fancy restaurant and then screw her, and leave her and Leo a hundred dollars richer. But a boyfriend? Not one of them came even close. Who would she choose if she could have anyone in the world? she wondered. Matt Dillon was cute, but he seemed a little dumb. Paul Newman was gorgeous and smart, but much too old. And forget Michael Jackson. She wouldn't go out with anyone who sounded like a girl. . . .

Lisa seemed lost in her thoughts, which was fine with Richard. He had problems of his own to consider. The cocaine in the jacket, for one thing. How did it get there? He tried to think it out logically. Steve gave him the jacket at the hotel in Bogota, which could mean his father knew about the stuff. Lisa certainly thought he did. But if Steve had bought the jacket in a store, how could he have known cocaine was in it? Maybe someone had tricked him. But still he must have known *something*, since he did come to the hotel last night to get it back. . . .

Richard tried to recall the short, violent scene but he couldn't piece it together. He just had pictures—him holding that long-barreled gun, Steve stepping toward him, a ringing in his ears and feeling faint. Last night Lisa said something about his trying to shoot his father, but that was absurd. He would never do a thing like that.

He looked down and saw a hot dog in his hand and wondered how it got there. He took a bite and followed Lisa to a stone step where they sat and watched the seals in their pool. One waddled to the edge of a concrete plat-form and slipped into the water.

"Aren't they beautiful?" She took a bite from her hot dog, then licked the mustard that squirted onto her thumb. "Some day, when I'm rich, I'm going to have a seal coat. Hey," she said, surprised at the thought, "I don't even know your last name! Mine is Frank. Lisa Frank."

"Richard Knowles."

"Pleased to meet you." She held out her hand and they shook. "Look," she appeared embarrassed, "I'd like to apologize about last night."

"For what?" Richard asked.

"You know . . ."

Richard knew. Talking about sex in the dark was hard enough; in the sunlight it was impossible. He traced a finger over a ridge in the concrete step.

"I came on a little strong. I'm sorry."

"Oh that! It was nothing."

"I hope it wasn't *nothing*!" She seemed hurt.

"No, no! I mean there's no need to apologize. It was . . ." he searched for the right words, ". . . a terrific performance."

"Yeah, but I shouldn't have grabbed you."

Richard found the rough grain of the cement fascinating. It went in little whirls, like galaxies or fingerprints. Then he became engrossed in the struggle of an ant carrying a crumb.

"Sometime you'll have to see me do it with music and my costume," Lisa continued.

He shook his head in wonder. "You know, it's amazing how ants can carry ten times their body weight. If I tried to lift even my own weight I'd probably get a hernia." He put out a finger but the ant refused to crawl on it.

Lisa seemed annoyed. She turned away and tossed a bit of hot-dog bun to two pigeons. Richard spoke without looking up.

"Do you really like doing that sort of thing? You know, dancing naked in front of strangers?" He tried hard to achieve a neutral tone. She gave him a quick, penetrating look, but didn't seem to get angry.

"Well, I like dancing," she answered. "And I'm not shy about taking off my clothes in front of people. So I guess I don't mind doing both things together."

"Huh!" Richard nodded his head, trying to show an understanding he didn't feel. When he first went to Pierce he would climb under the covers to change into his pajamas. Even now he felt uncomfortable showering with the other boys, after track.

"I just hate working for tips," she added.

"Working for tips?"

"What Sid wants me to do. It's not dancing. It's just spreading your legs and letting everyone have a look."

"And you don't like that?"

She didn't meet his eyes. "It makes me feel cheap."

And what about turning tricks? Richard was about to say, but he stopped himself. Lisa would just get angry at him again and he still wouldn't understand. At least he had kept his mouth shut this time. That was pretty good.

Lisa sensed the awkwardness. She got up and started to walk out of the zoo; he followed a few feet behind. The sun felt warm. They passed a family tossing Crackerjack to the monkeys in front of a "Please Don't Feed the Animals" sign. They saw a polar bear pacing restlessly by the fence of its enclosure, staring angrily out at a teenage boy who was taunting it by flipping pebbles at its face.

Lisa slowed down and they walked together, by a patch of daffodils. "What are you thinking?" she asked.

An old woman was uprooting the flowers by the handful, making a huge bouquet. Richard looked up and shielded his eyes from the sun. "I was thinking that in five billion years the sun will die and all life on Earth will die with it."

She gave him another funny look and they didn't speak again until they reached the model-boat pond, and the bronze tea party at its north end. As Lisa ran a hand over a three-foot metal mushroom, she asked if he knew who the figures were.

"They're from *Alice in Wonderland*," Richard answered, surprised she didn't know. "Didn't you ever read it?"

She shook her head. "We only had religious books in the house."

He found it hard to believe. He had spent his whole childhood reading. Characters in books were his closest friends. He told Lisa what he could remember of Alice's adventures after falling down the rabbit hole.

"It's a little like your story," he said when he had finished.

"What do you mean?"

"Well, you've sort of fallen down a rabbit hole, too, coming to New York and everything. How long have you been here?"

"Since last September. I ran away just after school started."

"Where are you from?"

"Pennsylvania. Where are you from?"

Richard thought about the question. "Nowhere, really. My father and I lived in a lot of places around the City. Then he bought a house in Rye. Mostly I live in Connecticut now, at school." His story was a bore. Hers was much more interesting. "Didn't your mom try to find you?"

Lisa laughed but there was nothing funny in it. "No, my mother didn't try to find me. She's happy I'm gone."

Richard couldn't understand. "But she must love you."

"Yeah, the way your father loves you."

"And what does that mean?" he wanted to know.

"If your old man had the choice of having you without the jacket, or the jacket without you, which would he choose?"

Richard turned to watch the model boats sailing in the pond. Sometimes he really liked Lisa, but sometimes he just wanted to punch her out. At least this time she realized she was being stupid because when she spoke again her voice was apologetic.

"What about your mother?" she asked.

Richard shrugged. "She left when I was a baby. My father doesn't talk about her. I don't remember anything about her at all."

"Wow," Lisa said.

Richard turned to her, sharply. "Why did you do that, huh? Why did you run away and leave your mother like that?"

"We had a fight!" she snapped back.

"Just one fight? And for that you run away and become . . ." He stopped himself just in time.

"Richard . . . !" she warned. They were in a minefield. One wrong word could trigger an explosion.

"Well, I didn't appreciate that crack about my father!"

"I'm sorry, but it's true."

"Well, what I said is true too. What kind of thing is that to do? Run away just because you had a fight!"

"Well, what about you?" She lowered her voice to a whisper to prevent anyone from overhearing. "You didn't have to run away just because you had some coke in your jacket!"

"I'm wanted by the police!" he whispered back.

"But you didn't do anything. You could just turn yourself in."

"They don't know that," he cried, softly. "I was on that plane alone. They think I smuggled it in!"

"And your father won't speak up and tell the truth?" She had a smug smile on her face.

Richard raised a finger and spoke in a stiff voice. "I've been thinking about that. My father never said he was the one who put the stuff in the jacket. Maybe he didn't know it was there and found out later, and now he's trying to get it back to the owner before I get into trouble."

Lisa nodded her head. "That's great, Richard. That's even better than Alice in Wonderland."

"Well, it could be true! He said he wanted to explain, and I never gave him the chance."

"Yeah, it could be true. And I could be Little Orphan Annie."

"Fuck you!" he said, biting off the words.

"Any time, big boy!" she shot back, putting out her tongue provocatively.

Richard blushed and looked back to the model boats. What seemed like an eternity passed before either of them spoke. Finally she broke the silence.

"We need a plan," she said for the umpteenth time. Richard could only nod his head.

11

I T took forty-five minutes for O'Hare to drive from the hospital to Pierce Academy. It was a bright April day and the Connecticut hills were covered with new grass and budding leaves. Suicide season, O'Hare thought. It used to puzzle him, all those spring suicides, but lately he understood. It was unbearable, feeling hopeless while the world was coming to life.

The headmaster received him immediately. He told O'Hare that Pierce Academy was very concerned about Richard, and would do everything it could to help. O'Hare then spoke to some of Richard's classmates, and visited the boy's room.

It was different from Pat's room, but not by much. Different posters covered the walls—a NASA shot of Saturn, Frank Shorter winning a marathon, Einstein on a bicycle, Bruce Springsteen in concert, an Earth rising over the bleak horizon of the moon. Pat had favored NFL quarterbacks and TV starlets.

He moved into the room and trailed a finger over the titles of the books on Richard's shelves. *The Book of Lists* (Pat had that one), *Dune, The Guinness Book of Records* (that one too), *Foundation and Empire, Continents in Motion, Swinging Sorority Sisters.* He leafed through a stack of magazines—issues of *Scientific American, Penthouse,* the *National Lampoon,* and *Byte.* Richard seemed to be a little more intellectual than Pat, but the pile of dirty laundry in the corner of their rooms could have been interchangeable.

It was noon, time to find a man named Mario Federici. Federici, the headmaster had told him, ran the athletic program and was close to the boy. If anyone knew where Richard might be it would be him.

O'Hare walked to the Federici house, a huge, white Victorian set directly across from the school. He felt a pang as he went through the iron gate. The yard was newly mowed. A flower garden had been planted and the crocuses were already up. An English sheepdog frisked about on the front lawn.

A short, plump, anxious-looking man strode from the house to greet him, while two children curiously peered out through the livingroom window.

"Lieutenant O'Hare, I'm Mario Federici." The man extended his hand.

O'Hare liked him immediately. The handshake was firm and the face showed care. "I hope I'm not taking you away from a class," he said.

"Not at all. It's lunchtime. Why don't we sit out here." Federici took him up to the porch and the faces in the window disappeared. "Have you eaten? Jo made some sandwiches."

"Thanks, I'm fine."

"How about a cold drink?"

O'Hare could see that the man was bursting to ask about Richard, but being a good host came first.

"I can offer iced tea or lemonade."

"A lemonade would be fine," O'Hare replied.

Federici took the dog inside with him and O'Hare had a moment to close his eyes. His house on the Island had been a split-level ranch, and his dog had been a collie, but the rest was about the same. Pat mowed the lawn. Anne took care of the garden. He did most of the rest of the chores. Of course Anne helped when she wasn't on duty, and Pat pitched in when he wasn't busy with football practice, or tinkering under a friend's car, or just doing the teenage work of hanging out and cruising around, which was most of the time. . . .

Federici returned with a tray holding two glasses and a pitcher. He poured the lemonade and came straight to the point. "Richard's in trouble, isn't he?"

O'Hare chose his words with care. "As I told the headmaster, all we know at the moment is that he's missing. Thanks." He accepted his filled glass gratefully.

"Lieutenant, in the past four years Richard has become a part of my family. My oldest, Paul, is his best friend. If anything has happened, we'd like to know."

O'Hare took a long drink. The lemonade was tart, squeezed from real lemons. He wanted to trust this man, but it was a risk. The more people who knew about the cocaine, the more dangerous it was for Richard.

"Richard has run away," he said. "We have reason to believe he's in Manhattan. What I'd like from you, or your son, is any idea of where you think he might have gone—"

Federici blinked, then interrupted. "He's at the Bo-Mond Hotel."

O'Hare looked at the man blankly.

"On Forty-eigth Street off Eighth Avenue. I had dinner with him last night."

O'Hare stared. "Dinner?"

"He called. I met him in the City."

O'Hare felt his face flush. Federici continued.

"He was in a state. Something to do with his father had upset him. He wouldn't come back to school with me, so . . ."

The gym teacher described what he had done, and O'Hare felt his flush deepen. "Damn!" he murmured, and stood up.

Federici got up with him. "I'm sorry, Lieutenant, I thought if I tried to force him to come home he'd just run away later. I didn't know what else to do."

"It's not your fault." O'Hare raged at his own stupidity. He had made one brief call to Pierce last night, learned Richard hadn't shown up, and let it go at that. If he had just sent Wilhite up to the school. If he had uncovered Federici's relationship with the boy . . .

"Can I use your phone?" he asked.

"Sure."

They started for the house. Wilhite was in Times Square checking video arcades and movie theaters. He could be at the Bo-Mond in ten minutes.

"Lieutenant, what's all this about? Please."

O'Hare trusted his instinct. "Richard came back from Colombia yesterday wearing a jacket stuffed with cocaine," he said.

"Cocaine?" Federici's eyes grew round as he quickly worked it out. "Steve Knowles! Jesus, and I phoned him—!"

"You didn't know," O'Hare interrupted. "You did what you thought was best."

In the front hall they were greeted by a beautiful woman with tanned skin and prematurely gray hair. She spoke immediately, with no introduction. "I hate to interrupt, Mario, but this is important."

"My wife, Jo," Federici introduced her. "Honey, this is Lieutenant O'Hare."

O'Hare nodded and saw the children standing in the livingroom. The fifteen-year-old, Paul, had a frightened look on his face. His younger sister stood next to him. She had a struggling two-year-old by the hand. Jo spoke to both her husband and the lieutenant.

"It's Richard," she said. "He just called. He's on the phone."

Federici moved fast for a short, heavy man. When O'Hare caught up with him he had the phone at an angle to his ear, so O'Hare could listen in.

"Richard?" he asked.

"Hi," the boy replied. "I said I'd call so I'm calling." He sounded wary, defensive.

"Good. Thanks. Great to hear from you. Are you okay? Did you reverse the charges?"

"Yeah. Is that okay?"

"Of course. Absolutely. You can always call me collect, you know that."

They were both nervous. O'Hare couldn't do anything about that. He caught Federici's worried look and tried to reassure him. Jo was watching from a few feet away with her arm around Paul. "How're you doing?" Federici went on.

"I'm doing okay."

"Money holding out?"

"Sure, no problem."

"If you need more I'd be happy to come in and meet you . . ."

Another glance at O'Hare who nodded his encouragement. Richard didn't take the bait.

"I'm fine," he insisted.

"You, uh, get hold of your father yet?" Federici asked.

Richard didn't reply immediately. "I haven't tried to reach him," he finally said.

"Oh. I was wondering if you would." The coach sounded almost casual. "I mean, you did tell me you were having a problem with him, and he must be worried . . ."

This time there was a long pause at the other end of the line.

"Richard?" Federici asked, unable to keep the worry out of his voice.

"I'm here," came the sullen reply. "Look, I have to go now—"

O'Hare instinctively squeezed Federici's arm and the coach interrupted. "Richard, I had a visitor today. A detective." He gave a quick, desperate look at O'Hare and shrugged his shoulders. O'Hare shrugged back. "He came to see me about you."

Another pause from Richard. Shock, O'Hare thought. "What did he tell you?" The boy's voice sounded surprisingly calm.

"Everything." Federici sounded calmer too. "This is serious business, Richard. I want to talk to you about it."

"Sure, I'll just sit down with you and the whole police force . . ."

"No, just me!" Federici broke in. "Please . . ."

"There's nothing to talk about!" The words were shouted into the phone. "The cops think I did it! They're going to put me in jail!"

"No, they don't."

"They tried to arrest me at the airport! They thought I smuggled in the stuff!"

"Richard, they don't think you're responsible. They just want to talk to you. The detective is here with me now. His name is Lieutenant O'Hare. We've been talking about you and he's very concerned. Will you talk to him for a minute?"

The pause this time had a different quality to it, and when Richard spoke there was wonder in his voice.

"You followed me!" he exclaimed.

"What?"

"You followed me to the movie theater. You waited outside, then followed me to the hotel and called my father. There's no other way Steve could have found me."

O'Hare took the phone out of Federici's hand.

"Richard, this is Mike O'Hare. Will you do me a favor? Will you listen to me for a few minutes. I just want to tell you a few things about this situation you're in, through no fault of your own. . . ."

He heard a click and his heart sank. The phone in his hand was dead.

12

RICHARD strode down Central Park West in a tight fury. His hands were thrust deep in his pants pockets and he was walking as fast as he could. Mario was the only person he had really trusted. Now he had no one. Well, they could all go fuck themselves, he thought. He didn't need any of them anyway. Not his father, not the school, not even Mario!

"Richard, will you slow down?" Lisa shouted from behind. She was jogging to keep up.

He slowed his pace and began looking inquisitively into the face of each passerby. Humans were so boring. Each wore the standard kit: an oval head covered by a million strands of protein fiber, two optical instruments for sight, two side vents to process sound, another pair of holes centrally located for breathing with one more below, adapted for making sounds and taking in gross, animal food. Such a primitive species. Somewhere in the universe, he knew, there existed a life-form of minds free of bodies, taking nourishment directly from a star, each sharing a consciousness with the rest, living eternally in peace, with perfect trust. . . .

Lisa's voice intruded.

"We have to sell some of the stuff, Richard."

He pretended not to hear.

"All I have left is twenty-one bucks. How much do you have?"

Nothing at all, he said to himself. Just some loose change. He fingered the coins in his pocket.

"Richard, are you listening? We need some money and we need a place to sleep tonight. We have to sell some of the stuff!"

"We can't," he heard himself say.

"Why not?"

"Because it's not mine."

"So what?" She didn't see the point. "It doesn't matter whose it is. We have it!"

Richard felt his head shake no and he began to walk a little faster.

"What are you going to do with it?" She had to run a few steps to catch up. "You're not going to give it back to your old man!"

He was confused. He couldn't logically explain why he didn't want to sell the cocaine, but he didn't. The weighted tubes in his jacket gave him substance. Selling even that little bit to the clerk had lessened him.

"Richard!"

Lisa had stopped. They were at Columbus Circle and Richard realized that if he kept walking she wouldn't follow. He slowed down and came to a halt a few yards away, examining the wares of a pretzel vendor, trying to look as though he didn't care.

"Richard . . ." She was speaking slowly and clearly. He couldn't ignore her now even if he tried. "I'm not going to stay with you if we don't sell some of the stuff."

He felt his pulse racing but managed to keep an unconcerned look.

"I'm serious. We can't live in this city without money. If we don't make some together, I'm going to make some myself."

"How?" he asked bitterly. "By going back to your pimp?"

"Maybe, or by working alone."

"Okay! Go ahead, if you have so little respect for yourself. See if I care!"

Dumb, stupid words! Of course she would go back to hooking. Of course he cared.

"You go to hell!" she answered back, and went to sit by herself on a stone bench. She didn't look at him at all, but took a small makeup kit out of her pocket and began to apply a pink gloss to her lips.

When she looked up it wasn't in his direction, but at a man passing by. He was blond and good-looking, a little like Robert Redford, Richard thought. She smiled at the man and Richard felt a knot in his chest. The man smiled back but kept walking.

Then, a few paces later, he stopped, putting up his foot to retie his shoelace. He casually turned his head to look back at Lisa and this time there was no mistaking the invitation in her smile. Slowly, with a noticeable swagger, he retraced his steps and sat down next to her. He must have said something funny because she laughed, and then touched his hand.

The knot in Richard's chest made it hard to breathe. They stood up and Lisa took the man's arm. Richard found himself running toward them, and shouting as he ran.

"Get your hands off her, you creep!" He pushed and surprisingly Redford fell back. "She's my goddamn sister and she's fifteen years old! You want to go to jail?"

The smile fell from the man's face. His head jerked left and right to see if anyone was watching. Richard felt a surge of power; there was fear in those movie-star eyes.

"I was just talking to her!" the man exclaimed in a high, un-Redford-like voice, and then he spotted an empty taxi. He reached it at a sprint and yanked open the door. A minute later he was out of sight.

Richard's breath was ragged, but the surge inside felt terrific. Then he saw Lisa's smug smile and wasn't sure if he had just won a victory or suffered a defeat. "Just one bag!" he panted. "We'll sell just one bag!"

Her smile broadened as she put her arm through his

and led them toward Eighth Avenue. On the way she explained what they had to do.

"First, we find a head shop and buy some cut, and a few bottles, and a scale, and maybe a screw-on funnel." She was filled with excitement and talking rapidly. "Then we mix the cut and the coke, about half and half, and we sell it for a hundred bucks a gram. That's all there is to it! I've seen Leo do it a hundred times!"

"Head shop? Cut?" he repeated with a sinking feeling.

"A head shop is a store that sells drug stuff," she explained as they came upon one at Fifty-seventh Street. It was a small newspaper and magazine store with marijuana pipes and tiny bottles and other drug supplies kept on a low shelf at the back of the store. "Cut is just a plain white powder that you add to the coke so you have more to sell."

"And who do we sell it to?" He didn't really want to know.

"I have customers. Don't worry about that." Her green eyes sparkled mischievously and Richard wondered how she could be so beautiful and so wicked at the same time.

The stuff came to twenty dollars and change.

"Great," he muttered glumly as they turned up Broadway. "Now we don't have any money at all!"

She threw an arm around his shoulder and whispered in his ear. "By this time tomorrow we'll be stuffing hundred-dollar bills in our shoes!" Then she giggled like a little girl. "Come on, let's go window-shopping to see what we're going to buy!"

By sunset they had seen every shoe store and boutique on Columbus Avenue, and they were tired and hungry. "What we need now is dinner and a place to sleep," Lisa announced.

"Yeah. With sixty cents between us. You have any ideas?"

"You know your problem, Richard? You have no confidence in me." She sounded hurt, and he didn't want to debate the point. They pooled their change. "Come on, let's go shopping."

"Sure, let's go shopping."

Richard quickly learned what Lisa meant by shopping. They made it into a Red Apple just as it was closing, and while he picked out a can of Pepsi she crammed two hard rolls and packets of cheese and salami into her jacket.

"Is that all we're going to buy?" she innocently asked at the checkout counter.

He glared at her and could feel the sweat under his arms. But the checker just looked bored and tired, and as he bought the soda she didn't seem to notice Lisa strutting through with a bulging jacket.

"Are you nuts?" he exploded when they were outside. "For a piece of salami you make us risk a million dollars worth of . . ." he lowered his voice and looked around, nervously. "I could have gone to jail for the rest of the century!"

"Cheese?" she asked sweetly.

His legs felt weak. She peeled off two slices of Velveeta and put them between halves of a roll, then added slices of salami. "Relax," she assured him, "I know what I'm doing."

"I'm glad one of us does."

She handed him his sandwich, then made one for herself. They were walking uptown. "Where are we going?" he wanted to know.

She shrugged. "I don't know. I'll know when we get there."

As good an answer as any, Richard thought. It fit right in with the rest of the day. A clock in front of a bank said nine o'clock. He had been on the run since five the previous afternoon and had no idea of where he was headed. All he knew was that he had to avoid the police, his father, Francie, now Mario . . . and no matter what, hold on to the cocaine.

He looked at Lisa. She seemed so happy; she was practically skipping as she walked. She knew the streets and how to talk to people—she was so different from him. She didn't try to think things out all the time the way he did. She didn't worry like him. She could just size up a situation and act.

"Hold on a sec!" She had stopped in front of a coffee shop and now was ushering him in.

"What's the matter?"

"I have to pee. You better go too," she warned. "I don't think we're going to have much of a chance tonight."

He went to the bathroom, then washed his face and even brushed his teeth with his finger. He sniffed under his arms. Nothing he could do about that, he decided. But she was no rose either after a day and a half on the run.

When he met her in front of the coffee shop she had redone her makeup and looked terrific. She *was* terrific. She was beautiful and exciting and had only one fault— she scared him shitless.

They walked uptown and suddenly the neighborhood changed. The uniformed doormen and neat brownstones and rich-looking stores had disappeared. Now they were passing storefront tenements and gutted buildings. And it stank— really stank—from the garbage strewn all over the street. Richard couldn't believe the litter, or the ripped-up furniture sitting on the sidewalk, or the stripped cars resting at the curb. He was about to ask her what they were doing here when she took his arm and pulled him down a side street.

"At least we don't have to worry about cops," she said with a forced smile. With the growing number of dark faces around, Richard had begun to think that a cop just now might not be totally unwelcome. She spied an abandoned-looking building, and led them to the unboarded front door.

"How about a cheap hotel tonight?" he asked with a shaky voice.

"No money. Tomorrow we can stay at the Plaza."
She looked up and down the block, then grabbed his hand
and pulled him up the stone steps. The front door swung
open and they were in. "We're in luck!" she whispered.

Yeah, we're in luck, Richard thought. He tried to hold
back his fear as he groped behind her through the darkness
and into a room. It was a bare, cavernous space lit only
by the streetlight that filtered in through dirty windows.
The ceiling was twelve feet high. A monstrous fireplace
was carved into the far wall. Two mattresses, complete with
blankets and pillows, lay on the floor.

"Holy shit!" Lisa whispered. She looked around, then
went off to explore the rest of the floor.

"Someone is living here," Richard moaned to himself
in a very soft voice. "Someone is living here, and they are
going to return, and find us, and if they don't kill us they'll
call the police."

"What?" Lisa said in his ear. Richard jumped a foot
at the sound of her voice. She took his hand and squeezed
it. "Isn't this great?"

"Someone is living here, Lisa," he repeated.

"Not for weeks."

He walked into the room and found a cardboard
bucket on the floor. Inside were chicken bones. He touched
one. It was moist. "Lisa . . ." his voice quivered.

"Don't worry! People crash in these buildings all the
time! The mattresses stay and they come and go. They're
just junkies and drunks." She walked around the room,
examining it.

"Oh, just junkies and drunks. Great."

"Don't worry. We don't have anything they want."

"No, nothing at all," he said miserably, wrapping his
arms around his jacket.

She was at his side again. "Well, they don't have to
know about *that*!" She flopped down on a mattress, took

the gun out of her pants, and pulled out the half-smoked joint and book of matches. "Come on, relax!"

"Okay, I'll relax." He sat on the mattress with his back stiffly against the wall. Relax. The word had no meaning anymore.

"I wish we had a TV." She puffed on the joint and passed it to him. "You know any more stories? I really liked Alice in Wonderland."

Richard took a puff. "How about Goldilocks and the Three Bears?"

"I don't remember that one. How does it go?"

"I don't remember it either." He thought he heard a noise outside and strained to listen, but it wasn't repeated. "Have you done this before?"

"What? Sleep in an abandoned building?" She seemed insulted by the question.

"I was just wondering how you knew to come here."

"Well, I didn't know about this particular building, but I know about abandoned buildings like this. I have a friend who sleeps in one."

"Oh yeah?" Richard said.

"Yeah. He's a drunk, and he's a little crazy, but he's really very sweet. His name is Andrew . . ."

Richard would have liked to hear more about Andrew, but just then the front door of the building creaked open. Lisa jerked her head straight up and froze, and Richard did the same. They sat absolutely still. There were steps and muffled whispers in the darkened hall.

Lisa reached across the mattress and picked up the gun.

"It isn't loaded!" he whispered frantically.

"Ssh!" she whispered back, and pointed the gun at the doorway as several sets of white eyes looked into the room.

13

LEVERTON drank a beer as she watched Steve Knowles sleeping on the couch. He slept on his back, his chest rising and falling peacefully. There was a gentle smile on his lips. By his right hand, resting against his thigh, was a .44 Smith and Wesson Special, and under the couch lay an Uzi automatic rifle. Steve Knowles wasn't going to be taken by surprise again. The weight of her own .22, strapped to her right calf, was a comfort.

He blinked in his sleep. He had slept most of the day, thanks to the Darvon prescribed at the hospital. Thanks also to the sixty milligrams of heroin she had injected into his arm when they first got home. He kept his smack in an Anacin bottle in the upstairs bathroom. For fast, fast, fast relief, he said.

His eyes opened and for a moment he looked bewildered. Then he remembered where he was and who she was, and tried to sit up.

"Son-of-a-bitch!"

He lay back and shut his eyes against the pain. Leverton sipped her beer. She watched him lick his lips; his voice came out in a dry whisper.

"Mary, do you suppose you could get me one of those?"

When she returned he had the TV on and was sitting up, adjusting his arm in his sling. She poured his beer and set it in front of him. It was an effort for him to reach for it, and another still to lift the glass to his lips. Satisfied for the moment, he rested his feet up on the couch, modestly covering his knees with his robe. A car chase flickered across the television screen.

"Senseless violence," he sighed, and shook his head disapprovingly. Leverton had to suppress a smile as he muted the TV with the remote control and turned toward her.

"You're older than you looked at the hospital. What are you, around forty?"

"Around," she replied.

"No offense," he assured her, "I meant it as a compliment. It's hard to tell a junkie's age. Most dry up young and blow away." He smiled, showing even, white teeth. "But you take care of yourself, Nurse Mary. You have muscle on your bones. Like me." He nodded and raised his glass. "No cotton in our veins!"

She joined him in a silent toast. To Mary Lewis, she said to herself, trying to remember all the careers Mary Lewis had had. She had been a bookkeeper, a call girl, a bank teller, a top aide in the Mayor's office—and now, in the event someone should inquire, Mary Lewis was registered as a nurse at Westchester General Hospital. A renaissance lady, Leverton thought with pride.

Knowles took a long swallow, then shook his head sadly. "I bet there are more junkies on hospital staffs than in all the methadone centers in the country." He seemed genuinely upset about the fact. "How did you get started, anyway?"

"A doctor I was dating," she replied.

He barked a short, unpleasant laugh. "Married? Kids?"

A pain stabbed through her. "Was," she answered quickly. "No."

She sat in a chair across from him and met his stare. He was handsome, there was no denying that. She had admired the grace of his features while he was lying unconscious on the carpet not twenty hours before. But what she had not seen then, nor in the hospital this morning, was the intensity of the man. Even drugged now, and in pain, energy seemed to flow out of him.

"How did you get hooked?" she asked.

"Vietnam. I was a Marine. Took some shrapnel at Khesanh. In the hospital I was in a lot of pain. They gave me all the morphine I wanted."

"And you're still in pain?"

"I've always been in pain, Nurse Mary. Pain is my woman, a faithful bitch, if ever there was one."

He laughed again and lapsed into an angry silence. Leverton did not break it, but sipped her beer, patiently. His eyes were back on the television screen—a helicopter chase this time.

"We're no different from anyone else in this country, Nurse Mary," he finally said, his tone almost philosophical. "Everyone's addicted to something. It's the new beast, addiction—the great white shark. Jaws!" he grinned, showing his teeth again. "What we do, smack, is nothing. It's harmless, really. How many junkies are there in this country? A few hundred thousand? And the ninety percent of us who are doctors and nurses and businessmen don't hurt anyone. Remember when everyone was terrified over the street junkie? You don't even hear about heroin as a problem anymore. Today it's *crack* that's ruining our children and destroying our civilization. Today it's the crazed crack addict who's the fin of the shark—that terrifying symbol that cuts the water and becomes a *New York Post* headline, an 'Action News' special. And how do we eliminate this abomination? It's easy. We 'Just Say No.'"

He chuckled grimly and his eyes flickered like candle flames. Leverton was impressed. He was speaking with the passion of a minister.

"But what the newspapers and TV don't want to acknowledge is that just below the surface is the back of the beast—all those addicts like you and me; addicts like the Hollywood producer who started with a snort of coke at a party, then went to an occasional pop, and is now injecting the stuff under his tongue, or into his prick, because he's blown out all the veins in his arms and legs; addicts like the Wall Street broker who started as a weekend snorter and now has a dime-sized hole where his nostril used to be. And what about pot, our 'nonaddictive' high? How many lawyers and teachers and accountants do you think come home after a hard day's work and light up to relax, to satisfy their 'nonaddiction'? Ten million? Twenty million?"

Leverton gazed at him in amazement. The sermon could have come from a televangelist.

"But the point is, Nurse Mary, that heroin and coke and pot really *are* harmless next to the killers that make up the body of the beast: alcohol, pills, tobacco—addictions that paralyze and destroy in numbers too large to count—addictions supported by law and billion-dollar industries. How many alcoholics are there in this country? How many deaths do you think can be attributed each year to alcohol? How many battered wives? How many abused children? And how many pill poppers and cigarette smokers are there? How many breweries and bars and liquor stores and drug companies and tobacco farmers and cigarette manufacturers grow rich and fat while their customers waste away and die?"

Leverton got the point. A lot of people were in pain. A lot of people were "on" something to reduce the pain. It was hard to argue with that. But Knowles was using that fact to justify his own addiction, and his smuggling, and the abuse of his son.

"We live in an age that has spawned addiction, Nurse Mary, and now it's everywhere, devouring everyone."

His eyes closed. He looked exhausted by the outburst. He even seemed smaller now, somehow, shriveled by years of bitterness and pain.

" 'Just Say No,' " he murmured with a faint smile on his face. "We're raising a generation of such impolite children. At least we should tell them: 'Just Say No Thank You.' "

He smiled broadly at the joke and then his mouth clenched in a grimace of pain. "Why don't you bring down the Anacin, Nurse Mary," he asked wearily.

She went upstairs and waited for five minutes. She passed the time by taking off her shoes and tiptoeing through the rooms of the floor. Only the master bedroom was furnished. The others were ghost rooms—bare walls and floors. One had a bed, Richard's room, she guessed, but there was nothing else in it to suspect that a fifteen-year-old even spent vacations here. She hurt inside. Pat's room had always been thick with the stuff of a boy's life— it still was. That was her craziness. She dusted around it all once a week. It wasn't there waiting for his return; she wasn't *that* crazy. It was there for her. As some kind of support.

She put her shoes back on and returned to the livingroom with a slow, easy stride and a sleepy smile she did not feel.

"I took care of myself upstairs," she told him, patting her handbag. "I have my own kit. I don't like to share needles these days."

He nodded his understanding. She knelt by the couch and put the rubber tie, spoon, powder, and hypodermic needle next to the candle on the coffee table. Then she lit the candle and cooked the powder in a spoon. He watched hungrily as she filled the syringe to the requested sixty-milligram level, and then he leaned back on the couch and closed his eyes. When she tied off his arm and injected the heroin he took on the appearance of a child on Christmas morning. A minute later, with his head lolled back and a sweet peace in his face, he began opening presents.

14

THE beam of a flashlight caught them full-face and reflected off the pistol in Lisa's outstretched hand. Richard heard a high-pitched squeal and someone cursing. Then there was a scuffle of feet and the light was gone. From the darkness a voice shouted at them.

"What you doin' there?" It was a woman's voice, angry and black.

Lisa pointed the gun into the darkness. "Who are you?"

"Who are *you*?" the voice challenged back.

Richard reached out his hand and found Lisa's searching for his at the same moment. They gripped each other tightly. "My brother and I are sleeping here tonight," she yelled into the hall.

"The hell you are!" the voice squealed with indignation. "This here's our place!"

"Not anymore," Lisa replied.

"What you talkin'?" the voice squealed again. "We been livin' here a week already!"

Richard shook Lisa's arm. "Maybe we should go," he said softly.

She brushed him off. "Sorry, lady, but we're here now," she called out.

"That's our damn bed stuff!"

"And this is our damn gun!"

It was a standoff. Richard spoke without thinking. "Listen, why don't you come in here and we'll talk about

115

it." Lisa pulled her hand out of his and glared at him furiously. What else is there to do? he wanted to say, but the woman's voice spoke first.

"You gonna put away that gun?" She didn't sound as sure of herself anymore.

"We won't use it," Richard assured her.

"Unless you make us!" Lisa added vehemently. She was still glaring at him. He shifted uncomfortably.

There were some hesitant steps, and then the light was on them again. Richard placed one hand on Lisa's arm, gently lowering the gun. The other came up to shield his brow. "Would you please get that out of our eyes?"

The light turned to the ceiling, and now, in the reflected glow, he could see a family of three—a young mother with a baby in one arm, and in front, protecting them, a ten-year-old boy with the eyes of the polar bear Richard had just seen at the zoo. He was holding a baseball bat in his hand.

"Hi!" Richard forced a smile. The black faces could have been carved in stone. Even the baby stared sullenly. "Want to sit down?"

"We wanna go to sleep," the mother answered angrily.

"I know. We do too." He looked at the mattresses. "Maybe there's room here for all of us."

The boy spoke. His voice was soft and high and his chin jutted out in defiance. "This is our house, muthafucka. We found it. We don't gotta share it with you."

"Yes, I know, but we need a place to stay too—"

Lisa interrupted him. "Goddamn it, we don't have to negotiate with these fuckers!" Her gun came up in a careless gesture, pointing straight at the mother.

With the speed of a whip, the boy whirled the bat and charged forward. Richard acted instinctively. He grabbed the gun out of Lisa's hand just as the boy was upon them and stuck it in his face.

"James!" the mother screamed.

The boy froze with the bat high over his shoulder. Richard's arm was fully extended, the end of the gun barrel just inches from the child's eyes.

"James!" the mother cried again, "you get back here, boy!"

James didn't move. Richard steadied the gun with both hands. He could see the question in the boy's face. Could the bat be brought down fast enough . . . ?

"James, I'm talkin' to you!"

The boy could not hold out against his mother's voice. He slowly stepped back, the bat still high above his head. Richard's arms were trembling as he lowered the gun.

"We'll go," he said. His voice cracked as he made the announcement. The black woman had her hand to her throat as though she was having trouble breathing. The baby's eyes were wide open, watching it all.

He turned to Lisa. He could see she had been scared, too. "Come on." He got to his feet. She pushed his hand away angrily when he tried to help her up.

"You childrens got no place to go?" the mother asked in a shaky but conciliatory voice.

"We'll be fine!" Lisa shot back quickly. "We don't need your damn house!"

Richard looked around. "There probably *is* room for all of us," he suggested.

"No way!" Lisa insisted. "We're going!" She started out.

"Lisa," Richard implored.

"There's room upstairs," the woman suggested. "You can take one of these here mattresses."

"Lisa, you hear?"

She stopped at the doorway but didn't turn to face him. She was really furious at him now, Richard knew. "How about it, huh?"

"I don't see why you bother asking me," her voice came back, coldly. "You seem to be making all the decisions anyway!"

"Well, we're here already, and it's late, and we don't have any money . . ." Richard gave up. Lisa was determined to be angry. Anything he said now would just make things worse.

"James," the mother commanded, "you give a hand and help take this here mattress upstairs."

"Shit, Ma," the boy protested, but the stern look on his mother's face stopped him. He hurled his bat against a wall, and angrily attacked the heavy double mattress.

Richard stuck the gun in his pants. "I'll take one end," he offered, but the boy snarled him off and wrestled the mattress out of the room.

"Come on," he said to Lisa, softly.

She didn't say a word, but angrily stomped out, following the struggling boy up the stairs.

As Richard left he nodded to the mother and she nodded back. The look between them felt very satisfying, somehow. They had begun as enemies and ended, now, almost as friends. And he had made it happen. It made him feel grown-up.

It was dark in the hall, and quiet. Richard bravely groped his way up the stairs, following Lisa's shadowy form and the soft thud of the mattress slapping against the steps. Suddenly the silence was interrupted by an ear-piercing shriek from below. Richard felt his heart pounding again, and grasped the bannister tightly. He wondered what could possibly be making such an awful sound. Then he remembered the frozen-faced baby in its mother's arms, and realized it had finally started to cry.

* * *

The second-floor room was brighter than the one down-stairs, with yellow light from the streetlamp pouring in through the shutterless windows. Richard sat with his back against the wall and watched Lisa curled up on the far side of the mattress, as far away from him as she could get. She hadn't said a word since they entered the room, and now she was acting as though she would never speak to him again.

The grown-up feeling had left him; he felt small and alone. He looked up at the peeling plaster and the sha-dows on the ceiling. They made interesting patterns, he thought. Squares of different shades of gray that now, as he watched, began to take on a weight and menace—became granite blocks perched so precariously above him that if he made a wrong move, even breathed a careless breath, he might upset their balance and they would come crashing down. . . .

Fighting the tightness in his chest, he held his breath for as long as he could, then slowly let it out. The boulders didn't fall. They weren't real. They were only shadows. He knew that, but he was still afraid. The line between what was real and what was not had almost disappeared.

"I could have handled it, you know!" Lisa announced, accusingly.

He had almost forgot she was there. She was still curled up, hugging her knees to her chest.

"You shouldn't have grabbed the gun!"

"I'm sorry," Richard replied.

"I know how to handle these things!"

"I know you do," he said. He knew why she was angry. For the first time he had taken over, and her pride had been hurt. He tried to make amends. "You've really been terrific so far. Honest."

Slowly, she began to straighten out and Richard felt a little relieved. Just by uncurling herself, it seemed, she was forgiving him. She stretched out her leg and lifted it, and then began exercising by lowering it, and lifting it, and lowering it again. He studied the line of her thigh widening into her hip, and rounding into her crotch, and he felt an unbearable yearning. Acting on an impulse, he crawled across the mattress and pressed himself against the length of her back. She turned her head.

"Cold," he said. She seemed to accept that and rested her head on his arm.

"You could have gotten killed," she murmured.

"Mmmmm." His face was in her hair, which smelled of sweat and shampoo, and made him dizzy.

"You want to give it to me now?" she asked.

"Huh?" He felt a sudden panic.

"The gun. You want to give it back? It's mine."

"Oh." His heart slowed and he nestled closer. "It doesn't have any bullets."

"I know." She sounded irritated. "I just want to have it. Like you want to have your jacket."

Richard didn't want to upset her. He reached behind and found the long-barreled revolver. He put it in her hand as he hugged her again.

"We have to get some bullets for it," she said.

"Mmmmm." She could have suggested they hijack a 747 and hide out in Disneyland and he would have agreed. He rubbed against her; she didn't move away.

"Tomorrow we have to sell some stuff, Richard."

"Mmmmm." He didn't want to deal with cocaine now. His left hand was resting against her breast. Slowly, he opened his palm and cupped it.

"Did you hear what I said?"

"Uh-huh." She didn't move away. She had to know he was there . . .

"And it's okay with you?"

He felt her nipple harden through the shirt. Anything was okay with him. The H-bomb could fall tonight. They could be killed in their sleep by that crazy kid with the baseball bat. Cocaine and tomorrow were a long way away. Her breast was in his hand.

"Whatever you say," he said.

Her head turned with a smile and her face was only inches from his. As he wondered whether or not she wanted to be kissed, she leaned forward and attached her lips to his.

Richard's first response was surprise. His second was discomfort. It wasn't sexy. It wasn't even pleasant. She was sucking his tongue so hard it hurt; then she bit his lip.

"Ow!" he complained.

"Take off your clothes!"

He didn't need a second invitation. He was barely able to keep up with her as they kicked out of their jeans.

"Here!" She guided his hand under her panties. She was wet and slippery and his finger slid into her without resistance. He was amazed. It didn't seem to hurt!

She pressed against his hand, her eyes shut, her mouth slack. Her fingernails stabbed into his shoulder painfully. Then her breath began to come in shallow gasps. She bit her lip and began shaking her head. No, she seemed to be saying. No, stop! He was hurting her! He tried to remove the intruding finger but her hand clamped over his, holding it in place, forcing him deeper in.

She fluttered under him and began to moan, and he understood. She was having an orgasm. He was dizzy with excitement as he took off his underwear and rolled down her panties.

"No, Richard!"

They were both naked; he was pressing stiffly against her.

"No, I mean it!"

He stopped, bewildered. "What do you mean?"

"I don't want to do it."

"Why not?"

"I just don't."

He didn't understand. She had just come! He was sure of it. He pressed against her again. Her response was sharper.

"Stop! I don't like it!"

She had withdrawn her body. Her knees were once again curled up to her chest. Her face was away.

"What do you mean, you don't like it?"

"I just don't!" She raised her voice as though that would explain her feelings.

Richard felt disoriented. "How could you not like it?" he asked.

She spoke softly, holding herself. "I never have and I never will."

He took a moment to digest this. There was something complicated about sex that he didn't get. She was a hooker, for God's sake! She'd done it hundreds of times! And when she wasn't doing it, she was dancing naked. Why, just last night she had put on a show for him, and a minute ago she had ripped off her jeans and . . .

"Do you understand?" she asked.

"Oh, sure."

"Really?" She turned her head and faced him. She looked like a ten-year-old child now.

"Really," he lied. "But what I don't understand is, if you don't like it, why do you do it so much?" He had asked the question in innocence and wasn't prepared to see the child's face harden into stone.

"Go fuck yourself, huh? Just do me a favor and go fuck yourself!"

She turned away. Richard lay quietly as her anger sank in. Damn! he cried to himself as the tears came again. He rolled to the side of the mattress and put all his energy into controlling the sobs. He thought he was doing a good job, too, until he felt her hand on his back.

"I'm sorry," she said.

He didn't answer. They had played this scene last night and that had been bad enough. The repetition of his vulnerability was unbearable.

"I can do something for you," she said softly. "I don't mind." Her hand massaged his back and the tears stopped. Responding to a tug on his shoulder, he rolled onto his back. He brusquely dried his eyes and looked again at the shadows on the ceiling. With a start of surprise, he felt her hand at his crotch.

"Actually, I like doing this," she whispered. "I want to make you happy. I just don't like to fuck. Can't you understand?"

Richard was beyond understanding. He was beyond any thought or feeling except for the simple enjoyment of her massaging hand. His body responded without confusion or concern.

"I like seeing you excited like this," she breathed. "It makes me feel all warm inside."

He closed his eyes and strained against her. The sensations came in waves, mysterious and unstoppable. "Come," she murmured in his ear. "Come . . ." And with the ease and inevitability of a wave rolling in on the beach, he did.

15 "MORNING."

Richard blinked the sleep out of his eyes. There was Lisa, fully clothed, sitting cross-legged on the floor a few feet away. In front of her was the balance scale and a one-gram bottle with the plastic funnel screwed on. In her lap she held a tube of cocaine.

"Lisa, what are you—?"

"Sssh!" she told him. She was leaning forward, her attention fixed on the scale and bottle. With a steady hand she transferred a small amount of white powder from the cup of the scale to the funnel. Then she tapped the side of the funnel to get all the powder down, took off the funnel, and screwed a plastic cap onto the full bottle. Richard saw nine other little bottles standing in a row, all filled the same way.

"Morning," he replied with a sinking feeling.

He had just had a dream, but he couldn't remember anything about it. Now, lying naked on a mattress in some abandoned building, somewhere in Manhattan, with Lisa measuring cocaine into little bottles, he felt as if he'd awoken from one dream into another. He found his underwear and put it on.

Lisa was rubbing her finger along the inside of the funnel and then against her teeth.

"What are you doing?"

"Leo does this all the time. It numbs the gums. Sort of like getting a shot from the dentist."

He climbed into his pants. "Do you like cocaine?"

"It's no BFD," she replied.

"BFD?"

"Big fucking deal. I do it once in a while with Leo, to keep him company, but it doesn't really make me feel good. And the postnasal drip—you know what a postnasal drip is? It's like having a cold in your head, with snot continually dripping into your throat. And people *pay* for that! Hungry?"

"I was until a minute ago."

Richard closed the plastic tube of cocaine, pleased to discover how little Lisa had used—practically none, as far as he could see—and slipped it through the open stitches of the collar and into his jacket lining. Lisa wedged the gun into her pants, put the ten miniature bottles in one jacket pocket and her tools in the other, and led them out of the building. It wasn't until they were on the street, stepping over garbage, that he remembered the black family from last night.

"Where did they go?" he asked.

She shrugged. "Don't know. They were gone when I woke up." They approached the north end of Central Park, where Lisa took a drink from a water fountain. "I guess they're a welfare family or something, or maybe kicked off welfare. Or maybe they were evicted from their apartment, or burned out. There are a lot of people on the streets. They just live where they can."

Richard took a drink too, then waited as Lisa found a suitably overgrown area and went behind a bush to pee. He hadn't even thought about the family not having a home. He had taken it for granted that everyone had a home, somewhere. But of course they didn't. That's what the fight was all about. It was awful, now that he thought about it.

"Where are we going?" he asked when they started walking again.

"Downtown. To the Exxon building. We're going to

see a vice-president named Charles Abbot Sprague, and we're going to sell Charley ten grams of stuff for a thousand dollars."

"Oh," Richard said, "just like that."

"Why not? He buys from Leo all the time."

Richard thought about that as they walked to the East Side. "Then he's a customer of yours?" he said in a casual voice.

"Uh-huh."

Lisa didn't look at him. She acted as though the question wasn't important. Branches of magnolia trees, growing in the park, hung over the stone wall on Fifth Avenue. Richard picked a blossom and removed the petals, one by one, until he came to the inner, private parts of the flower.

Lisa stopped. She stood close to him and put a hand on his chest, under the blue jacket. "I didn't like doing it with him," she said. It felt as though she had his heart in her hand. "In some ways it wasn't even me doing it." She looked puzzled. "Does that ever happen to you. Do you ever feel separate from your body—like your body is doing something, but you're just watching?"

His eyes opened wide and he dumbly nodded his head. She had just described half his life! She kissed him on the cheek. "I like you," she smiled.

He floated for two blocks. She said she liked him! Which meant she must have liked his touching her last night, and touching him! But so much was still confusing.

"Last night, when you said you didn't like it . . ." he ventured.

"When I said I didn't like what?"

"You know, sex. What did you mean?" They walked in step together. Richard's stride was naturally longer so he shortened it, to keep perfect pace.

"Everyone wants to fuck me," she said softly. "I let them because they pay. But I don't like it. I don't enjoy it."

It didn't make sense to him. He couldn't imagine not enjoying sex. "Do other girls like it? Your girlfriends?"

Lisa shrugged. "I guess some of them do. When they do it with their boyfriends, or something. I guess when you do it with your boyfriend or with your husband it's different."

She took his hand and seemed very sad. He decided to stop worrying about it. If Lisa was confused about sex, he didn't stand a chance of figuring it out.

There was a security guard in the lobby and the thought of what they were about to do gave Richard a sudden, sharp pain in his stomach.

"You okay?" Lisa asked.

"Yeah. Never been better."

She signed the register and the guard gave them two stick-on badges. Lisa's said Guest of Exxon 67, and Richard's, Guest of Exxon 68.

"You know what sixty-eight is?" Lisa asked in the elevator.

"What?" he replied.

"You do me and I'll owe you one."

She laughed, so Richard knew it was a joke, but he didn't get it. He laughed anyway, though. He didn't want her to think he was a *total* jerk. They stepped out at the twenty-seventh floor and into a small lobby with a desk at one end. The woman behind the desk looked them over quickly and was coolly polite.

"Can I help you?" she asked, obviously not meaning the words at all.

"We're here to see Mr. Sprague," Lisa told her.

"Do you have an appointment?"

"No, but he'll see us."

The woman looked doubtful and furrowed the two

penciled lines above her eyes, where her eyebrows should have been.

"We're his children," Lisa confided. The penciled lines shot up in surprise. "By his first wife. Actually, they were never legally married." She lowered her voice dramatically. "You see, we're illegitimate."

Richard felt another spasm in his stomach. The receptionist seemed suspicious but didn't say a word. Instead she dialed her phone.

"Trudy, there are two youngsters here to see Mr. Sprague . . ."

"Lisa Frank," Lisa announced.

"Lisa Frank," the woman echoed. After a moment, her eyebrows arched up again. She was clearly unhappy with Trudy's reply, but she pushed a button and pointed them toward a set of translucent glass doors.

On the other side the carpet was thick and white, the walls soft shades of blue and aqua. A white glow radiated from fluorescent lights in the ceiling and surrounding Richard, in stereo, was the muted sound of a string orchestra playing "I Want to Hold Your Hand."

A tall, distinguished, perfectly groomed man with graying hair was hurrying down the corridor to meet them. He had the kind of face that Richard had come to identify with the fathers of the boys at Pierce—a prominent jaw, chiseled brow and cheeks, and a nose that was squared off at the tip as though by a surgeon's scalpel, an effect Mario once described as "Presbyterian circumcision."

"Hi, Charley," Lisa said brightly.

Charles Abbot Sprague had a tight smile on his face. He ushered them into a small conference room and closed the door.

"Nice seeing where you work, Charley," Lisa continued. But then she stopped talking. The features on the man's face had begun to change; they seemed to melt together and reform, like special effects in a horror movie. Sprague's eyes had widened so that a ring of white showed all around the watery blue pupils, and shot through the white were angry streaks of red. His nostrils were flared like an animal's. His entire face had turned purple. When he finally spoke his voice sounded as though he were being strangled.

"What the hell are you doing here, you bitch?" His fury was directed at Lisa. He didn't even seem to see Richard at all. "You know not to come here! Are you crazy? Now you get your fucking ass out of this building and never show up again, you understand?"

Lisa reacted as though she hadn't heard a word. "Nice seeing you too, Charley. This is my friend Richard. We're here to do some business with you."

Charles Abbot Sprague looked dumbly at both of them as though he didn't understand. Then a stream of obscenities erupted out of him, the likes of which Richard had never heard, even from the most foul-mouthed twelfth-grader at Pierce. He just stood there, amazed and embarrassed, until Sprague finished his outburst.

"So if you're not out of here in thirty seconds," the man concluded, "I'm going to call the fucking police, and fix it with a judge so that your hooker ass rots in jail until you start collecting social security! You understand?"

Lisa understood. "Sure, Charley, you want to call the cops? Let's call the cops!" She acted as if she didn't have a care in the world as she moved to a desk phone and picked it up. "I'm fifteen years old, and you've been screwing me for six months. Come on, here's the phone. Your wife's going to love it. Your kids will be very popular in school. You want me to dial for you? I can tell them about your vasectomy scar, and your hemorrhoids, and that cute game you like to play with the diapers and baby powder."

Richard was amazed again. More special effects. The color in Sprague's face turned from purple to a sickly shade of green.

"What do you want?" he croaked.

"First I want you to sit down, Charley, and not have a heart attack."

Sprague sat woodenly at the table and Lisa took a seat opposite. She motioned Richard into a chair beside her.

"We want to sell you some coke, Charley. High-grade stuff. A hundred dollars a gram."

Sprague was looking at them closely. Richard felt uncomfortable under the scrutiny. "I don't need any," Sprague told Lisa.

"Well, we need to sell it, Charley."

"I just bought half an ounce from Leo."

"And now you're going to buy some from us."

Sprague seemed to consider this. Then he jerked his head toward Richard. "Who's he?"

"A friend," Lisa answered.

Richard smiled uncomfortably. "Hi," he offered. But Sprague just looked right through him.

"You've caught me at a bad time," he said to Lisa. "I have plenty of stuff and I'm short of cash."

"Ten grams," Lisa interrupted. "You're going to buy ten grams for a thousand dollars."

"You're crazy!" Sprague cried.

"Charley, I've seen you snort a gram in an hour. And money is no problem for you. Don't be difficult."

Sprague was thinking fast. "I'd have to taste the stuff first," he began, but before he could finish Lisa had a bottle on the table and was unscrewing the lid.

"Jesus!" He bolted out of his chair and locked the conference-room door. "Are you crazy? Bringing that here?"

"It's good stuff, Charley. I wouldn't rip you off." She had laid out an ample line on her compact mirror and was offering him a cut-down straw.

"Jesus!" Sprague repeated. He stood, undecided for a moment, then grimaced and took the straw. With a quick, experienced motion he snorted the line.

"Well?" Lisa wanted to know.

"Not bad." He sniffed twice. "I've had better."

"Cut the shit, Charley." She started unloading gram bottles from her pocket.

"Lisa, put that away! I told you I haven't got any cash. You want to take American Express?" For the first time that morning Sprague managed a weak smile. Lisa stopped taking out the bottles.

"How much do you have?"

The man shrugged and took out his wallet. He counted to a hundred and twenty.

"Toss it here," she ordered.

"What is this, a deal or a mugging?" He had the trace of a smile on his lips as he threw his wallet on the table. Lisa riffled through it and from a fold in the leather plucked out a one-hundred-dollar bill.

"You missed this one, Charley. I make it two-twenty."

"My mistake," Sprague said in a low, menacing tone.

Lisa took the hundred and five twenties and tossed back the wallet. "I'll leave two bottles and we'll be back this afternoon with the other eight. Your bank is open, right?"

Sprague didn't answer. The back of his throat was working, but no sound came out.

"It's just eight hundred dollars, Charley. No BFD. Shall we say noon?"

"Not here." Sprague finally responded. "It's too dangerous." He licked his lips nervously.

"Where then?"

"The Donnell Library. On Fifty-third. I'll be in the reading room."

"We'll find you." Lisa sprang out of the chair and jerked her head. Richard followed, a deep dread growing within him. As they walked out he could hear the executive muttering something at them. But he just kept going. He didn't want to hear what.

16

MARIO Federici made an unhappy face as he separated his bun and looked at the meat patty inside.

"Can't get a decent hamburger these days," he grumbled. "Remember when we were kids? Hamburgers as thick as your fist, costing all of twenty-five cents?"

O'Hare warmed his hands against his coffee mug. The coffee helped relieve his morning lightheadedness, but it was hard concentrating on what Federici had to say. He kept thinking about how badly he wanted a cigarette.

"You think I'm crazy, coming to the City like this," Federici continued. "But I was really going crazy up at school. Just thinking about Richard—and worrying. I had to come down here and talk to you. Later I'll walk around the streets for a few hours. Maybe I'll run into him."

"I understand," O'Hare offered.

"That a man could do something like that to his son . . ." Federici's voice trailed off and he shook his head sadly. Then he reluctantly bit into his lunch.

"I've seen worse," O'Hare replied. "A man who used his twelve-year-old daughter as a prostitute. A woman who smothered her baby because the kid cried too much." The waitress passed by with more coffee. "I've seen worse," he said again.

Federici looked up. "I'd hate to have your job," he admitted.

"Yeah, me too."

They shared a joyless laugh. Federici had dark circles under his eyes. No one's been sleeping well these days, O'Hare thought.

"Are you married?" the track coach asked.

"Separated."

"Oh." Federici's face fell. He seemed to take O'Hare's sorrow as his own. "I'm sorry. There's so much of that these days. Children?"

The innocent questions, O'Hare thought. "Yeah, I had a son who died."

Federici looked up in shock. O'Hare had to continue.

"Patrick. He was at a party. There were some drugs going around. Joints, ludes, a little coke. At midnight he was being driven home by three friends. The driver lost control and the car skidded off the Long Island Expressway into a concrete wall. The driver and Pat were immediately killed. A third boy, sitting in the back, died a week later. The fourth survived."

He recited the details by rote, he knew them so well. But the pain was as fresh as ever.

Federici's eyes were filled with tears. With a small motion he pushed his lunchplate aside.

"You have three kids?" O'Hare said, trying to keep the conversation going.

Federici nodded. "I come from a large family. Italians, you know. Lots of kids."

"I wanted to have two or three, but after we had Pat my wife wanted to go back to her career."

Federici was searching for words. "I would think a tragedy like that might bring a husband and wife together."

"Yeah, you would think that, wouldn't you." O'Hare was surprised at the bitterness in his voice. "It closed us off in separate worlds. I don't know why. We just stopped talking . . ."

And then stopped touching. And then Anne stopped feeling anything for him at all.

The waitress reappeared to take away Federici's plate. O'Hare forced himself back to the present. "Do your kids do drugs?" he asked the coach.

"I told Paul if I ever found him with a joint I'd break both his legs." Federici formed a weak smile and then gave a helpless shrug. "I'm sure he's tried pot, at least. And the others will too. How can you stop that? Jo and I let them know the risks; they'll make their own decisions no matter what we say. You just have to do your best, and trust them, and love them no matter what."

"We knew Pat was drinking a little, and smoked cigarettes out of the house. Hell, I did when I was his age. But . . ." O'Hare felt tears beginning to form and looked away. "Anne and I were so involved in our work. Maybe if we had watched a little more carefully, given him a little more attention . . ."

"Don't do that!" Federici raised his voice and O'Hare felt the man's hand on his wrist. "It was an accident! You and your wife didn't do anything Jo and I haven't done! For Christ sake it's awful enough without blaming yourselves . . ." Then, awkwardly, he stopped, as though he had accidentally trespassed onto private property, and removed his hand. "What are you doing today?"

Richard. O'Hare had almost forgotten about the boy. "I guess I'll hit the Bo-Mond first and try to get ahold of the night clerk there, the one who saw Richard."

"Let me go with you," Mario asked.

O'Hare shook his head. "Thanks, but if you really want to help, go back to school. Richard may call you again, or maybe even show up."

They parted on the sidewalk with a warm handshake. "You have to take risks," Mario Federici said. "You can't care for people without taking risks."

O'Hare made his way up to a fourth-floor room of the Bo-Mond where he found the clerk sleeping in bed. The room stunk from alcohol—a bottle of Wild Turkey stood open on the night table—and from the stale smell of pot. The shade was drawn to block the morning sun. The only illumination came from a game show flickering silently on the TV.

O'Hare shook the clerk roughly.

"Huh? Whazzit?"

The man turned his head and opened his eyes. His face was a mess. His left eye was a narrow slit lost in a swelling the size of a small egg; his lips were split in two places and encrusted with dry blood. O'Hare flipped open his shield and identified himself.

"I'm looking for a boy," he told him, taking out the passport picture. "Name is Richard Knowles. You seen him in the past few days?"

The clerk studied the snapshot for a moment, then slowly shook his head. "Nah."

O'Hare wasn't fazed by the bruises and the dried blood—it was the man's face itself that made him sick. He had seen it a thousand times in his career: behind the desks of hooker hotels, in ticket windows of porn movies, handing out leaflets in front of sex clubs—it was the same pasty, pockmarked mask that drifted through nothing jobs with only the predator's eye for an easy score. Only this one had had a piece of bad luck. This one had tangled with an angry Steve Knowles.

"What happened?" O'Hare inquired pleasantly.

The clerk groaned. "Got mugged at the desk the other night." He spoke like a bad ventriloquist who moved his lips just enough to ruin the illusion. "Coupla niggers came in, junkies, I guess."

He started to lie back on the bed and something inside O'Hare snapped. He grabbed the clerk by the shirtfront and with one hand lifted him from the bed, holding him half a foot off the floor and against the wall. He brought his face close up to the clerk's and spat his words into the terrified eyes.

"Now listen to me, asshole! You saw this boy two nights ago when he came in for a room. And then you got into a fight with his father who did that job on your face. If you think you've got a few bruises now, you just keep telling that stupid fucking story and you'll know what real unhappiness is!"

The clerk began talking. Words tumbled out of his mouth faster than his split lips could manage. O'Hare took it all in, reasonably satisfied with how it meshed with his own information. When the man had finished, O'Hare reluctantly lowered him, controlling an impulse to smash him just once against the wall.

"Okay, asshole. You see this boy again, you dial this number, you got that?" He gave the clerk a card.

"Sure, Lieutenant." The man tried to smile and a scab on his lip began to bleed. "I don't want no trouble. You can count on me."

"Yeah, I'll bet my pension on it." O'Hare threw the man back on the bed. Then, feeling like he'd been handling garbage, he wiped his hands on his pants and left.

When he stepped out of the hotel, the bright sun hurt his eyes. The clerk hadn't given him much that he didn't already know, but he comforted himself with the fact that he had his first witness against Knowles. The clerk could testify that Knowles had tried to steal the jacket. It was a start.

Wondering what to do next, O'Hare turned to see a pint-sized pimp, black as coal and dressed in cowboy leather, crossing the street in his direction. As O'Hare watched, the pimp collided with a man getting out of a double-parked car.

"Watch where yo' fuckin' goin', man!" the pimp mouthed. Then he brushed himself off, strutted past O'Hare, and disappeared into the Bo-Mond. More scum, O'Hare thought. New York attracted them like a magnet. After seventeen years on the job, the City was no better a place to live. If anything, it had got worse.

"Huh!" O'Hare exclaimed to himself.

He was puzzled now. The man who the pimp had bumped into was looking straight at him and walking purposefully toward him with a smile on his face, as though they were friends. He was short and squat with thick, peasant features. Russian-looking, O'Hare thought, but no peasant. His suit was expensive and perfectly tailored, and he wore gleaming black shoes. O'Hare racked his memory. He was certain he didn't know the man.

"Lieutenant O'Hare? If I might have a word . . ."

He spoke as though he had sandpaper in his throat and grinned an oily smile. O'Hare didn't like anything about him. His car, a white Lincoln Continental, glided to the curb a yard away. O'Hare glanced at the chauffeur, an intimidating man with an enormous head and thick neck, and blond hair that glistened in the sun.

In a moment of sheer intuition O'Hare knew who they were. He quickly recalled Anne's sketchy description over the phone and confirmed his intuition. These were the goons who had carved their way into Steve Knowles's house and put him in the hospital. He took a step back to keep them both in the same line of sight.

"My name is Casper," the short, bullish man rasped, holding out a surprisingly soft, white hand. "Milton Casper. I'm a businessman and I'd like to talk business with you."

17

O'HARE did not take Casper's outstretched hand. "I'm a policeman," he replied with a manufactured politeness, "not a businessman. I don't do business with anyone."

Casper ignored the slight and continued to smile. "I know that, Lieutenant. Please forgive my brusque introduction. It's only my way of saying I think we can help each other."

"And how's that?" O'Hare asked.

"What do you want?" Casper looked straight at him with unblinking gray eyes?"

"What do I want?" O'Hare repeated, not understanding.

"Everyone wants something, Michael," Casper explained with simple directness. "Some want love, some want sexual gratification, some want money, some want power. Some are happy just sitting on a bar stool holding a bottle."

O'Hare held his face in a blank stare. He couldn't believe the unabashed directness of this squalid, little gangster.

"Everyone wants something they don't have," Casper continued in that same pleasant manner. "It's human nature. For instance, I want something I don't have," he admitted happily. "Something that you might help me get. And in return I would like to help you get something you want but don't have. We don't have to call it business. Let's call it simple cooperation between people of good will with a mutual interest."

Casper had finished for the moment. His face was pink and glowing. O'Hare felt a little warm himself. He undid a top button of his collar. It couldn't hurt to play along with Casper for a bit, he thought. To get him to reveal a little more. "What is it you want that I can help you with?" he heard himself ask.

Casper looked disappointed. "I had wanted you to tell me first, but if you insist— It's a jacket, Michael. More precisely, a parcel within a jacket. A boy's blue jacket with a nylon exterior, to be exact."

O'Hare chose not to respond. Casper went on calmly.

"Well, it appears that the jacket has been misplaced and I believe we are both looking for it. Now it strikes me that if I find it before you, I am in luck and you have nothing. Whereas if you find it first the situation is reversed. What I am suggesting, Michael, is that we come to an understanding. Why should one of us be totally satisfied while the other is sadly disappointed? Why can't we both benefit, no matter which of us finds the jacket."

Casper came to a full stop, this time waiting for a reply. O'Hare couldn't believe the man's nerve. The fact that he was attempting to bribe a lieutenant of the New York City Police force seemed of no concern to him. But what was O'Hare to do? Oh, he could run him in for attempted bribery and hold him for a few hours, but that was bullshit. There was nothing in evidence but a conversation. The idea was to build up a case against slime like this that would stand up in court. The idea was to put men like Casper away for a decade. It rarely worked, but that was the idea.

His head was beginning to throb in the bright sun as he searched for an appropriate response. Finally, he settled for the obvious. "It sounds as though you're trying to bribe a police officer, Mr. Casper."

"Oh, Michael, what an old-fashioned way of looking at things!" Casper pretended to be hurt. "We all work together these days, Michael—the police, the government, private business. How many men and women in the Department do you think are *not* cooperating with someone in the private sector?"

O'Hare's head ached painfully now. It was the glare off the finish of the white Lincoln, stabbing through his eyes. He half-closed them and rubbed his scalp with his fingers. Casper was right enough. There would always be corruption. Serpico and the Knapp Commission were long gone.

"I know about you, Michael. I know a lot more about you than you think. I know about the tragedy of your son."

That woke him up. He looked intently into the flat, gray eyes.

"I know you've cut down your smoking from three packs a day to one pack a week. Very commendable. I envy your willpower." He took a box of Balkan Sobranies out of his jacket pocket and put one between his lips, then offered one to O'Hare.

O'Hare shook his head stonily. Little pinpricks of light swam above his nose.

"I also knew you were coming to this hotel today," Casper continued, "and that Richard spent the other evening here. How do I know these things, you must be asking yourself? The answer is painfully obvious, my friend. I have someone in your precinct who sells me information."

He lit the cigarette with a gleaming, gold lighter. "You are working very much alone, Michael. I sympathize with you. I hope you accept my offer of cooperation in the spirit in which it is intended."

O'Hare struggled to think clearly. It should not have come as such a surprise. Information was bought and sold by the police all the time. But a man in his own precinct?

Selling information about Pat? He leaned heavily against the hood of the Lincoln and the white-haired chauffeur scowled at him.

"Michael, let us enjoy a little speculation for a moment, shall we? Let us suppose that this jacket we are looking for contains cocaine. Now we both know how the world works, Michael. We both know that really, in this world, cocaine is very small potatoes. I'm not talking about the money. Coke is good business. Even big business. We wouldn't be having this discussion if it wasn't. And I'm not talking about dealing crack to some crazy punk on the street. Truthfully, Michael, cocaine's a bullshit drug. It's for rich people who want to play at being naughty. So they buy a mixture that's sixty percent milk sugar, and they pay a C-note for it, and then they make a straw out of another C-note, and they toot. They're having a party. And we're talking bankers and lawyers and congressmen here, Michael, not scum. So who the fuck really cares? Do you think a hundred years from now the tobacco companies won't be selling joints? Do you think the drug companies won't be marketing cocaine just as soon as the moral climate allows them to? It will happen, Michael. We're just living in a transition time. So why should we bust each other's chops? Why not help each other out, instead?"

O'Hare was lost. Between his pounding head and Casper's smooth, hypnotic voice he felt as though he might faint. And even with a clear mind, he wasn't sure he could argue against this man. Casper was citing facts. Corruption *was* everywhere. If you lived with a moral code, that was a personal choice. No one was going to give you a medal for it. A year ago he would have reacted differently. A year ago his strength and will were firm. But now . . . ? He groped for something to say.

"How do you know I'd keep my end of the deal?" he managed. "How do you know I won't keep your money and the cocaine too, if I get it?"

"Because I trust you, Michael," Casper replied with seeming sincerity. "I trust cops. I *like* cops."

O'Hare almost laughed through his pain.

"You think that's funny, Michael, but I got two daughters. You think I want them molested by some creep while they're walking home from school? I give to the PBA!" Casper beamed, and for one terrifying moment O'Hare thought the man was going to hug him.

"Michael, we're similar people, you and me. We're honorable. We're not junkies like Steve Knowles. And Michael," Casper lowered his voice to a conspiratorial hush, "we're doing the same job. You know what I'm saying? There's a lot of shit out there. Creeps and crazies. They got no control over themselves. Last winter in my own neighborhood, Michael, a nice old gentleman was killed by a shithead punk who was high on crack. The old guy was stabbed in the heart for two fucking dollars! That's the kind of trash I'm talking about, Michael. You try to control it. That's your job and I bless you for it. But I control it too. That boy? That shithead punk? The police never found him, Michael, but I did. He's in a wheelchair now with a broken back. He'll never kill again."

"Terrific." O'Hare spoke with a ringing in his ears. "Maybe we should give you a shield." He heard Casper laugh and felt a chill of sweat at the back of his neck.

"I'm not trying to build myself up into a saint, Michael. All I'm saying is that someone's going to do the business I'm doing. If you managed to bust me, a dozen crazy kids would be killing each other to take my place. Who would be better off? You? The City? Think about it, Michael. A deal between us isn't such a crazy idea. What do you say?"

He took out his handkerchief and wiped his neck. His answer had to be simple. He had no ability for complicated thought. "Sorry, Casper, I'm a cop, not a philosopher. My job is to arrest people when they break the law . . ."

Casper interrupted with enthusiasm. "Okay! You want a collar? You got a collar! Of course it's not going to be me; I wouldn't do anything stupid enough to give you the chance. So let it be Knowles. I'll set him up and deliver him, wrapped in a bow. You get your arrest and, let's say, forty thousand cash. The DA gets his conviction. You take a few ounces of the stuff for evidence, the rest ends up in the backseat of this car. What do you say, Michael? It's a good deal for everyone. The DA does it all the time, only he calls it plea-bargaining."

O'Hare saw his chance. If he could use Casper to deliver Knowles, then just possibly he could turn Knowles against Casper. . . . The thread was getting too difficult to follow. Right now he didn't see the harm in playing along.

"Can I have a cigarette?" he asked.

Casper grinned and took out his Sobranies. He handed O'Hare the gold lighter and opened the car door. "Come inside for a minute," he suggested. "It's air-conditioned."

Air-conditioned! O'Hare was in no mood to argue. Casper slid in and he followed, lowering himself onto the crushed-velvet seat. The dark coolness was an immediate relief. The ringing in his ears stopped. The back of the car was a combination office–livingroom with a telephone, desk, bar, and small TV. Casper's Lincoln was more luxurious than the room he lived in. He watched the gangster take a thick envelope from the desk. It was stuffed with new one-hundred-dollar bills.

He lit the cigarette and sucked in the rich tobacco. It tasted like wine. The leather armrest was sensuous under his fingers. He began to feel much better. His headache dwindled to a slight throb. From what he could see, there was twenty or thirty thousand dollars in the envelope Casper was counting from. O'Hare cleared his voice and pointed to the front seat. Casper immediately understood.

"Mr. Downey, would you mind stepping out for a moment?"

Mr. Downey stepped out without turning his head. Casper continued to count. When he reached twenty he stopped. He held the money in his hand and looked at O'Hare, expectantly.

"All I asked for was a cigarette, Casper," O'Hare said.

Casper laughed heartily, then stuffed the bills into O'Hare's jacket pocket. "Consider this a token of my good faith, Michael. You can always return it if you want. Am I a reasonable man or not?"

"Oh, you're a reasonable man," O'Hare said, handing back the lighter.

Casper wouldn't accept it. "No, that's for you. A gift. Whether you accept my offer or not."

"No—really, I can't."

"Of course you can. You risk your life for citizens like me every day, Michael. You deserve the best. Besides, didn't I tell you I like cops?"

O'Hare climbed out of the car still holding the lighter in his hand. It was heavy. Solid gold, for sure. His head was spinning, but now it was from excitement at this turn of events.

Now what? he wondered. A drink at Stanley's would be just the place to think it over.

18

"LISA, people are looking!"

She was dancing up Fifth Avenue. Richard was pleased to see her so happy, but concerned that they might be attracting attention. "We have two hundred dollars!" she whispered in his ear.

"I know." He wasn't as happy about the fact as she was.

"And we have this!" She held up a shiny brass key.

"What's it for?"

"You'll see," she laughed mischievously. "What do you want to buy?"

He shrugged. They were in front of Tiffany's and she pulled him over to a window that looked out on the street. Her eyes sparkled with excitement.

"Look at that fucking diamond!"

"We can't afford it."

"I bet we can, too!" She put her arm around him and squeezed the stuffing in the jacket. "We could dump one of the bags on the counter. Wouldn't they just shit?"

One block north they found F.A.O. Schwarz. Richard had never been in the store, but it was one of Lisa's favorites. She pulled him through the doors into what looked like a child's paradise. Hundreds of stuffed animals! An African scene of giraffes and tigers and antelopes drinking at a water hole! Model trains speeding along yards of track, over mountains and across trestled bridges. An entire space station hung overhead!

She skipped over with a full-sized chimpanzee. "Can I have it, huh?" she asked. Her face looked six years old.

"Lisa . . ." The chimp was tagged at a hundred and forty dollars.

"Please?" She leaned closer and breathed in his ear. "If you let me buy it, I'll give you something tonight!" She looked around, then let her fingers press firmly against the front of his jeans.

"Lisa!" He felt himself blushing furiously. She was clucking her tongue and looking down at him.

"You better hold this in front of you," she suggested, handing him the stuffed chimp. "You don't want to embarrass us." She batted her eyes and walked him to the cashier.

It was a roller-coaster ride! Richard thought with dismay. Being with Lisa, he didn't have any control over his life. Not over the speed they were going at; certainly not over the direction. It was all he could do to hold on, hoping they wouldn't derail.

And who knew at what moment they would? Selling the coke was dangerous. And besides, it was all they had. What would they do when it was gone?

They. He shifted uneasily as Lisa gave the stuffed animal to the cashier. When had they become a *they*? But there was something nice about that, too. Nothing had been said, but they were together now, for the moment. Sort of like a team, helping each other out.

The cashier was examining Lisa's one-hundred-dollar bills when Richard felt a tap on his back. He turned to see a steel-gray revolver in his face.

"Aaagh!" he screamed, knocking the gun out of the hand. The six-year-old boy who had been committing the armed robbery looked shocked for a moment. Then the blank little face burst into tears and went howling to find its mother.

Richard's legs felt like Jell-O. He leaned against the counter for support. "I'm sorry," he stammered.

"He was just a little boy!" the cashier scolded, and angrily rang up the sale. Lisa declined any wrapping. She took the chimp in one hand and Richard by the other, and walked them out of the store.

"It looked so real . . . !" he tried to explain, but Lisa was laughing.

"You should have seen your face!"

She had tears in her eyes, and he began laughing, too. And then he was running. Laughing and running at the same time, his legs weak, his chest heaving uncontrollably.

She took off after him. "Bang!" she shouted from behind. "Bang! Bang!" He turned around and saw her shooting at him, her forefinger pointed forward and her thumb straight up. "Bang!"

It wasn't funny! She had a real gun in her pants and he had a million dollars worth of coke in his jacket. But he couldn't stop himself. Finally he fell to the sidewalk, roaring so hard he thought he was going to throw up. When she caught up she fell on top of him.

"I'm starved!" he finally gasped, gaining some control over the silliness.

"Me too. Let's knock over a McDonald's!"

They were helpless for another five minutes.

Lunch was a hot dog each at a Sabrett's stand, two slices of pizza with sausage at the Pizza Parlour, two pretzels from a street vendor, and a cherry vanilla ice cream cone for her and a double fudge swirl for him.

"It's no good for you, you know," Lisa said as they walked down Madison Avenue, she carefully stepping over the cracks in the sidewalk.

"What's no good for me?"

"Chocolate. It'll give you pimples."

"That's not true."

"Is so."

"It is not! I read a book about it."

"Shit, you read a book about everything."

"Acne comes from viruses."

"What are you talking about?"

"Germs. Pimples come from germs, not chocolate."

"You're full of it. I wash my face every day and I have this zit right here that won't go away!" She pointed to a red blotch on her neck.

"Hormones," Richard said authoritatively, moving from his germ theory without losing a beat. "It's because you're an adolescent. You're experiencing an increase in your hormone level."

She looked at him suspiciously, sucking a cherry out of the ice cream, then playing with it with her lips and tongue. For some reason it made him uncomfortable.

"How come you don't step on the cracks?" he asked.

She shrugged her shoulders. "I don't know. It's bad luck. You know—step on a crack, break your mother's back." Richard followed, carefully avoiding the cracks. He wasn't superstitious but they certainly didn't need any more bad luck.

"Hey!" she exclaimed, and he followed her finger. It pointed to a square of sidewalk ribboned off to protect newly laid cement. No official-looking person was in sight.

"Lisa, no!"

But it was too late. She was at the cement and on her knees. When he got there she had already made a capital "L".

"Keep a lookout, huh?"

It was either that or drag her away. He kept a lookout, but every few seconds turned back to see what she was doing. When she finished the cement read: "Lisa & Richard—1989." She started to get up, but then leaned down again to put a heart around it. "It doesn't mean anything," she quickly assured him. "It's just the way it's done. Sort of tradition."

"Yeah." Unaccountably, he could feel his heart beating. "Like not walking on the cracks."

"Yeah." Her hand found his as they rounded Fifth Avenue. They didn't speak for a whole block. "It'll be there forever, won't it," she finally said.

"Maybe not forever, but a long time."

"After we're dead?"

"Probably."

She sighed. "It's spooky to think that some day, after we're dead, some kid might read it and wonder who Lisa and Richard were."

She held the chimp a little closer and Richard's hand a little tighter as they approached the massive facing and spires of St. Patrick's Cathedral. When she saw it Lisa stood still, staring at the building with awe. "I want to go inside," she said.

"I don't think we can, with the monkey and all," Richard answered uncomfortably.

"We don't have to go in. I just want to look from the door."

They climbed the steps and looked into the vast, vaulted space. "Do you believe in God?" she whispered.

"No," he replied.

"But there has to be a God!"

"Why?"

"Because who made us if not God?"

"We evolved, Lisa. From little one-celled animals."

"But who made *them* if not God?"

Richard didn't try to explain. Actually, he wasn't sure he could. But there was a scientific explanation for the beginning of life, he was certain of that. That was the beauty of science. It explained everything. Except for people, of course. Nothing could explain people.

Outside the church, they sat on the stone steps. Lisa's mood had turned serious and she hugged the chimp tightly. "My father went to Arizona to look for God," she said unhappily.

"Do you miss him?" Richard asked.

"Sometimes. Do you miss your mother?"

Richard thought about the question. It was tricky, and he had to search for the right words to explain his feelings. "I don't miss her exactly. I mean I never knew her, so how could I miss her?" Though, of course, he did wonder about her a lot. And he was a little jealous on parents' day, at school, when all the other fathers and mothers showed up. "What about you? Do you miss your mother?"

"She doesn't miss me," Lisa answered promptly.

"How do you know? Have you spoken to her recently?"

She shook her head.

"It's been all winter," he continued. "Maybe she does miss you now."

"She has a boyfriend."

"But that doesn't mean she doesn't miss you. Or want to hear from you. Maybe she feels awful now about your running away. Maybe she realizes she really loves you and wants you back. Maybe she's been looking for you for months now, but can't find you. . . ."

For a moment Lisa let herself give in to Richard's fantasies, but then she pulled herself back. "That's enough!" she finally told him. "You weren't there. You don't know!"

"I'm not saying I was," he replied. "I'm just saying that if you haven't called your mom in all this time, maybe things have changed. I mean, it's *possible*."

"Yeah, it's possible," Lisa answered bitterly. "Anything is possible. Prince Charles could divorce Lady Di and marry me, and I could be Queen of England. In the meantime let's get over to the Donnell. We don't want to keep Charley and his money waiting."

She headed them toward the library.

"But maybe your father came back," Richard persisted. He said it in a nice way, but he was getting under her skin. "Maybe he got lonely or bored in Arizona."

"No way! He was nuts. Everyone knew that. He left a note saying God had spoken to him and told him to go into the desert, just like Jesus."

"Okay," Richard went on after a moment's thought. "But maybe once he got there God sent him another message, telling him to go back home."

"Give me a break, huh?"

Lisa was upset, but this time she had to admit that Richard had a point. Since her father was nuts, there was no telling what he would do. He *might* have come back.

"And maybe your mother now realizes that she loved him all along."

"Yeah, that's a good one!"

Now he was being stupid again. It had taken twenty-four hours for her mom to remove all traces of Philip Frank from the house—the Jesus pictures, his religious books, his clothes. . . . "You know, the week after he left she dyed her hair orange! *Orange*, for Christ's sake!"

Richard shrugged. "Sometimes when people are upset they do weird things."

"Yeah, my mom was upset all right. And Jack was right there to comfort her."

Richard fell quiet for a moment. "Jack was her boyfriend?"

"Yeah, Jack was her boyfriend."

"Well, you know, being alone and all, it was only natural that she would find someone else."

"Jack moved in two days later!" Lisa spat out the words and could see the surprise on Richard's face. "My father left on a Sunday. My mom threw out all his shit on Monday. And Jack came over for dinner Tuesday night. It was the first time I'd ever even heard his name!"

That shut him up. It even made her feel good, somehow, shocking Richard like that.

"She introduced him to me, saying he was an old friend," Lisa continued. She wanted to shock Richard some more. "He sure seemed to be. At dinner the two of them drank and joked like they had won the lottery. Then, the next morning, when I came down for breakfast, there was my mom in her slippers and a robe, acting like it was just another normal morning, making scrambled eggs like she always did. The table was set for three, like it always was. Only the man sitting in my father's chair was Jack."

They walked in silence together for a block. Lisa hated even thinking about Jack. It made her feel too angry, and anyway, he was out of her life now.

"Well, maybe he's moved out," Richard suggested. "You know, my father had some girlfriends who lived with us, and none of them lasted more than a few months. Maybe your mother finally got tired of him and kicked him out."

"Nobody kicks Jack out of anything!" Lisa replied sullenly. "He's a truck driver and weighs about two hundred pounds. I couldn't even keep him out of my room!"

That got him again. Richard's eyes opened wide as he started to understand. "You mean he tried—?"

"Of course he tried! All men try, don't they? They just keep trying and trying until you give in!"

She answered his question even before he had the chance to get it out. "No, I never let him screw me. But he was at me all the time, whenever my mom wasn't home. 'What's the big deal?' he would say. I could have my other boyfriends too. And he had money. He could buy me things. And really, I should be grateful that he was taking

152

care of my mom and me. I should show him how grateful I was!"

"But didn't you tell your mom?" Richard asked.

"Are you kidding? Jack said he would deny everything. And who do you think my mom would believe?" It really hurt now, like a bad stomachache. "All he wanted was for us to be one big happy family!" she said softly, bitterly.

Richard could see Sprague's chiseled features through the reading-room window. He was sitting, leafing through a magazine as though he didn't have a care in the world. Richard had hoped the man wouldn't show up. Sprague was no idiot. They could be walking into a trap. But Lisa was so confident, and she had been right up until now.

"Hold the chimp," she said. "I want both hands free."

"What about me?" Richard wanted to know, taking the monkey and following her through the revolving door.

Sprague stood up as they approached. His hands rolled the magazine into a tight cylinder. Lisa ran up to him and kissed him on the cheek.

"Hi, Uncle Charley! We had such a wonderful morning. We went shopping, we had lunch, we even went to church. And look what we bought!" She pointed to the stuffed animal in Richard's hands.

Sprague nodded without saying a word, then jerked his head for them to follow. He led them toward a stairwell that led to the bathrooms in the basement. At the top he stepped aside to let Lisa go first. Richard's stomach churned. Sprague was in control. Lisa was still babbling about their great morning until she turned a corner at the bottom of the stairs and screamed "Leo!"

At the same moment, Richard felt Sprague's bony fingers clamp around his upper arms and shove him forward.

At the bottom of the stairwell was a short, black man in cowboy clothes with his arms clasped around a struggling Lisa.

"Let me go, goddamn it!" she demanded.

"You make any noise, girl, you gonna be hurt!" Leo twisted Lisa's arm until she cried out in pain. Then he looked up at Richard with round, angry eyes. "Greetings, my man! You must be runnin' up quite a bill with my lady, here."

Lisa twisted in an attempt to bite his arm but with one hand he pinned her to the wall, his fingers around her throat. "Please, Leo," she moaned.

Richard still couldn't believe it. The man was maybe five feet tall and trying to dress like John Wayne with a ten-gallon hat, buckskin jacket, leather pants—with fringe, for God's sake—and cowboy boots! But he also had muscles the size of grapefruits. He looked like he could strangle Lisa with one hand. He reached into her jacket and grunted as he came out with a fistful of small, powder-filled bottles.

"I told you!" Sprague whispered triumphantly, his head twitching, looking around nervously. Leo slipped the bottles into his own pocket, then opened Lisa's jacket and found the gun.

"You out of yo' mind, girl?" he hissed furiously. "You out of yo' fuckin' mind? Stealin' my piece? Rippin' off my stash? Runnin' away with this child? What the fuck you think you doin', girl?"

Lisa flashed a desperate look at Richard and he understood. Leo didn't know about the cocaine in Richard's jacket! There was no mistaking the message in her face. The jacket had to be protected!

Leo turned her around with a slap. "You look at me when I'm talkin' to you, girl!"

"I'm sorry Leo," she cried.

"You sho' are! An' you gonna be a whole lot sorrier when we get back."

Sprague was licking his lips with a sharp, pointed tongue. "I can't stay here, Leo."

"I unnerstan', my man. I thank you fo' bringin' this matter to my attention. I owe you one."

Richard felt his arms suddenly released. When he turned around a moment later, Sprague was gone.

"Well, what you waitin' on, boy? Get yo' ass out of here!"

He backed up a step and looked at Lisa. Go on, she nodded. He made his way up the stairs, stopping finally in the reading room where there was a guard and a lot of people. A moment later they emerged. Leo had Lisa firmly by one arm, but it wasn't necessary. She wasn't resisting. When they went out the side door he tipped his ten-gallon hat at the security guard. Lisa followed him, limply. Her cheeks looked hollow, her eyes vacant. Richard had never seen a face so utterly lost.

Now he was alone. He looked around, forlornly.

Libraries had always been favorite places for him. When he was nine and ten, after school, he remembered running home to check in with the housekeeper, and then walking the half-mile or so to the closest library. He was always happy in those great, quiet rooms.

This one felt like a tomb. He sat at a table with a lifeless chimp by his side. An old woman looked at him suspiciously, then hooked her withered arm around a small stack of books and slid them closer to her. Don't worry lady, I won't steal your lousy books, he wanted to say.

He had to do something. He had to find Lisa. He had to rescue her from Leo.

He really needed her, too. She was smart. She could keep them away from the police. And besides—he liked her. He wanted to hold her again. He wanted to have sex with her. Maybe he even loved her.

He would begin by making a list. He went to the librarian and borrowed a stub of a pencil and a piece of paper. Across the top he wrote *RESCUING LISA*. Under that, on the left side of the page, he wrote *ASSETS*. He checked his pockets and realized that Lisa had all their cash. Under *ASSETS* he wrote "75 cents." He thought for a moment, then wrote "surprise." That was in his favor—they wouldn't be expecting him. He couldn't think of any more assets, so he began two more columns, *OFFENSE* and *DEFENSE*. Under the first column he wrote "weapon?" Under the second he wrote "disguise?" Then he thought for a moment and wrote "protect stuff!"

His plan seemed simple and direct. He thought it probably wouldn't work, but he didn't know what else to do. He quickly jotted down the supplies he would need and then the stops he'd have to make—a department store, a supermarket, a bathroom, the Port Authority Bus Terminal, a pizzeria. . . .

19

THE morning was going well for Leverton. She had had no trouble with Knowles during the night. After his fix he fell asleep on the couch; she slept upstairs, in her clothes, on top of the bed. She slept more deeply than she had expected, and was surprised to find him already up when she awoke, nervous but energetic. Breakfast was on the table.

She couldn't help but remark on the square hole, low in the kitchen wall.

"Junkies," Knowles explained. "Local punks. They know I keep stuff in the house. They must have come looking for it while I was in the hospital. Speaking of which . . ."

His body was tense; she could feel his need. She went upstairs to get the Anacin bottle. Then she prepared his morning fix and injected it into his arm.

"What about you?" he asked, breathing deeply now, more relaxed, his eyes closed for the moment.

"I keep it to one a day."

He nodded, seeming to accept that. But apparently he wasn't accepting everything. After breakfast, when Leverton examined her purse she found the contents rearranged. While she was sleeping Knowles had examined her driver's licence and credit cards. He had seen her pictures of Pat. But most important, he had checked out her kit: syringe, disposable needles, and the few grams of high-grade heroin supplied by the Department.

In half an hour Knowles was out of his stupor.

"How about giving me a hand with this, Nurse Mary?" he called to her. He was on his haunches, looking closely at the hole in the kitchen wall. "Power tools," he told her. "They knew what they were doing." He went into the garage and found a plywood square. She helped him nail it over the opening.

"This won't really keep them out," he shrugged philosophically. "But at least it'll cut down on the drafts."

Then he pulled the BMW into his driveway and began a thorough inspection. First the interior, then the trunk, and finally, lying on a low dolly, the job made slow and laborious because of his broken arm, the underside of the car.

"What's the problem?"

He didn't answer. Probably looking for a transmitter, she thought. It would be nice if the Department *had* some sophisticated equipment. She wanted to tell him not to bother.

"You know how to drive a stick shift?" he asked, coming out of the house carrying something wrapped in a light blanket. He put it in the trunk, next to the spare tire. Its form showed through; it was the Uzi automatic. Nor did he really try to hide his .44, tucked into a holster by his left armpit.

"Yes, I can drive a stick shift."

"Then let's go to town." He handed her the keys and got into the front passenger seat. She slipped behind the wheel but didn't start the car.

"You know, I accepted this job as a nurse, not as a bodyguard," she said.

"There won't be any trouble that I can't handle, Mary. I just need some help with the driving."

"And the arsenal?" The Uzi was making her nervous as a cop; it would certainly have made her nervous as a nurse.

He didn't try to insult her intelligence. "I assume you

understand the nature of the business deal I mentioned last night?"

"Yes, I think so."

"I have to protect myself, Mary. I can't call the police."

"I understand that. But what I don't understand is why I should take this kind of risk for what you're paying me."

He laughed. "What are you suggesting?"

She smiled. "You're a businessman. You understand contracts. I contracted to be your nurse for an agreed price. It seems to me that if you want me for another job now, a job for which you stand to make a lot of money and I assume some risk, we should negotiate another contract."

He laughed again. "You have balls, Mary. I like that. Okay, let's renegotiate. If I'm successful with this deal I'll give you a bonus of, say, one thousand dollars."

"Say five thousand," she replied, not missing a beat.

He didn't laugh this time. "Two thousand, and I suggest you say yes, Mary."

She took a breath and started the car. She was pleased. That was just the way Mary Lewis would have handled this situation. "Where are we going?" she asked.

"Midtown. There's someone I want to look up. I have a few questions to ask, and a small debt to repay."

The BMW hugged the road, responded instantly to her touch. Driving it was a joy. And they say crime doesn't pay, she said to herself, bitingly. What crime does not pay is taxes, and so it can enjoy the little luxuries of life, like this snappy car.

She waited ten minutes before asking the question.

"So what's the deal, anyway?" She kept her voice light and casual. He didn't respond. "After all, if we're in this thing together—"

"We're not in anything together, Mary," he interrupted brusquely, setting her straight in no uncertain terms.

"I work alone. At the moment you're a high-priced chauffeur. Got it?"

She didn't press for more.

They entered through the glass doors of the Bo-Mond Hotel and took the narrow flight of stairs that led to the second-floor lobby. Leverton knew this sort of building well. It was one of many in the Times Square area that were originally built as small apartment houses above storefronts. But now, with just a bit of conversion, they had become much more profitable as hotels for transients, and for the hooker trade.

Knowles put on an impressive show of anger for the manager, barely controlling himself when the man told them he knew nothing about renting a room to any fifteen-year-old boy. Knowles finally calmed down when the manager gave them a room number on the fourth floor. The night clerk who had been on duty at the time was sleeping there just now, the manager said. Francie Cobb was his name. Maybe he knew something about it. Knowles thanked the man and they walked up to the fourth floor. Leverton figured that her presence as the distraught mother by her husband's side didn't hurt.

They found the room and Knowles motioned her to stand back. He drew his gun and measured a pace from the door. Then, in one continuous movement, he raised his right foot and kicked through the lock.

The door shattered open. The night clerk was sitting up in bed, watching TV. When he saw Knowles his face went slack with shock.

"Oh, shit," he moaned.

Knowles stepped into the room. "I'm Richard's father," he said. "I think we've already met."

Francie Cobb pulled himself forward, bringing his feet to the floor. "Yes, I remember," he began bravely, but the gun in Knowles's hand caught him flush on the side of the face, knocking him off the bed. He shrieked in pain, then continued in a high-pitched wail as he quivered on the floor, holding his battered jaw.

"That was for the bite," Knowles said calmly. "Now let's talk about Richie." He looked quickly at Leverton. She kept her face neutral.

Francie quieted down into a low moan. Knowles pulled him up onto the bed by his shirt collar. Blood trickled down his chin. With a shaky finger, he pointed to a bottle of bourbon on a nightstand. Knowles handed it to him, and watched disgustedly as he sucked on it like a newborn calf.

Knowles went and closed the door, then sat next to the clerk on the narrow bed. "Now about Richie?" he asked again with the same measured calm. Leverton sat in a nearby chair.

"I was gonna tell you about him, honest," Francie cried through the pain in his mouth. "You didn't give me the chance!" Knowles raised his gun to indicate his disbelief and the man cringed. "No, please, I wanna help. I wanna make a deal with you."

Knowles seemed almost amused. "What kind of deal?"

"We can work together," the clerk pleaded. "We can be a team. I can help you find your boy and the jacket."

"How?" The gun dangled ominously.

"Through the girl," Francie said. A sudden animation filled his face. "I can help you find him through her. I know her. And all I want is a quarter share of the stuff. How about that? Twenty-five percent."

"Sure, Francie," Steve Knowles agreed. "Now how are you going to find this girl?"

"I'm real tight with her pimp. What I'll do is use him

to find her. He don't have to know nothing about the stuff. Twenty percent! Just twenty percent. That's reasonable, huh? I don't want to be greedy."

"What's this pimp's name, Francie?"

"Charley Fong," Francie said.

"Charley Fong?"

"He's a Chink, but a real tough dude. Knows karate. Black belt and all that shit. Runs with a gang in Chinatown. You don't want to mess with them Chinks, Ace. They're mean fuckers. You just leave him to me . . ."

There were footsteps in the hall. Francie started.

"In fact, why don't you and your friend get some lunch or something, and I'll go see Fong."

The footsteps stopped at the door. Knowles crossed his arms, hiding the gun, but keeping it trained on the entrance.

"How about ten percent, Ace? If I help you find the stuff? Sort of like a finder's fee. I couldn't be more fair than that, could I?" Francie sounded very nervous.

The broken door swung open and the doorway framed a black midget all done up in cowboy clothes. Leverton saw a puzzled look on the leathery face.

"Hey man, you got trouble with yo' door?" the midget said to Francie. Then he saw Leverton and Knowles. "Oh, sorry, man. I didn't know you was entertainin'. Jus' wanted to show you somethin'. He pulled out a long-barreled revolver and grinned from ear to ear. "An' guess who I found with it?"

Francie seemed to be having some kind of attack. He was muttering words and holding up his arms, waving them as though trying to ward off evil. But the dwarf cowboy pressed ahead. He reached out and pulled into view a pale, limp, blonde-haired girl.

Leverton couldn't hold back a gasp. It wasn't the puffy lip and purple bruise on the girl's cheek that shocked her. It was the look of utter emptiness in the child's eyes. They didn't focus. They didn't care. Leverton was used to seeing that in old people ravaged by senility and neglect. But not in a teenage girl.

"You!" Steve Knowles said. He was staring intently at the girl. For an instant there was a flicker as her eyes rested on him. Then they went blank again.

The cowboy looked puzzled. "You two know each other?"

"You must be Fong," he said to the midget, obviously the girl's pimp, and then shot a quick, angry look at Francie who was cringing on the bed, sucking furiously at his bottle.

"Fong? What you talkin' 'bout, man?"

"Please come in. I'm Steve Knowles, Richard's father."

"Oh yeah, the boyfrien'!"

The pimp shoved the girl through the doorway onto the floor, and followed her in. Leverton had to control her own angry response to the casual brutality of the man. Without a sound, the girl picked herself up and sat dumbly on the bed next to Francie, blocking out everyone in the room by gluing her eyes to the TV. The pimp addressed Knowles in a tone of righteous wrath.

"That boy yo' son, man? How you bringin' up that boy? Lettin' him run in the streets? Takin' up with ho's? Stealin'? Gettin' in trouble? That boy should be in school, man!"

Wonderful, Leverton thought. A brutal, midget pimp, dressed in leather, lecturing Steve Knowles on child-rearing.

"An' gettin' my girl into trouble?" The pimp turned his attention to the girl. "You crazy or somethin', Lisa? Rippin' off my snort?" He took a fistful of gram bottles out of his jacket pocket and held them in her face. "Tryin' to deal to one of my ace clients?"

A stillness fell over the crowded room and Leverton

caught a series of quick glances. The girl, alive for a moment, turned from the TV screen to look at Knowles. Knowles's attention was on the pimp, trying to figure out exactly how much the man knew. The clerk held out a trembling hand toward Knowles.

"Yeah, you're crazy, Lisa," Francie said out of the side of his mouth, desperately trying to catch Knowles's eye. "Imagine, stealing Leo's coke and trying to sell it!" The message was clear to Leverton. Francie had told the pimp nothing of the cocaine in Richard's jacket, and now he wanted Knowles to go along with the deception. The coke was for them to share. When Knowles finally turned his head the clerk attempted a hideous wink.

The pimp missed it all. He was still trying to figure out an earlier confusion. "An' what's all this Fong crap?" he asked Knowles.

"Just a little joke," Knowles answered. "Francie here was just telling me that your name was Charley Fong."

The anxious expression on Francie's face turned to a look of horror. Knowles showed a sadistic pleasure as he continued through the clerk's frantic signals to stop. "He told me you were a Chinaman."

"I ain't no Chink!" the pimp said with growing anger. "What the fuck's wrong with you, Francie? You got a twitch or somethin'?"

Knowles answered for the clerk. "The girl and my son weren't dealing your coke, Leo. They were dealing mine."

"Yo's?" Leo was now completely confused. Francie moaned a low, painful moan.

"Mine," Steve Knowles said. "Francie found it on Richie and tried to grab it for himself, but I interfered. It was in the lining of my son's jacket." He looked quickly at Leverton again. She didn't blink. He returned his attention to the pimp. "Was it Francie who told you what happened?"

"No, Francie didn't tell me nothin'!" the pimp said,

glowering at the clerk. "I got a call from a customer tellin' me Lisa was tryin' to deal him some coke, so I come here to ask fuckface what was goin' down. He tol' me Lisa an' some boy had ripped off my piece an' my stash. Maybe he even lifted a ounce hisself, jus' to make the story stick."

He brought his face menacingly close to Francie's. "You got somethin' to say, fuckface?"

A noise that sounded like a rattle came from Francie's throat and he lifted the bottle for another drink. It never reached his mouth. Leo swung his arm and the revolver caught the bottle flush on the side, knocking it out of Francie's hand and shattering it into a thousand pieces. An instant later Leo's gun was against his forehead.

Every pore on the clerk's battered, pockmarked face seemed to open at once and he glistened with sweat. "Leo, you wouldn't," Francie croaked.

But apparently Leo would. The pimp's finger slowly closed around the trigger. Leverton's heart pounded. How could she allow a murder in front of her eyes? She crossed her legs and reached down to the cuff of her pants.

"Leo, for God's sake!" Francie cried.

"Leo . . ." Leverton warned. Her fingers grasped the handle of her gun.

Leo pulled the trigger. With the sound of the click, Francie fell onto the bed in a dead faint.

"Turkey!" the pimp muttered, blowing away an imaginary puff of smoke from the end of the barrel. "I ain't never had no bullets for this sucker. Can't get 'em. It's a fuckin' antique."

Leverton sighed deeply and uncrossed her legs. The pimp sat on the bed next to Francie's body and burst forth with an explosion of questions for Knowles.

"How much stuff does yo' kid have, man? We got a deal if I get it fo' you? We gonna split it? I'll make her talk, man," he gestured at the girl, "if we got a deal."

Suddenly, as the realization dawned, Leo's face grew

angry. "Shit! I had the fuckin' kid in my hands! I coulda had the jacket an' the stuff!" He turned to Lisa with mounting rage. "You knew, you little bitch! You knew an' didn't tell me! You gonna cooperate right now! You gonna tell me where you been with yo' boyfrien', an' what plans you two was makin', an' where you think he is right now!"

Lisa had returned her attention to the TV. "Fuck you, Leo," she said tonelessly.

He struck her face with his open hand. The slap sounded like a pistol shot and it turned Lisa's head around.

Leverton's response was reflexive. She grabbed the pimp's wrist, braced one foot against the bed, and yanked. As he rose toward her she chopped at his throat with the edge of her palm. Leo emitted a gargled scream, then hit the opposite wall and crumpled to the floor, gagging and coughing.

Knowles and Lisa were staring with open mouths. "Sorry," Leverton murmured. "I don't like to see kids get hit," she said weakly.

"Holy shit!" the girl exclaimed, and for the first time Leverton saw some life in her. The pimp was still choking.

"What you do that fo', woman!" he gasped. "I didn't fuckin' hit you!"

Knowles reached down and helped the pimp up, but his eyes were on Leverton. "Where did you learn to do that?" he asked. "Nursing school?"

"Shit, she ain't no nurse!" Lisa muttered.

"I once took a course in self-defense," Leverton explained. She looked at the floor, angry at herself now for the outburst.

"Self-defense?" The pimp furiously grabbed for his ten-gallon hat that had flown off when he hit the wall. "You wait 'til yo' fuckin' attacked befo' you use that self-defense, lady! Shit! She's my damn girl an' I'll beat on her whenever I like. An' if you wanna make somethin' of it, you can start right now!" He chopped a crease back into the hat and defiantly put it on his head. Then he clenched his hands into tight fists.

"Mary doesn't want to fight with you, Leo." Knowles soothed. "She took you by surprise, that was all. I'm sure she realizes that in a fair fight she wouldn't have a chance. Isn't that right, Mary?"

"Of course, Leo," Leverton replied. "You're a man. How could any woman stand up to a man?" Her sarcasm was lost on the pimp, but Lisa picked up on it and smiled.

"Fuckin' right!" Leo said. "So don' you tell me how to treat my girls!" He reached into his pocket and pulled out a knife. With a flick of his wrist, a four-inch blade snapped open. Leverton jerked back, her hand drifting down to her right ankle again.

"Leo, why don't you put that away?" Steve Knowles said.

"Fuckin' cut off her tits, she tries that again," the pimp glowered, paring his fingernails.

"Leo, I'm willing to make a deal with you," Knowles continued. "I'll give you five thousand dollars if you deliver the coke within the next twenty-four hours."

"Shit man, five grand ain't squat for what that boy is carryin'." A light rap on the door cut him off. "What?" he shouted in annoyance.

The reply was garbled. Leo got up, pulled open the door, and stepped back in surprise. There in the doorway was a teenage boy, his face white as chalk. He wore a blue nylon jacket and held a cardboard pizza box in one hand. In the other, a small, black revolver shook nervously.

"Richie!" Steve Knowles whispered.

20

"**NOBODY** move!" Richard ordered. His voice was high and squeaky, and the gun in his hand jumped from the midget cowboy to Steve. "I'll kill anyone who moves, I swear!"

"No one's moving, Richie," his father said. "Just relax."

"Yeah, man, relax." The pimp grinned nervously, taking a step back.

Lisa jumped up and ran to Richard. She touched his arm, as though to be sure he was real, then turned and stood next to him, facing the others.

"Back up, Leo!" she demanded. "All the way to the window!"

"Now you be cool, girl."

"You heard her!" Richard shouted. He waved the gun with a jerky motion and Leo moved back. Lisa scooped up the gram bottles that were lying on the bed. "Let's get out of here," she said.

"We're going," Richard announced, "and I don't want anyone trying to follow us—"

His father interrupted. "Richie, we have to talk."

"We have nothing to talk about!"

Steve stood up. Richard's heart pounded. His father seemed so large. "Out in the hall. Just you and me."

"Sit down!" Richard demanded. He pointed the gun at his father's chest. Steve sat back down.

"All right, Richie, I know how much you hate me."

"I don't hate you!" Goddamn it! he thought. His eyes were beginning to tear.

"You tried to shoot me the last time we met."

"I did not! That's a lie!"

"Richard . . ." Lisa was tugging at his arm.

"After all those years of caring for you, bringing you up all by myself . . ." Steve continued.

"You never cared for me!" he shouted back at his father. "You never brought me up! I brought myself up!"

"I did the best I could, Richie. And this is how you repay me? By not even letting me explain what happened? By not even listening to me?"

"Richard!" Lisa was pulling harder.

"Stop it!" he told her, and shrugged her off. *He* had the gun now; *he* was in control.

He looked around, for the first time really seeing who was in the room. Francie was lying on the bed, blinking his eyes, staring hungrily at the blue jacket. But his face was a mess. He looked too beaten up to be much of a threat. Leo, by the window, *was* dangerous. But luckily he seemed scared of the gun.

Then he noticed the woman. One of his father's new girlfriends, he supposed. He was certain he had never seen this one before. She was pretty, but older than the others, not really Steve's type. Her face was too soft. Anyway, she was a woman. He didn't think he had to worry about her.

Steve was the one to worry about. His father was always the one to worry about, Richard thought. But something had happened to him and his arm was in a cast. That was a bit of luck. Having only one good arm would make it hard for Steve to try anything tricky.

"All right, explain!" he said to his father.

"Richard!" Lisa said again, but he ignored her. His attention was fully on Steve.

"I have some business friends in Colombia, Richie," Steve began. "They gave me the jacket as a gift. As a present for you. I didn't know what was in it, I swear. It wasn't until I got home that they called and told me what was in the jacket, and ordered me to get it from you as soon as you came through customs. Unfortunately, when there was trouble at the airport, I didn't think straight. I'm sorry for that. But since then all I've been trying to do is get it back from you so you'll be safe."

"Bullshit!" Lisa cried.

"Trust me, Richie," Steve insisted. "Come home with me. Everything will be all right."

The room became still.

"He's lying, Richard," Lisa said in a low voice. "He's lied to you all your life."

Richard swallowed so that he could speak. He had come to a decision. "Who's she?" he asked, pointing the gun toward the woman.

"A friend of mine, Richie. Her name is Mary. She's a nurse. I hired her to help me take care of my arm, after Francie broke it in our fight."

Richard slipped his left arm out of his jacket.

"What are you doing?" Lisa whispered.

He transferred the gun to his left hand and took the jacket off. Lisa looked upset, but he couldn't do anything about that now. He held the coat out to the woman, but kept the gun pointed at Steve.

"Take this to the police," he told her. The woman didn't move. Steve looked bewildered.

"What are you doing, Richie?"

"It's not your cocaine," Richard replied. "You're not responsible for it. Those guys tricked you as well as me. We don't owe them anything. When the police get it we'll both be safe. Go on," he said to the woman, "take it!"

She took the jacket.

Then she took one step toward the door and the room exploded.

Steve bolted out of his chair and collided with the woman, who slammed into Richard, knocking the gun out of his hand, and sending them both crashing against the wall. Richard felt the jacket against his ribs and reflexively curled an arm around it. There were shouts. Curses. Lisa was pulling at him and the jacket as Leo's body came hurtling across the room in a flying tackle that just missed Richard, but decked Francie.

Then suddenly the jacket was out of his arms. Lisa had grabbed it. She was tugging hard at him but he couldn't move. He looked down and saw that Leo had both hands around his ankle. He shouted to Lisa, who stomped on Leo's hands with the heel of her shoe. Leo screamed, and Richard's ankle was free.

Now they were running again.

It was a dream—a nightmare. Richard's legs felt like rubber. The carpet in the corridor sucked at his feet. When they reached the stairwell he felt as though he were falling, tumbling, into a pit. The shouts behind them were from monsters in the night.

They hit the street. The sunlight made him blink, and the dream-feeling ended. They were running for real now. He headed them toward Broadway.

"Come on!"

He wanted to sprint, but Lisa was running as fast as she could. Behind them he could see Francie and Leo and then his father teeming out of the hotel.

She was already winded. The three men were catching up. Richard pulled at her and she stumbled, but regained her balance. Leo had sped past Francie and was almost on top of them now. Steve was just behind.

"Give me that!"

Richard tore the jacket out of Lisa's hands. He swung

his arm and the coat flew in a high arc into the middle of the street.

It worked! Leo skidded to a halt. Steve ran directly into the pimp and they both fell to the ground. Behind, Francie veered off into the street, making a beeline for the jacket.

Now they could stop for a moment. They were at the corner of Broadway and Lisa was doubled over, sucking in deep lungsfull of air. He pulled her next to him, behind a parked truck, and together they peered out.

Francie had scooped up the jacket and was running with it, but the lining had ripped open and plastic tubes were falling into the street. He stopped, frantically trying to gather them up, but Leo was immediately on top of him. They fell to the ground, wrestling, as Steve arrived. One of the tubes was torn and Steve bent down to look at it. Then he picked it up.

"Let's get out of here," Richard said. He dragged Lisa around the corner and pulled her by the arm as they jogged several blocks more until he felt sure they were safe.

"Boy, that was close!"

His heart was thumping with pride. His rescue had worked! Lisa sat silently at the curb. She was breathing hard and looked ready to cry. He knelt down next to her.

"I got the idea from the kid in the toy store," he told her happily. "I figured if it worked on me it could work on Leo. But I didn't have any money, so I had to shoplift the gun from Woolworth's. Then I had to get into the hotel, so I got this empty pizza carton and told the man at the desk I was delivering a pizza to a guy named Leo. But there was no one in Leo's room, so I walked around until I heard voices . . ."

"Shut up!" she shouted, and suddenly she was crying and hitting him at the same time.

"Shut up! Shut up! Shut up!"

He had to put his hands over his face; her punches really hurt.

"Do you think it matters now?" she cried. "Do you think anything matters now?" She stopped hitting him, and he was able to grab her hands and hold them.

"What do you mean?" he asked.

"Do you think you're some kind of hero? Huh? Do you think you're a big man because of what you did? You're stupid, Richard! You're a stupid kid and I never want to see you again!"

He didn't understand. He thought she would be grateful to him for rescuing her. "But Leo had you . . ." he began weakly.

"I could have gotten away from Leo anytime I wanted! You gave them the jacket!"

"But they were going to catch us just now," he choked.

"You could have gotten away with the jacket, and I could have gotten away later. We could have met, somewhere. All we had was that jacket, Richard, and now we have nothing! I hate you!" she finished miserably, and turned away.

Richard had never felt so awful in his life. He had risked his life for her and now she hated him. He sat back down on the curb with his back propped up against a wire garbage basket and buried his head in his arms.

"Oh, shit," he heard Lisa mutter.

A bus nearly ran over his toes. It honked angrily at him and he didn't care. He didn't care about anything anymore. He wished a bus would run him over.

"We can't just sit here," she said. He felt her pull at his arm.

"Go away," he told her.

"Richard, I'm sorry."

"No, you're not!" He raised his head and stared at

her angrily. "You're not sorry about anything! I risked my life to help you and what do I get? A thank-you? One nice word?"

And now, stupidly enough, he began to cry. He wiped away the tears with his hand and pulled himself to his feet. "Why don't you just go back to Leo, okay? Why don't you just leave me alone!" He began walking away. She had to take running steps to keep up.

"Richard, stop for a minute. Please. I *am* sorry, really."

He stopped. She sounded as though she meant it. They stood face-to-face and just looked at each other. Her lower lip was quivering and her eyes were brimming with tears. A droplet slid down her cheek. "And Richard . . . ?" she went on.

"What?"

"Thank you."

She couldn't control her lower lip anymore; she was blubbering like a baby. She hid her face by burying it in his shoulder. People were watching, but Richard didn't care. He put his arm around her, tentatively, awkwardly. She looked up and he brushed his lips against hers, then kissed the wetness of her cheek. It tasted salty.

Finally she stopped crying and managed a little smile. "I guess we need another plan." She wiped her face on the sleeve of his shirt.

"Yeah, I guess we do. But maybe first we should go and get the cocaine."

She looked at him blankly.

"You didn't think I would actually risk bringing the stuff into the hotel, did you? You didn't think I was *that* stupid."

Slowly, the astonishment in her face widened into a huge smile. The next minute she was laughing so hard that she fell over, onto the sidewalk.

21

O'HARE scratched down some figures on a cocktail napkin. Just for fun. Just to see the bottom line.

Two kilos of coke—that was the customs agent's guess at what the jacket held. That would be almost four and a half pounds. Now, at sixteen ounces to the pound, and twenty-eight grams to the ounce . . .

He quickly did the arithmetic. There were almost two thousand grams of pure cocaine in the jacket, which, when cut, would yield four thousand grams of sellable product.

He picked up his wide-rimmed glass and took a swallow of Jameson's Irish. It was dark in Stanley's, and cool. And the whiskey had done its work. His headache was almost gone.

Four thousand grams of product. Worth one hundred dollars a gram at the going street price. That was the bottom line. Four hundred thousand dollars. Four hundred thousand tax-free dollars.

There were so many ways to play it.

He could play it straight. Until this morning O'Hare had never taken so much as a free meal. In a country where a president once boasted about having no trouble raising a million dollars to pay off jailed blackmailers, where congressmen starred in movies that showed them peddling their offices, O'Hare had played it as straight as a parson. Well, he could continue on that path. He could take the two g's down to the station and voucher it. He could write in his report that he had agreed to the payoff in an attempt to get both Casper and Knowles. He could live in his furnished room, maybe move to an apartment if he could find something for under a grand a month. He could stay at his job, beating on the scum of New York, and in three years retire with a pension that, after taxes and inflation, might leave him a little above the poverty line.

Or he could take Casper's offer. He could "do business" the way Casper said everyone did business. Forty thousand dollars was a substantial sum, even with today's cost of living. He could do business with Casper and other "businessmen," and in a few years have his own private pension to add to the Department's.

Or, he could go the whole nine yards. With a little nerve and luck he could walk away with the jacket itself. The thought made his pulse race. Of course there would be an investigation. He might have to disappear to some Caribbean island, a not totally unpleasant thought. But—he would never see Anne again. He wondered how much of a loss that would be, if seeing her now caused so much pain.

And what would his sin be if he went that route? he wondered. Surely it wasn't a question of a black mark in God's ledger. God died for O'Hare the day Pat did. So who was he being virtuous for? For Anne? She didn't care what he did. For himself? He sipped his drink and smiled at the thought. He had no morality left, just anger and pain. At the moment he simply couldn't see anything wrong with confiscating a few pounds of refined coca leaf, assuming he didn't get caught. In fact, who deserved it more than a hard-working cop who had spent seventeen years risking his life to protect others? Surely he deserved it more than a slime like Casper, more than the venal underground within the Department that would probably rip it off the day it was vouchered in the property clerk's office.

But then, if he did grab the coke, what would be the difference between himself and Milton Casper? The thought worried him. There *would* be a difference, he knew that. Seventeen years of honest police work could not be wiped out by one transgression. But O'Hare was having trouble understanding exactly what that difference was. He would think about it all again—when he was sober.

He had just come to that decision when Wilhite walked in. The tall sergeant took a moment to adjust to the dim light of the saloon, then walked over to O'Hare and slid into the other side of the booth. Whilhite began his report as though there was nothing irregular about this meeting, as though it had been scheduled as just another event on the day's agenda.

"Leverton called in," Whilhite said. "She had to make it short. Richard showed up at the Bo-Mond half an hour ago. He's been with a girl, a teenage hooker named Lisa who we might be able to trace through her pimp at the hotel. Knowles got the jacket, but the stuff wasn't in it, and Richard got away. He still has the coke. He's probably still in the neighborhood."

O'Hare took the news with a sip of whiskey. "Where's Leverton?"

"Still with Knowles. She says she's doing fine. She thinks they'll be heading back to Rye."

O'Hare nodded and emptied his glass. "You want one?" he asked. Wilhite shook his head no. O'Hare signaled, and the bartender came over with a bottle. Wilhite had contained himself admirably to this point, but he lost it when the bartender left.

"What the fuck are you doing, Mike?" he demanded.

"I'm having a drink, Ernie. What does it look like I'm doing?"

"It looks like you're fucking burying yourself!"

O'Hare shrugged. They didn't even have to discuss how Wilhite had found him. Stanley's had been his bar for sixteen years. Until he swore off ten months ago.

"Why, Mike?" Wilhite was asking the question with his arms outstretched. He looked like he wanted to shake

177

O'Hare. "You didn't have to take this case. You sure as hell didn't have to work with Anne."

"I want Knowles," O'Hare replied mechanically.

"Fuck Knowles!" Wilhite was angry. "I don't give two shits about Knowles. What about you? You're worth a dozen Steve Knowles! So we get Knowles. You think that's going to do one rat's ass bit of good to anyone if you go down the toilet? We got to take care of ourselves, Mike! Sure we do a job, but first we got to take care of ourselves."

O'Hare felt a warmth inside, and not just from the liquor. Wilhite did take care of people. He took care of his ex-wife and his two kids. He took care of his mother who lived in The Bronx. He took care of his kid brother, who, in his teens, began to show psychotic symptoms, and now was a full-blown schizophrenic. Whether or not the LSD the boy had taken had contributed to his illness would never be known, but he had to be cared for, and Wilhite had placed him in a private institution, and visited regularly to monitor his treatment.

"Alcohol is a great preservative, Ernie."

"Yeah, for corpses. It's called formaldehyde."

O'Hare laughed at the joke, then gestured at the bartender for a pack of cigarettes.

"You want to go look for the boy?" Wilhite asked.

"Sure," O'Hare said, not moving. His eyes stared downward, examining the napkin. "By the way, I had a little conference this morning." He looked up into his sergeant's eyes.

"Yeah? With who?"

"With a businessman named Milton Casper." Wilhite's face was blank. "He's the banker who foreclosed on Knowles the other night."

Wilhite took a moment to digest the information. "He just walked up to you? Just like that?"

"Just like that," O'Hare replied.

"What did he want?"

"He wanted to buy me."

The bartender came over with the cigarettes. O'Hare opened the pack slowly, taking off the cellophane in one piece. Wilhite had nothing to do with his hands. He clasped them together on the table, thumb pressed against thumb.

"Fuckers think they can buy the world," he said.

"Fuckers have bought the world," O'Hare replied.

"What burns my ass is the cars they drive!" Wilhite turned to a safe topic. "I got an eight-year-old Rabbit that's busting my balls."

"Rabbits suck," O'Hare agreed.

"I bet he bought that Continental for cash."

O'Hare nodded. It was as though he had never mentioned the bribe offer. But cops were often jittery when it came to talk of corruption. It didn't mean anything. You just never knew who might be doing a little business on the side. You didn't want to know. He brought the subject back to Casper.

"He said he'd give us Knowles."

Wilhite raised his eyebrows.

"Of course, not until he gets the stuff."

"Scumbags!" Wilhite exclaimed. "Not an ounce of loyalty among them!"

"Yeah, not like cops." O'Hare searched the sergeant's face and found nothing but puzzlement. "You know where he found me? In front of the Bo-Mond. He knew the boy had stayed there. He knew I would be there this morning. He knew how many fucking cigarettes I smoke each week." O'Hare opened the pack and took one out.

"How the hell did he know that?" Wilhite demanded angrily.

"I don't know, Ernie. What do you think?"

Wilhite answered immediately, his tone anguished, his face saddened. "He's got someone in the precinct on his payroll."

"Yeah, that's what he told me." O'Hare searched Wilhite's face. If betrayal was there, he couldn't see it. But who could it be besides Wilhite or Leverton? Who else knew the information Casper had acquired?

"Fuck!" Wilhite said softly.

"Yeah, fuck."

O'Hare had intentionally chosen Wilhite for this assignment because Wilhite's life, too, had been maimed by drugs. Wilhite would never betray him to a dealer. It was inconceivable.

"Ernie," O'Hare continued softly, "how did you know it was a Continental? You've never seen the car." O'Hare was afraid that if Wilhite hesitated for even a second he would burst into tears.

Wilhite answered in an even tone of voice, without missing a beat. "It was in Leverton's report. Of the night Casper visited Knowles."

Of course. O'Hare exhaled with relief. He found himself nervously rolling the cigarette between his fingers.

"Both Leverton and I have been filing reports, Mike. Lots of cops at the precinct have access to them."

"Yeah," O'Hare said. It was true. Anyone interested *could* have picked up the information. Two drinks on an empty stomach were making him paranoid.

"You want to look for the kid?" Wilhite asked again.

"Yeah." O'Hare finished his drink and stood up. "And maybe one of us should back up Leverton."

One of us, O'Hare repeated to himself. Guess who? He felt that his need was transparent. It was stupid, backing up Leverton. It would be a waste of manpower. She had come up with the idea—she had to take the risks. And if she did get into trouble, what could a backup do? But suddenly he was worried about her. And, as always, he wanted to be near her.

On the way out of the saloon he lit the cigarette. The gold lighter felt warm in his hand, and solid, and powerful.

22

I T was impossible! Lisa thought, when her laughter had subsided. Her mind was a jumble, making it hard to listen to what Richard was saying.

"So since I didn't want to take the stuff into the hotel, I needed some sort of plan. I tried to figure out what you would do in the same situation."

They were walking across Forty-second Street. He was talking rapidly, and his pace matched his speech. She took his arm to slow him down.

"So I shoplifted some powdered sugar at a supermarket, along with some plastic bags and safety pins, and I made the switch in the men's room of a Chinese restaurant. At first the waiter wouldn't let me in, but I told him I was sick, and I would throw up in front of all his customers if he didn't."

It was fate, she decided. There was some supernatural power at work. Maybe God really did exist and had planned it all.

"Then I had to hide the stuff, so I thought the safest place would be a locker at Port Authority."

And here they were now. The Port Authority Bus Terminal. The convention center for every hustler and pusher and drunk and freak in the city—where there were more cops under one roof than anywhere else in the world. And Richard thought it was safe.

"I just had seventy-five cents," he was saying, "exactly what the locker cost! It was like a miracle."

It was. He opened the locker and her chimp was sitting inside, looking as though it had been operated on by a very bad surgeon. Safety pins fastened a slit that ran from its throat to its belly.

He handed it to her as a gift and she cried out in pain. One of the pins had unsnapped and pricked her finger. A bead of blood formed. She put it to her lips and watched curiously as Richard took the open pin and, looking a little embarrassed, carefully fastened it to her shirt, just above her breast. With a start, she realized what he had just done. She had seen it a dozen times in high school. She had just been pinned!

Her head was whirling. None of this made any sense. Not the feeling that she and Richard had been destined to meet, not the surge of emotion a few minutes ago when they cried and kissed each other on the street . . . How had it happened, she wondered, that at the age of fifteen years and ten months, after dancing naked for pimply college kids and fucking her brains out for horny businessmen, she was suddenly pinned?

Well, she had to thank him somehow. She could feel her face flush as she kissed his cheek. He looked so proud. *Pinned*, for Christ's sake!

The chimp was heavier with its new stuffing. She held it tightly against her chest, hiding its scar from prying eyes. Port Authority was no place for them to be now. *New York* was no place for them to be now.

"Richard, I still have over a hundred bucks. We could get on a bus and go to Boston or Philly . . ."

He was shaking his head.

"There are a lot of people looking for us here. We could get an apartment or something in another city. I could dance or model while you went to school—"

He interrupted her dream. "I can't," he said.

"Why not?"

"I just can't."

182

She knew it had something to do with his father, but she wasn't sure what. "You don't owe anything to your old man, you know. You saw how he tried to con you."

"He said he didn't know about the stuff in the jacket."

"But he was lying, Richard. You proved that when you gave the jacket to that lady. He attacked you. He doesn't want to help you or protect you. He wants the stuff!"

Richard was shaking his head in slight, rapid movements. "No, he was just angry at me. He was angry at me for not trusting him."

"Oh shit!" Lisa muttered.

A cop had spotted them and was slowly walking over.

He would be looking for a boy alone, with a blue jacket.

Richard wasn't alone, and they didn't have the jacket anymore. But the first thing he'd do was ask for some ID.

She had to think fast.

She held the chimp tightly and ran to meet him.

"Officer, am I glad to see you!" she cried out with great relief.

"What's the matter?"

Her voice quivered slightly. "It's my brother!" She grabbed the policeman's hand and led him back to Richard whose face had gone white. "He's lost his wallet!"

"Oh, Jesus . . ." the cop sighed.

"We just got off the bus from Philadelphia. There was a crowd by the escalator. I guess that's where it happened. Mickey didn't even know it was gone until a minute ago."

"Are you kids here alone?" he asked.

"Yeah. We came in for the day to visit our uncle."

"You got any identification?"

It took him long enough to ask.

"Sure."

And of course "Mickey" didn't. His wallet had been stolen. She gave the cop hers, and thanked God she had

kept her old G.O. card, and library card, and her gold-edged card for perfect attendance at Sunday School.

"Where's this uncle of yours?" the policeman asked.

"We're supposed to meet him at his office. He's going to be furious at us."

"No, he won't. These things happen all the time in New York. You got enough money to get there?"

"That's no problem," she smiled. He looked ready to let them go. "It's just a little uptown. We can walk over. Is there any chance of getting Mickey's wallet back?" She thought she should be more concerned about that.

"Not if you didn't even see the guy who took it."

"Oh." She put on a show of disappointment. Then an idea came to her. It was weird, but kind of wonderful at the same time.

"Do you think you could take us over to Uncle Charley's?" she asked. The policeman looked unhappy. Richard looked like he was about to faint. "I'd feel so much safer if you could. I could call him and have him meet us downstairs, in front of his building. I just know he'd be very grateful . . . Please?"

The cop nodded reluctantly. Lisa turned so he couldn't see her face, then raised her eyebrows at Richard and flashed him her most mischievous smile.

This is too much, Richard said to himself. This is definitely too much.

He sat stiff as a rod in the backseat of the patrol car. Lisa was in front holding the chimp, holding a million dollars worth of cocaine, on her way to meet Sprague to complete the deal, and chatting happily with the policeman. She was crazy, that's all there was to it. If she didn't get them killed they would spend the rest of their lives in jail.

"There he is!" Lisa cried out.

Sure enough, Sprague was there, standing by the entrance to his building. He spotted the police car and looked like a ghost. Lisa thanked the cop and got out. Richard joined her on the pavement.

"Hi, Uncle Charley," she shouted, waving to Sprague. "Want to meet our new friend?"

Sprague came over. He didn't have much of a choice. He was walking stiffly and had a tight smile on his face. He blinked his eyes and nodded at the cop.

"Mickey got his wallet stolen," she explained unhappily, "and this nice policeman was kind enough to drive us over. Thanks again," she said to the cop.

"No trouble," the officer assured her. He smiled respectfully at Sprague, then cautioned Richard. "It's better to keep your valuables in your front pocket, son. It makes it harder for anyone to steal them."

Richard nodded vigorously. "Yeah, I'll do that from now on," he said.

The cop drove off and Richard felt unsteady on his feet. Sprague looked the same way. Lisa could not have been more pleased with herself.

"You think Leo can stop us?" she crowed softly. "You think you can stop us? Or the cops? We're the A-Team, Charley. We're the dynamic duo!" She put her free arm around Richard's waist. He was grateful for the support. "Now, about that trip to your bank . . . ?"

Richard sat slumped in the backseat of the taxi as Lisa quietly counted out the money—eight one-hundred-dollar bills. She held her hands low, so the driver couldn't see through his rear-view mirror. The chimp was on the floor by her feet.

"We can't do this again," he said softly.

"We'll see," Lisa murmured.

"He said he'd kill us if he ever saw us again. He said he'd hire a professional hit man and have us shot. He said that would be cheaper in the long run . . ."

"Here!" She pressed four one-hundred-dollar bills into Richard's hand. "Does this make you feel better?"

"Not especially."

It didn't. Selling the stuff to Sprague was dangerous. Selling the stuff to *anyone* was dangerous. As more people knew they had cocaine, more people would be after them. And it seemed that everybody in the world was after them already. And it wasn't even *right*, selling the stuff. It wasn't his. But if they didn't do it, Lisa would go back to hooking.

"Come on, smile," she cooed. She was watching out the window, but leaned back and let her hand rest in his lap. One finger traced over the zipper of his fly.

"Lisa!" he murmured, uncomfortably.

She whispered in his ear. "All this money makes me horny!" Then suddenly she leaned forward. "Stop here!" she told the cab driver. It was the third time she had made him stop. Once again she dashed out of the cab and into an old, seedy building, only to reappear a few minutes later and get back in. "Keep going," she ordered.

The driver turned in his seat. "Do you know what you're doing, miss?" he asked. A very good question, Richard thought. The meter showed fourteen dollars and forty cents.

"Yes, I know what I'm doing." Lisa handed him a one-hundred-dollar bill. "Does that make you feel better? Now will you keep driving? And slowly, please."

He started up again. They were definitely in a slummy part of the City. Bums in the street would come up to the car when it stopped at a light and clean the windshield, looking for a handout. It was pathetic, Richard thought. People shouldn't have to do that for money. He felt a little sick just watching them.

"What *are* you doing?" he whispered to Lisa.

"It's dangerous for us walking around like this," she whispered back. "We're too conspicuous. We need a father."

"A father?"

"Stop!" she shouted again.

The cab swerved to the curb. She was looking at a drunk lying against a building, sleeping, with his hands folded like a pillow under his head. She ran out of the cab and shook the man awake, then pulled him into the taxi. He offered no resistance. He hardly even woke up. He followed Lisa like a dirty, fuzzy old sheep. He smelled like a sheep too, Richard thought.

"Miss . . ." the cabby began.

"He's our Uncle Andrew," Lisa interrupted. She leaned forward and spoke as intimately as she could over the front seat. Not that she had to worry about Andrew overhearing. He had already curled into a ball and was snoring.

"He goes off and gets drunk a lot, and my brother and I have to find him and bring him home," she sighed heavily. "It's very sad."

"Where's home?" the cabbie wanted to know. Richard wanted to know too.

"Central Park West and Seventieth Street," Lisa told him. "You see, mostly we live in Arizona. Dad's an evangelist—got his own television show and everything. But we come to New York a lot so dad keeps an apartment here."

Lisa leaned closer and lowered her voice, as though revealing a great confidence. "As you can see, Uncle Andrew never really amounted to much in life, while dad is doing great. So when dad comes to town Uncle Andrew gets depressed, and goes off on these binges . . ."

The cabbie waved his hand, giving up. The only thing

187

he seemed to understand was the address, and he headed for it. Lisa leaned back in her seat with a satisfied smile on her face.

Amazing, Richard thought.

He was amazed again when they pulled up in front of an apartment building on Central Park West and Lisa produced her shiny brass key.

"Charley keeps an apartment here," she whispered to him, collecting her change from the cabbie and grabbing hold of the chimp. "For his weekend fun. His wife doesn't even know about it. I swiped the key when I went through his wallet."

Richard whispered back. "Lisa! He really will have us killed!"

"He won't even know we've been here. He never uses the place on weekdays. Come on, I've been here a dozen times. The doorman knows me."

That was true enough. The doorman grinned broadly when he saw Lisa, but his face hardened into a scowl as he caught sight of Andrew, asleep on his feet, being supported by Richard who was using all his strength to keep the man vertical.

"Sad, isn't it?" Lisa confided to the doorman. "I'm sure you know about Mr. Sprague's work with the Catholic Committee to Help the Homeless. No?" She showed surprise at the doorman's ignorance. "It's sponsored by the church. Every Easter each member is required to bring home a derelict and give the bum a bath and a hot meal. I think the idea is to keep the bigshots humble—sort of like the pope washing a peasant's feet once a year, you know? Mr. Sprague gave me his key." She showed it off. "He'll be by later this evening to administer the bath personally." She fished a ten-dollar bill out of her jeans and gave it to the doorman, who suddenly was more than happy to help Richard maneuver Andrew across the marble-floored lobby and into the elevator.

Lisa pressed eighteen.

"Lisa," Richard sighed, "have you ever thought of working for the CIA?"

Andrew suddenly started. His bloodshot eyes opened long enough for him to realize where he was.

"Fourth floor, ladies lingerie," Andrew announced, and pressed a couple of buttons before Richard could grab his hand. Then he closed his eyes and went back to sleep.

Richard's amazement didn't end after Lisa let them into the apartment. They deposited Andrew on a living-room couch and Richard looked around with his mouth hanging open. This was a hotel suite out of the Playboy mansion, for God's sake! These were rooms that would normally be reserved for the President of the United States, or Frank Sinatra!

The livingroom alone was thirty feet long! One entire wall was a sheet of glass, and from eighteen stories up Richard could see miles of the Hudson River, with two fragile looking bridges at either end. He could see the high-rise apartments lining the New Jersey shore. And beyond them, through the layers of smoke and exhaust and pollution, he could see the dull, reddish blot of the setting sun.

"Not bad, huh?" Lisa whispered. She had come up behind him and was sharing the view. "This is sure different from last night."

Richard couldn't remember for a moment, then it all came back—the abandoned house with the black family, sleeping on a mattress on the floor . . . "Yeah, just a little," he agreed.

She gave him the tour.

"As you see, we have a kitchen complete with all my favorite foods, and two bedrooms, and two bathrooms with dressing rooms . . ."

And velvet couches, and a plush carpet, and soft lighting, and a TV.

"We should be out by nine in the morning," she warned him. "The doorman will get suspicious when Charley doesn't show up. But don't you see, it'll work!" She gave him a hug which didn't ease his worries.

"What'll work?" He was back at the window. Cars looked like toys, and people on the streets crawled as slowly as ants.

"We'll get Andrew washed up, buy him a new suit, and he can be our father. We can tell people that we're from Texas, and that our dad is an eccentric millionaire, and we're up here getting him treatment at Bellevue. We can be a family, Richard!"

"Yeah, we can be a family."

She put her arms around him and hugged him again, and this time Richard felt the kind of tingle he got from putting his face close up to the surface of a glass of freshly poured ginger ale.

Well, she had a point, he thought. They were as good a family as many he'd seen. So the father was a drunk and a little nuts. A lot of fathers were drunks and a little nuts. So the daughter was a hooker. A lot of people prostituted themselves in this world. So the son was wanted by the police for smuggling cocaine across two continents . . .

"And we're a perfect team," Lisa was saying. "You've got the stuff. I've got the connections to sell it. And Andrew makes us legitimate!"

Andrew must have heard his name because he suddenly sat up on the couch. "You're gonna like us, Tee Double-You Aay," he sang out to no one in particular, and fell back asleep, gently snoring.

"Legitimate," Richard repeated to himself, and watched bubbles of spit form on their "father's" lips.

"There's enough stuff in your jacket for us to live for years while I study to be an actress or a dancer or a model, and you go to school!"

Lisa was in a cloud. Richard couldn't have brought her back to earth even if he wanted to.

"And by the time the stuff runs out I'll be making good money with my dancing, or modeling, and you'll have a job as a scientist or something. And Andrew is really very sweet. You'll like him once you get to know him."

Richard sighed. Maybe he should believe her, he thought. Maybe with her experience and his brains and Andrew as their cover, the three of them *could* live together as a kind of family. Lisa had worked miracles up to now. Look at where they were. Safe for the time being, in a gorgeous apartment a thousand feet over New York City. And since he met her, he had performed one or two miracles himself. Maybe it *would* work out. With Lisa anything seemed possible.

The windows of a building to the north had become golden mirrors, brilliantly reflecting the light of the setting sun.

She kissed him quickly on the cheek. "Don't worry," she breathed into his ear.

"What, me worry?" Richard said, forcing a smile on his face.

23

L E V E R T O N was furious with herself. Her performance with the pimp in the hotel room had been stupid. She hadn't done the girl the least bit of good, and she had focused unnecessary attention on herself. And then, when the boy walked in, the whole ugly mess had been handed to her as a gift and she had blown it! Fooled by a plastic gun!

Pathetic, she thought.

The aftermath was as ridiculous as a slapstick comedy with the night clerk and the pimp clawing each other in the street over the plastic tubes of powder. Knowles hadn't even tried to stop them. He had already tasted the stuff. Francie and Leo would have all the powdered sugar they could use for the next year.

Knowles seemed to take it remarkably well, though. During the ride back to Rye he just kept his eyes shut and didn't say a word. He didn't seem angry that he had been outwitted by his son; he didn't even seem suspicious of her. Maybe her stupidity with the pimp hadn't been as obvious as she thought. After all, why couldn't a nurse be an expert at judo? Maybe she had been lucky this time. Maybe she had no problem with Steve Knowles at all.

"How about another beer, Nurse Mary?"

Knowles was lying on the couch. She sat in the easy

chair a few feet away. The same positions they had been in last night. The same request. It had already become a pattern.

Leverton tried to imagine what life would be like, living with this man. Impossibly frustrating, she decided. There was a fierce, almost sexual energy inside of him that excited her, but it never surfaced. Moment to moment, Steve Knowles was a bore. All he really wanted to do was spin dreams, and wait for his next fix.

She stood up and went to the kitchen.

Nurse Mary, he had said. He had called her that three times in the last hour. Was she imagining the sarcastic tone, that slight emphasis on the word *nurse*? Or was she just being paranoid?

The girl had known it instinctively. "She ain't no nurse!" the child had cried.

Knowles had to be suspicious, she now decided. It was his business to be suspicious. If she was a little paranoid, he would be ten times worse. It was stupid to think she had no problem with him. He was watching her every move. She couldn't afford another mistake.

She poured a cold beer and returned. He took the glass and began examining her with an obvious, intrusive stare. He was doing it deliberately, trying to make her uncomfortable. She sat very still and considered her options. She could always abort the assignment—just get up and walk out. He wouldn't even know what she was doing until she was out the door. But then what about that lost girl, the damaged boy . . . ? Who would protect them if she walked out? And who would destroy vermin like Steve Knowles? No, her job was here. She returned his stare with a cool confidence.

"How about we take care of ourselves, Nurse Mary?" he finally said.

"Take care." Knowles's euphemism for getting high. It was a couple of hours early, but . . .

193

"Sure, why not?" She stood up, relieved to break the growing tension.

"And I want you to join me this time." He had a mischievous smile on his lips. "I want to watch you do it." He could have been a little boy suggesting a dirty game.

Anxiety swept through Leverton, but with it came a strange sense of relief. The scrutiny was over. He had decided upon a test.

"All right," she said. The calm certainty of her response surprised her.

She would have more time to think about it upstairs.

She took the steps slowly—a deliberate effort at controlling her racing pulse. Was it worth it? she wondered. There was no guarantee Knowles would find his son again, no guarantee or even likelihood that they would be able to build a case against him for anything.

She picked up his kit. She was well prepared to play the role of a junkie. She had done it before. A Department doctor had taught her how to give both subcutaneous and intravenous injections. An ex-junkie had shown her how to cook heroin. She had learned what a normal dose was, and how to tie off a vein. But up until now she had only played the role. Until now the only substance she had shot into her bloodstream had been a ten-percent glucose solution.

She examined the kit with a practical interest. One thing in her favor—Knowles's junk would be clean. He would be cautious enough in that respect. And she didn't have to shoot the sixty milligrams he took. She could insist on the standard junkie dose of ten. That wouldn't knock her too far on her ass. Actually, that might even be interesting to try.

The admission sent a shiver down her spine.

Coming back down the stairs she was lightheaded with anticipation. It took all her concentration to cook the spoonful of heroin over the candle, and her fingers trembled as she filled the syringe with his dose. She picked up the rubber strap to tie off his arm, but he stopped her. He had that same naughty smile on his face.

"Ladies first," he insisted sweetly. "I told you, I want to watch."

She put down his syringe and studiously began preparing her own dose. Her mouth was dry. "I take ten milligrams," she explained.

"No way," he told her, playing the role of generous host. "I want us to take the big ride together."

There wasn't a junkie in the world who would have refused.

She didn't have to go through with it, she said to herself as she prepared her syringe, carefully filling it to the sixty-milligram level. Even now she could put down the needle and walk out the door. Instead, she wrapped the tie around her arm and secured it. The needle slid easily into her vein.

She had prepared for this assignment as thoroughly as possible, but nothing could have prepared her for the feelings now sweeping through her body. Warm foam flooded her stomach, her womb, her breasts. The euphoria opened as a morning glory at dawn, reaching out with its petals and folding her into its honeyed well. She threw back her head and laughed her first full, nerveless laugh in a year.

"Jesus Christ!" she murmured, over and over again, and in the distance she heard Steve Knowles laughing, and then the sound of a bell.

O'Hare sat in his car and sipped. He timed himself to one tug at the bottle per five minutes. He needed the numbing effect of the alcohol, but couldn't allow himself to get drunk. His eyes rested heavily on Knowles's house.

Five minutes passed and he took another swallow. He stared at the cracks of light that came through the edges of the livingroom curtain. He didn't know what to do. He couldn't sit here all night, and he couldn't go in.

Then he thought about it for a minute and wondered why not? Why couldn't he go in? All he needed was a pretext, and now that he thought some more, he didn't even need *that*! There were no secrets between him and Knowles anymore. The cat-and-mouse game was long over.

"Fuck Knowles anyway!" he said aloud. He didn't need an excuse to knock on that asshole's door!

He got out of the car and stopped. He needed an excuse for Anne. She would take it as an invasion of her assignment if he came in, a lack of trust in her competence. Well, fuck her too! If she really was some junkie nurse whom Knowles had picked up he wouldn't be doing these mental somersaults to justify his behavior. He had every right to forget she was a cop. It was his duty to forget it! It was perfectly natural for him to keep the pressure on Knowles.

He walked quietly up the path. There were sounds from inside. A woman's laughter. He rang the bell. The door opened and Knowles stood before him, surprised for a moment, but then bursting into a show of delight.

"Come on in, Lieutenant," Knowles invited, graciously. "We're having a party."

O'Hare walked in.

Syringes, cellophane packets, spoon and rubber tie sat on the livingroom coffee table. Anne sat obscenely in a deep, stuffed chair, her legs splayed out, her arms dangling loosely over the sides. She had her head stretched back and her eyes were half-closed, and she was laughing a deep, rollicking laugh as though someone had finally explained the meaning of life to her, and she had just got the joke.

He looked at her flushed face and nearly two decades fell away. Anne Leverton, fresh out of college, new to New York, was laughing happily over landing a small role in an off-off-Broadway musical.

They were at a party; they had just met. They had

danced a few dances, then talked for hours about life, politics, sex, and what a coincidence it was that he was a policeman since her father and uncles were cops, too. Her grandfather had been a cop! Her whole damn family were cops! One thing was for sure, she told him that very first night, she wasn't going to marry any cop! She was going to be an actress! She was going to have her own career, maybe go to Hollywood and make movies after she trained for the stage.

He met those willful green eyes and agreed that her decision was smart. Cops made lousy husbands, and, to be perfectly honest, actresses didn't make such terrific wives. She laughed and gave him a ticket to her show. When O'Hare saw her onstage that next night—a slim, sexy, redhaired elf in black leotard and tights, dancing just a beat out of step and singing slightly off-key, he knew this was the girl for him. He began proposing that week. . . .

She looked no less beautiful today, O'Hare thought. The lines in her face and the gray strands in her auburn hair gave a depth to her beauty that no twenty-year-old could match. She was laughing quietly now, but was more deeply flushed. Her face glistened with a thin film of sweat. He picked up an empty cellophane packet and put it to his tongue. Heroin. She had shot up with Knowles. O'Hare's insides coiled into a knot.

It wasn't hard to understand what had happened. Anne thought she had to either shoot up or risk being made as a cop. She would never walk out. It was easy to understand, but shatteringly wrong. As wrong as his sitting in the car just now and sucking on a bottle? As wrong as his fantasies of stealing the cocaine himself?

Her laughter finally subsided and she opened her eyes. She looked up dreamily and didn't recognize him at all.

How had they come to this? he wondered numbly. They had survived the disappointment of her acting career not working out. They'd had Pat, and had bought a house on Long Island. O'Hare had thought they had it made. He had a challenging job, a bright and brawny son, and Anne seemed happy in her role of mother and wife and homemaker. But when Pat started school she became uneasy. She wanted more out of life. O'Hare suggested community theater; Anne came home with the news that she had passed the exam and was going to enter the Academy. She was going to be a cop!

She stared at him with dreamy eyes, then shut her lids. Her attitude was unmistakable. He was a downer, the high-school principal at the prom. If she closed her eyes he would disappear, and she could keep on dancing.

Knowles was enjoying it all thoroughly. He let out a small chuckle of amusement.

O'Hare took out his revolver and put it against the drug dealer's head. Knowles stopped laughing, but kept an annoying half-smile on his face.

"Control yourself, Lieutenant," he said in a soothing voice. "If you kill me your career is over. Maybe you go to jail. You've got a decent life. Don't do anything stupid."

A decent life. O'Hare looked at Anne. She was breathing softly and regularly now. She might have been sleeping, enjoying a sweet dream.

"What's the matter?" Knowles asked. "You never saw a junkie before? You never saw smack? It's no big deal. The lady's no virgin."

"Shut up!" O'Hare pressed the barrel against Knowles's face. Anne was humming a tune. He strained to hear, but couldn't make out the melody.

Knowles shrugged. "Okay. So what are you going to do? Bust me for possession?" His tone was straightforward and he wasn't even smirking. "Are you going to take a case worth half a million in coke and turn it into a bust for a few grams of smack?"

Knowles was right. It was laughable. What was on the table wasn't even felony weight. O'Hare moved to the couch.

He made a show of examining the heroin, but only wanted to be closer to Anne. He still didn't recognize the tune.

"Can we put this into some sort of perspective?" Knowles asked. "Can I give you a little history on the subject? A hundred years ago morphine was legal. Did you know that? It was sold over the counter, in drugstores and grocery stores. It was sold through the mail as cough mixtures and pain killers and consumption cures and for 'women's ailments.' It was treated like booze—not exactly respectable, but all right if you kept it under control. Men who sipped it with their lunch weren't fired from their jobs, and women didn't leave their husbands over it. There were more morphine addicts then than heroin addicts now, but they weren't put in jail. They were respected members of the community. They went to church on Sunday. The drug wasn't seen as a problem, so it didn't become a problem."

"Yellow Submarine." That was it! She was humming a goddamn Beatles' song. "We all live in a yellow submarine, yellow submarine, yellow submarine . . ."

She looked so helpless but didn't seem to be in pain. O'Hare wondered how different her shooting up *was* from his sitting at Stanley's and tossing back half a bottle.

"And another thing, Lieutenant . . ."

Knowles was still buzzing bullshit in his ear. It felt like a mosquito O'Hare wanted to swat.

". . . did you know university studies have shown that a heroin addict, given his normal dose, is a medically well man? Heroin doesn't damage body tissue or brain cells. Those cigarettes you smoke cause cancer. Booze destroys the liver. But there is no demonstrated physical damage from heroin or morphine. Did you know that?"

Knowles was leaning toward him, smiling. O'Hare swung his free arm and caught him flush on the side of the face, knocking him onto the carpet. When Knowles sat up, O'Hare cocked the hammer of his gun and pointed it at his heart.

"No, I don't know that, Knowles. But what I do know is you were resisting arrest when I busted you for possession. You went for your gun and I had to defend myself. There's hardly going to be any investigation at all."

Knowles picked himself up and rested on one knee. He touched his face to see if he was bleeding. He hadn't lost his smile. "Lieutenant, do me a favor. Either pull the trigger or put the piece away."

O'Hare wanted to scream. Knowles didn't care! He could live for another fifty years or be dead in a minute, it was all the same. The fucking Yellow Submarine! he raged, lowering the gun.

"Listen," Knowles was saying, "why don't we work together? Why don't we go after the man I'm working for?"

O'Hare gave him a quick look.

"I'm serious. His name is Milton Casper. I'm already screwed. You're sitting on me, and Casper wants me dead. Even if I managed to come up with the stuff, what would I do? Run halfway around the world to start a new life? I've got my home here. I've got a job, and Richie. The best I can do now is deal with you. We can work together—you get the coke and Casper, and I walk. What do you say?"

What did he say?

He had been a hair's breadth from pulling the trigger. Knowles had been a split second from dying. Now Knowles was calmly trying to deal.

O'Hare took a moment to calm his pounding heart and assess his position. As a cop he was sitting pretty. He had Knowles and Casper turned on each other. With luck he might get them both. But as a man—with his wife spinning opium dreams and treating him like furniture, with his only child dead, with his finger clutching the trigger of his gun, wondering whether to commit murder or negotiate justice with a junkie who was destroying his own boy— as a man O'Hare was hanging by a thread.

What did he say?

"You'll wear a wire against Casper?" he said wearily.

Knowles grinned from ear to ear. "Sure. I'll set up a meeting. I'll tell him I have Richie and the stuff and demand my cut. You'll have to get a few ounces of pure Colombian for me to convince him. If he pays, we have him cold."

O'Hare suddenly felt nauseous. Whether it was from dealing with this piece of scum in front of him, or from Anne's relentless humming, he couldn't tell. But he had to get out. He could pull her out with him, he thought, but then what? She had taken the smack voluntarily. She wanted to stay on the assignment. If he yanked her she would despise him even more than she already did. But how could he leave her here?

Her eyes fluttered. She recognized him this time, he was sure. "Who is he?" she said to Knowles.

"He's a cop, honey," Knowles replied.

"Then I guess he doesn't want to join our party."

She closed her eyes, a weary queen dismissing a no-longer-favored courtier, and O'Hare's question was answered. He swept the cellophane packets and hypodermics into a thick palm and headed for the kitchen. Knowles was right behind.

"Hey, what are you doing?"

He shredded the packets into the sink. The powder trickled down the drain like fine sand. Knowles was furious.

"I thought we had a deal!"

"This isn't part of it."

O'Hare snapped the needles and strode to the door. He was going to be sick and didn't want it to happen here. The tune followed him out. "We all live in a yellow submarine, yellow submarine, yellow submarine . . ."

It was still in his ears as he knelt by the side of his car. He retched till he spat up blood.

24

H A R D rolls. White bread. A packet of Velveeta cheese. Slices of salami, baloney, roast beef, and turkey roll. Containers of potato salad and macaroni salad. A bag each of potato chips, bar-b-q chips, and tortilla chips. Hostess Twinkies. Dipsy-Doodles. Yodels. Three pints of ice cream. Two bottles each of Pepsi, Diet Pepsi, Dr. Pepper, and root beer. A six pack of Yoo-Hoo. Twelve Milky Ways. A bottle of wine for Andrew. . . .

They were setting up a picnic on the carpet, by the livingroom window. Lisa's idea. After all, she argued, they did have the best view in the City. And besides, Andrew wasn't really ready for a restaurant yet.

"You just take whatever you want, Andrew," Lisa offered, getting out some plates.

"No siree bob!" Andrew exclaimed.

He was more awake now and seemed, for the moment, sober. But he was still weird.

"Food's no good for you," he informed Lisa. "Don't you know that? Breeds germs in your gut. Alcohol kills germs. Makes you pure inside." He happily patted the bottle of wine they had given him.

The view from the livingroom window was sensational. Richard went to it and felt as though he were standing on the edge of a cliff. It was a different planet out there, now. The plumes of smoke and jet trails and bands of pollution were gone. The sky had turned dark purple with just a spot of red on the horizon to mark the sunset, and the river was black. The City wore a hundred necklaces of light.

Lisa joined him. She pointed north. "That's where we stayed last night," she said. Somewhere out there was the abandoned building, the black mother, the boy with the baseball bat, the baby that wouldn't cry. Richard put his palm against the window and covered them with his hand. Then he sat down on the carpet. She sat down next to him and sprawled out on her stomach. He sprawled out too. The carpet was soft and springy.

"That's where the Bo-Mond is," he said, "and Leo and Francie."

"And your father," she added.

"Yeah." He wondered where Steve was right now, and what he was doing. He suddenly felt sad.

Her hand went further south, to the horizon. "And my mom . . ."

Her voice trailed off and she rested her head against his shoulder. Even with the sadness, Richard felt a moment of perfect peace. If he could only freeze time, he thought, right at this moment, forever.

There was a noise from the kitchen and Lisa was on her feet.

"What are you doing, Andrew?"

She bounced in and Richard followed. Andrew had his bottle of wine in one hand and was holding a knife in the other.

"It's got a goddamn cork in it!" He stabbed fretfully at the top of the bottle. "What's a cork doing in a wine bottle, anyway?"

Richard gently took the bottle away, and opened drawers until he found a corkscrew.

"It's French wine, Andrew, and French wines have corks," Lisa lectured. "And it's very expensive so drink it slowly and enjoy it."

Andrew grunted and gratefully took back the open

bottle. He gurgled a mouthful. "Good," he judged, wiping his lips with his sleeve.

Lisa sighed and began laying a tablecloth by the window. Richard helped. Andrew watched them, sipping his wine.

"Chemicals," Andrew commented, "that's the ticket! Chemicals kill germs—prevent decay."

The man was losing it. Richard began to feel uneasy.

"It's a fact of life! Corpses ain't rotting no more. We're all lying in our coffins now-a-days fresh as Wonder Bread. Know why?" Andrew blinked both his eyes together at once. "You got it! Preservatives!"

He laughed and drank and looked around. A trickle of wine ran down his chin. Lisa was arranging the cold cuts on a plate, trying to ignore him.

"Better living through chemistry, that's what I say!"

"Andrew, how would you like to live with Richard and me?" Lisa suddenly asked.

"Live with you?" Andrew seemed confused.

"Live with us," she repeated. "We could be a family. You could sort of be our father."

Andrew seemed to think about this for a minute. "Live with you," he said again, and pondered the thought. "Of course that means you would be living with me, too."

"Yeah," Lisa replied, patiently. "I was thinking we could rent an apartment. You wouldn't have to sleep in hallways anymore, or in those abandoned buildings, or those god-awful flop-houses."

"You mean I would be sort of a father to you," Andrew said, slowly working it out.

"That's right. Richard and I have enough money . . ."

"And you would be sort of a daughter to me."

"Right, and Richard would be your son. We'll buy you some nice clothes, and if you got sick we'd take care of you . . ."

"I already got a daughter, you know," Andrew informed them.

That got Lisa's attention. "No, I didn't know that," she answered.

"Oh, I certainly do, yesiree bob!" Andrew took a long pull at the bottle. "She lives with her mother, somewhere in California, I think." Andrew's face turned puzzled, then sad, and then a dark anger began to stir behind his eyes.

"Well, if you'd ever like to invite her to come visit us, I'd be happy to meet her," Lisa continued, oblivious to Andrew's changing mood. The man exploded so suddenly that Richard nearly dropped a plate of macaroni salad he was holding.

"You go home, girl!" Andrew thundered. His face was bright red, and the wine in the bottle shook to a froth. "You go home to your mama where you belong! Do you hear me?"

Lisa didn't seem to hear him at all. She continued calmly folding paper napkins into perfect triangles. "You have to stop drinking, Andrew," she finally said. "We shouldn't have given you that wine, even to celebrate."

"You go home girl!" he boomed again. "Your mama misses you!"

"My mother doesn't give a shit about me!" she flared back. Then she took a breath and spoke to the man as though he were five years old. "We're family now, the three of us. We'll take care of each other. We don't need anybody else. You'll see."

"Family . . ." Andrew echoed. Then a dull, blank look came over his face and he walked out of the room, into one of the bedrooms.

"He'll be okay in the morning," Lisa said, not looking up. There was a quiver in her voice. Richard helped her put out the silverware.

"Fucking wine!" she cried. "It's just like Jack and his

beer! He'd sit in the livingroom and drink a six-pack every night, and then he'd want to kiss me goodnight, and squeeze my ass, and he'd stink like garbage! How my mother could put up with it . . ."

Richard spoke softly and evenly. "You remember when we were talking in front of the church? We thought he might already be gone." He waited a moment to see if she'd heard, but couldn't tell. "You could call your mom and find out."

She wasn't listening. She was too angry. "Everybody's drinking or smoking or shooting up or snorting! Everyone has to get high! Well, fuck them, you know? Fuck them all!" The tears finally came and she threw herself on the carpet, away from him.

He understood. He couldn't count the number of times he had said fuck them all. He picked up a plate and sprawled out next to her.

"Salami?" he asked softly.

She shook her head and dried her eyes with a napkin. The sky was black now, and freckled with stars.

"Look." He pointed out the window. "It's taken the light from those stars thousands of years to reach us. We're actually looking back into history. We're watching those stars the way they were when Christ was alive, when the pyramids were being built."

Lisa sniffled. "So?"

Richard felt something he couldn't put into words. "The universe is only twenty billion years old, Lisa," he began, struggling to express his feeling.

She shrugged. She couldn't understand twenty billion years. He guessed she was having enough trouble with her own fifteen.

"Before that there was nothing."

"What do you mean, nothing?"

"Nothing," Richard repeated. "There wasn't any matter, there wasn't any time. There wasn't even any space."

Lisa scrunched up her nose. "You're crazy. How could there not be space? Even if it's empty, there has to be space." She took a slice of salami and began picking out the peppercorns.

"There wasn't!" he insisted. "All there was was one drop of stuff—plasma they call it, no one knows how big. Maybe the size of a galaxy, or a star, or this building . . . or that piece of pepper in your hand. But in that one drop was all the matter of the universe."

"Sounds like Alice in Wonderland again," she murmured.

"It's scientific fact, Lisa. What happened was this little drop exploded, and from that explosion all matter was made. Electrons, and protons, and neutrinos—even anti-matter. And eventually the stars were formed, and the planets . . ."

"So what's the point?" She nibbled at her piece of salami.

"The point is, Lisa, that the universe is still expanding from that explosion. And it will keep getting bigger and bigger until one of two things happens." She looked mildly interested, so he plunged ahead. "Either it will expand forever until all the stars die and all life in the universe ends, or it will stop expanding and start collapsing again, and get smaller and smaller, until it all goes back into that one little drop."

He fell silent. The darkness enveloped them.

"So what's the big deal?" Lisa finally wanted to know. Richard sighed.

"The big deal is," he patiently explained, "that when you look at the universe that way nothing really matters very much. I mean, the cocaine, your mother, my father —when you think of the death of the universe, none of it really matters at all."

"You know why I don't need to call my mother?" she said suddenly, as though that was the topic under discussion all along. "Because I don't need her anymore. I don't care if Jack is still there or not. I don't care if my father never comes back." She put her head in his lap and took a piece of turkey roll. "I have my own family now."

That again!

It was crazy, Richard thought. As though they could really be a family! As though nutty, drunk Andrew could go and rent an apartment!

"Okay," he replied. It was a lot easier going along with Lisa than trying to argue with her. "So why don't you call your mother and tell her that? Why don't you just call to say that you're okay, that you're doing fine on your own."

Lisa seemed to brighten a little. "I *could* do that," she said, sitting up. "I could just call to say 'Hi, I'm doing fine.' I could just call to wish her a happy Easter."

"Sure!" Richard said.

"Sure!" she echoed. "Why not?"

He reached over and picked up the phone. "Do it now!" he said, holding it out to her.

"Now?" Suddenly she seemed scared.

He lifted the receiver. "What's the number?" Lisa told him and he dialed. Then he handed her the phone.

He sat back, away by the window, and began to make a roast beef sandwich.

"It's ringing," Lisa said softly. She listened and waited, plucking nervously at the fuzz of the carpet. Nobody was answering.

"It's past dinner time," she started to explain. Richard could hear the uneasiness in her voice. "Maybe she went out for the evening. Maybe—" Suddenly she stiffened.

"Mom? Hi, it's me."

Her eyes were round and soft and far away—scared again, like a lost little girl. "Yeah, I'm still in New York. I just called to wish you a happy Easter."

Her hand holding the phone trembled, while the fingers of the other slowly combed through her hair. "Yeah, I'm doing okay . . . I'm a secretary . . . for a vice-president of an oil company . . ."

She didn't blink. She just stared straight ahead, as though in a daze. "I learned how to . . . yeah, and I may go to school next year, to college maybe, and study dancing or modeling . . ."

She listened for a moment and her face hardened. "Good," she replied, a little too loudly. "So the two of you are doing okay. I'm glad." Richard felt the warmth drain out of him. "And no word from dad?"

He leaned forward. He could just hear the thin crackle of reply.

"He's gone, honey. We have to forget about him. He's probably dead by now anyway. Listen, you need anything? Jack and I ain't doing that well, but we could send you fifty bucks or something if you needed it."

"No, I don't need anything from you," Lisa said in a tight, measured voice.

"Well . . ."—there was an uneasy pause—"it was great hearing from you. I'm glad you're doing so good. We should keep in touch more often, huh?"

"Yeah, we should."

Richard leaned back. He didn't want to hear any more. Lisa was rubbing her forehead with her hand as though she had a headache. "Okay . . . yeah . . . 'bye, Mom." She hung up and slumped forward, both hands pressing against her head.

Richard didn't understand. It wasn't supposed to work that way. Her mother was supposed to be happy to hear from her. She was supposed to want Lisa to come home. Fathers could be pricks, but mothers were supposed to love their children. "Lisa," he began unhappily, "I'm sorry . . ."

But he didn't get to finish. She swung her arm and hit him as hard as she could, knocking him into the picnic. By the time he picked himself out of cold cuts, she had locked herself in the bathroom. In the silence of the apartment he could hear her muffled sobs.

He felt hot, almost on fire. Radiation was burning into him from all sides now—from the stars above, from the neon bulbs below, from the monkey on the chair behind him. The cocaine was as charged and as powerful as a nuclear core. It made everyone exposed to it sick. Lisa had been a little burned by it; Francie and Leo were scorched half-crazy. And Sprague . . .

But not him. For some reason he was immune to the sickness. He wasn't really interested in the money he could make from dealing the cocaine, and he had no desire to snort the stuff. Really, thinking about it now, he was the perfect person to be holding it.

The thought became a tremor. Maybe he had been entrusted by fate, or by some higher power, to hold the cocaine and protect the others! That would explain his being immune to its effects. The more he thought about it, the more sense it made. *He* was the rightful guardian of the cocaine, not Lisa, not Steve, not Francie or Leo, not even the cops.

But then, if the cocaine really belonged to him, he would have to decide what to do with it!

He rubbed his throbbing head, picked up the phone, and dialed a familiar number. Jo Federici answered on the second ring.

"Richard! For goodness sake! Do you know how worried we've been about you?" Her voice was as warm and rich as chocolate pudding. He didn't answer, just closed his eyes and listened. "Are you all right? Will you let us help you? Where are you, anyway?"

The questions came in great waves of care and then Mario was on the phone. "How are you?" he asked.

"I'm fine," Richard said reflexively. "I just called to say hello." And to hear your voice, and Jo's voice, and speak to someone who wasn't sick with radiation.

"Where are you?"

"In Manhattan."

"Can I come and talk to you?"

"Maybe tomorrow."

"Richard, the police know you're innocent. You don't have to be afraid of them. They just want to see you safe."

"Mario, I want it over! I do!" The cry came from his heart, and then Lisa appeared. She had washed her face and stood by the archway to the livingroom, looking at him with wide, frightened eyes. She seemed almost afraid to come in.

"I'll call you later, Mario," he said.

"Richard, please give me a number where I can reach you! Just so we can talk! I swear I won't tell the police . . ."

"I'll call you later!"

He hung up and Lisa came to him with tentative steps. She lay down next to him and buried her head under his T-shirt. The bulge of his stomach almost made him laugh.

"You happy in there?" he asked.

She nodded.

"It must be dark."

"I like it. I can hear your heart beating. I'm sorry I hit you," she said.

"Oh, that's all right. I'm sorry . . ." he didn't know exactly how to name his sorrow, "I'm sorry about your mother."

"They're all shits," she said angrily, coming out of the shirt. "What your father's been doing to you gets me so furious."

Richard tensed. He didn't want to answer, but

couldn't stop himself. "I don't know if it's all my dad's fault," he began. "Remember, in the hotel room he said there were two guys who gave him the jacket—"

Lisa interrupted with a scream. "Damn it, why are you so blind? He used you, Richard! He used you to smuggle in the cocaine and all he wants now is to get it back. He doesn't give a shit about you! You just don't want to see it, that's all!"

She was furious at him and threw herself on a white velvet sofa, burying her head in the cushion. He was furious at himself, too. It was stupid trying to defend Steve to her!

"Lisa, we can't fight. We need each other." He sat beside her on the sofa and put his hand on her back. "We're family, remember?" It was a dream he was repeating. Her dream. "And maybe you're right about my father. Maybe he did use me. He never really wanted me, you know. He was never home when I was growing up, and he stuck me in Pierce as soon as he could. Maybe he did put the stuff in the jacket . . ."

He began trembling and turned away. He had said it all as a harmless lie, to make Lisa feel better. But it didn't come out as a lie. It came out as the simple truth. His hands were suddenly cold and he rubbed one atop the other, on his chest, and then held them under his armpits and shivered.

He felt her hand on his arm. When he turned she began kissing his face with warm, moist kisses.

She pressed against him, forcing him down on the sofa, kissing his neck now, and wrapping her legs around his thigh. He pressed back hungrily and suddenly she stood up. Her lips were pink and puffy, her face flushed, her fingers nervous as they smoothed her hair. "I'll be right back," she said, and disappeared into the bathroom.

He went to the window and pressed his nose against the glass. He wasn't cold anymore. He didn't feel any physical sensation at all. A helicopter was passing over the river and he held it between his fingers. He went back to the sofa and pushed it up, close to the window, as Lisa returned.

She was naked, but wrapped in a towel. She had gone into the bathroom to undress. This girl who had danced nude in front of a thousand men was embarrassed, now, to undress in front of him. With eyes half-closed she dropped the towel, stretched out her arms, and pressed herself fully against the window. Richard watched, paralyzed. She rubbed against the glass slowly, sensually, as though she was making love to the whole world below.

Then she melted back, onto the sofa.

He came to life and quickly slipped out of his jeans. Her eyes were closed, her lips parted. Her hands reached out and touched him, held him, guided him over her and onto her and into her. He moved slowly, not daring to breathe, gliding, sliding. . . .

She held him around the waist and grinned. His laugh exploded with joy and relief.

"Like it?" she asked.

He was tingling too much to answer. She squeezed him from within, holding him closer, shivering beneath him. He closed his lids and had a searing vision—the tubes of cocaine, eight pulsating tubes of plasma, each sending out waves of radiation, each burning his father's flesh.

He drew out of her, limp and unspent. She looked up at him, puzzled.

"I'm okay," he said, and kissed her on the forehead. She closed her eyes and in a moment she was breathing deeply. He got up from the couch and covered her with the towel. Then he headed for the kitchen.

25

THE honey in Anne Leverton's veins had thinned, and thoughts floated by like helium balloons.

The heroin had been overwhelming, nothing at all like booze. Booze took time to do its work, and left behind a rotten stomach and a pounding head. Heroin was instantaneous. Heroin was magic. Heroin was swimming in marmalade, being sucked by sugared fruit, breathing liquid oranges. The wonder was more people weren't hooked. The wonder was that anyone successfully kicked it.

For the first time in a year she didn't feel the pain of Pat's death. Liquor hadn't drowned it, and grass hadn't smoked it out. Nor had movies successfully loosened its clutch, nor parties. Nor had men, since Michael moved out, provided anything but the most temporary relief. . . .

Michael.

Where had her feelings for him gone? She didn't know and didn't care to look. Perhaps the marriage was never there. They were attracted to each other at the beginning —that she could remember. There were talks, and walks, and weekends in bed. But was it love? After the marriage they lived well together, or well enough. They rarely argued. They made decisions jointly. Michael was attentive in his fashion, but was that love? They both loved Pat, that was true. And when she joined the force they had their work in common, but there was competition there too. Finally they became friends more than lovers—friends whose bond was in the past, whose present delight in each other had been allowed to lapse. When Pat died the one strand that still connected them was gone. . . .

Her head spun. She felt the pang of paradise ebbing. She opened her eyes to a slit. Knowles was sitting beside her, watching. He must have seen the flutter of movement because his hand went out and touched her thigh. It didn't matter about Michael, she thought. Michael had become a voided man. The emptiness in him matched the emptiness in her. Love, if ever there, was gossamer-thin and gone.

And now, here was this short, hard, evil man touching her body, bringing her to her feet, leading her upstairs. She didn't have the will or desire to resist. In the bedroom, when he pressed her against the door and attacked her mouth with his, she tightened momentarily but then relaxed and allowed the invasion. He had an animal force that she could suck in to fill the void. His tongue probed and his hand pressed between her legs. There wasn't a subtle phrase in the man's grammar. His mouth was a nuisance. She wanted him in bed, inside her, filling her, replacing with his own heat the lost warmth of the heroin.

She gently pushed him away.

"Give me a minute," she murmured, and headed for the bathroom. With the door locked, she put her right foot on the toilet seat and unstrapped the holster fastened to the inside of her calf. She looked around, then buried the holster and revolver in a hamper of dirty clothes. It would be safe there until morning. Then she washed the sweat off her face.

She looked in the mirror and was startled by the woman who looked back. Her skin was flushed and puffy, her eyes sunk into deep hollows with pupils as dilated as any junkie's on the street. It didn't require much imagination for Leverton to see in that face any of a hundred tired, aging, Eighth Avenue whores.

She lay on the bed, naked. On her back. Not ashamed and not afraid. Not trying to cover her body and not trying to entice him with it. She stared at him dispassionately, and watched his anger form.

He had wanted to undress her, to feel slight tremors of resistance and murmurs of denial, to seduce her. She shouldn't be lying there so shamelessly, he was thinking. So expectantly.

He cursed softly. With the use of only one hand the job of unfastening his clothes was difficult. His frustration pleased her. When he took off his pants she saw the patchwork of scars on his legs—his war accident, she remembered. His introduction to morphine. He seemed embarrassed, and quickly got on the bed.

He left his shirt on, though. The buttons were hard, thin-edged shell and could dig into her. His cast too was a potential weapon. She felt as though she was going into battle.

He climbed between her legs and without a moment's hesitation, plunged. She was sure he wanted her unready, dry, so that he could force his way in. But she was wet, and open, and enveloped him hungrily. He pounded and tried to bruise her with his thrusts, but she turned every blow into a whirl of pleasure. His frustration mounted. The shell buttons scraped. The cast pressed against her shoulder.

A sudden pain startled her. He had dug his fingernails into her breast. With a strength and quickness that surprised her, she raised onto one hip, pivoted, and flipped them both over.

He was still inside of her, but now she was on top. She held his wrist with one hand and the cast with the other, and worked her pelvis in short, tight arcs. He was astonished. His thoughts seemed easy to read. No woman had ever done this to him before! No woman had ever been on top! He could easily turn her over again. Even with the use of one arm he was stronger than she. He just needed a moment to regain his strength. . . .

It never came. What started instead was a warm pulse high in his scrotum.

"No!" he cried.

It was a child's cry and he shook his head and bit the corner of his mouth. He didn't want to come. Not this way. She couldn't help a grim smile as she worked him, worked herself, tightly, rhythmically. . . .

He couldn't stop. He screamed and jerked and cried like a baby. She milked him mechanically, her own need met, her body already cooling. She was already beginning to feel ashamed. He was still throbbing as she climbed off and went to the bathroom. The muck was upon her. She needed a shower.

She was just closing the door behind her when the phone rang. She spun around and put her eye to the crack of the door. Knowles was sitting up, stiffly. He looked at the phone, then looked quickly at the nearly closed bathroom door. He answered the call on the second ring.

"Richie!" she heard him say. Her body froze. Every auditory nerve focused on the conversation outside.

"Yes, I want to see you too!"

She widened the crack a quarter-inch. Knowles was facing away now, tense, hunched over the phone as though wanting to pour himself into the line to reach his son. She didn't exist for him anymore. His sexual humiliation seemed all but forgotten.

"Where are you? I'll come get you!"

Apparently the boy wouldn't go for that. Knowles listened for a moment.

"Yeah, I know where it is," he said softly. He quickly turned toward the bathroom again and she narrowed the crack. She barely made out the whispered words. "Okay, tomorrow . . . I'll see you then."

He hung up and cast another quick, bitter look in her direction. Then he grabbed a blanket and headed for the door. Leverton could still read his mind. He wasn't going to sleep in the same bed with that bitch, he was thinking. He had happier things to think about—Richie's calling, seeing his son tomorrow, getting the cocaine. . . .

In the shower she tried to focus on her stroke of luck in overhearing the call, but it brought little relief. The heroin had left her emptier than ever. The sex had soiled her. With needles of hot water purifying her body she realized that in three weeks she would face the anniversary of Pat's death. It was unthinkable that a year could have passed. It was impossible that she had survived.

And now she felt a new ache, distinct from her grief for Pat. With a shock she realized it was the pain of having no one in her life to love.

She almost laughed. Of course she hadn't! With Pat dead and Michael gone, with each new man she met a body without a name . . .

The spray of the water washed away the tears as they formed. She thought if she could just raise the volume to drown out the sobs, she would hardly know she was crying.

Richard settled back on the couch as quietly as possible. Lisa didn't actually wake, but her arms went around his waist and she pressed her body to him. His heart was still pounding. He had done what he had to do. He had even called back Mario and told him about the meeting at the Planetarium. It wouldn't hurt to have a friend around when he confronted Steve.

He kissed Lisa on the forehead and she made a small happy sound. After tomorrow she'd probably never talk to him again. Where would she go? he wondered. What would she do? He didn't want to think about that. Instead he tried to lose himself in her body. She was holding him tighter now, pressing against him in a more purposeful way. He closed his eyes and tried to etch this moment into his memory. He wanted to have it for the rest of his life.

His pulse beat differently now—stronger, less fluttery. He was aroused, rubbing gently back. Was she awake? Her eyes were closed but she had a smile on her lips. Her thigh pressed firmly against him. He turned until he was half on her, not knowing if it was right. He didn't want to take advantage. He didn't want to do it while she was asleep. As he pondered his dilemma she moved under him, adjusted her thighs, and suddenly, without thought or intention, he was in her.

It was different this time. There was no distracting vision of his father. She was warm and he could feel her throbbing around him. He didn't move at all. He didn't have to. It happened all by itself. He just pressed harder, deeper, and she pressed up until he shook, caught his breath, felt a moan in his ear, and dissolved into her like a bar of soap dissolving in a bath, a thin white sliver turning into lather and circling in wide, dizzying whirlpools, down and down and down. . . .

26 **THE** morning dawned gray and cold, and Richard watched banks of clouds stretch across the horizon. Lisa slept next to him, breathing softly. On one side he felt her nuzzling warmth. On the other, the City made him shiver.

He looked at his watch. Eight o'clock. He patted Lisa on the shoulder. She made a sleepy sound and buried her face in the hollow of his neck.

"We have to get up," he said.

She shook her head no and reached down to touch him. It was an effort to force himself away.

"We have a lot to do."

She opened her eyes, still full of sleep, and smiled dreamily. He sat up, busying himself with the job of climbing into his underwear and turning his jeans right side out.

"I guess we do," she yawned. "I just wish we could spend a lazy day and do nothing at all. I'm tired of all this running around."

"Me too," Richard murmured. He slipped into his pants.

"I'll go through my book and find someone else to sell some stuff to, someone who won't be as difficult as Sprague." She was speaking as if she were still in a dream. "And then we'll buy some clothes for Andrew, and go to a real-estate agency and get us our own apartment . . ."

Richard broke in. "I called my father last night." She came out of her dreamy state with a hard, questioning look. He avoided it by concentrating on his shoelaces. "After you fell asleep," he explained. "I'm going to meet him this afternoon."

Her voice was harsh, prying. "Why?"

"I have to!" The left lace slipped its loop and became a double knot. "Shit!" He tried to work it loose.

"You saw him yesterday. You saw him the day before."

"I have some questions to ask." He succeeded in loosening the knot and now gave serious attention to making the bow.

"You're not going to give him the stuff!" she cried.

"No," Richard quickly replied, "I'm not giving him the stuff." There was nothing further to do with his shoes. He lifted his head and met the onrush of her anxiety.

"Everything will be all right," he said, lying terribly, and then, giving way to a sudden impulse, he leaned forward to kiss her. She turned her head at the last instant and he landed on the corner of her mouth. It felt like a slap.

"Get dressed," he said unhappily. "I'll look in on Andrew."

Andrew slept like a corpse—still, hardly breathing, with no color in his face except for the gray stubble of his beard. He rolled his watery eyes as Richard poked at him and tried to go back to sleep.

"Lisa," Richard called. "Give me a hand?"

She wasn't talking to him, but she did help stand Andrew up and start him moving. In the elevator he regained consciousness.

"Coffee," Andrew whispered desperately, and Richard obliged by finding a breakfast place on Columbus Avenue. Three cups brought Andrew back to life, but didn't help his mind much. He pocketed two packets of saccharin and a slice of buttered toast. Lisa didn't say a word. She just held the chimp on her lap as though it were her child, and angrily ate her pancakes.

It wasn't until they were leaning into the wind that she finally spoke.

"What questions?" she wanted to know.

"Huh?"

"What questions do you have to ask your father?"

"Oh, all sorts of things." It was cold and Richard didn't have his jacket anymore. He folded his arms around his chest and held himself for warmth. "I'd like to know if he really did put the stuff in the jacket."

"Jesus Christ . . ." she muttered softly.

"Lisa, we can't keep running the rest of our lives, and this business of being a family and getting an apartment—"

"You *are* going to give it to him!" she cried out, clutching the chimp fiercely to her breast.

"No!" he shouted back, and for a moment it seemed that she was going to run—away from him forever. But she didn't. She stood up to him and looked him straight in the eye. Her lower lip trembled.

"If you do, Richard, I'll hate you for the rest of my life! So help me God!" With one finger, she drew a cross over her heart.

She didn't have to do that, he thought desolately. He believed her. In an hour everyone would hate him, except maybe for Andrew who was too out of it to know what was happening. Andrew was happily feeding his slice of toast to the pigeons. They walked in silence.

After a few minutes, Andrew smacked his lips and asked, "Anyone else thirsty?"

"Andrew, I don't think you should—" Richard started to say, but Lisa interrupted.

"If he wants a drink, let him have a drink!"

He didn't argue. They found a liquor store and An-

222

drew selected a bottle by shape, one that would fit snugly in his jacket pocket. They arrived at the Planetarium early.

"Why don't we kill some time at the museum?" Richard suggested. Andrew was working on his whiskey, and Lisa had retreated into her own thoughts again, so he led them into the building. In a dark hall, filled with real-life stuffed animals, Lisa spoke again.

"If you're telling the truth," she said, "then you can meet your father alone. Without me and without the stuff. I'll wait outside with Andrew. He's not getting a chance to grab it again."

Andrew had wandered over to a nine-foot Alaskan brown bear reared up on its hind legs. He seemed hypnotized by the creature, and stared at it intently. Richard was wryly amused by the sight—four glassy, unseeing eyes locked in a test of will.

"Are you listening, Richard?"

"I heard you."

"Andrew and I will sit on a bench together, outside, and I'll have a taxi waiting. If you come out alone there won't be any trouble. But if you come out with him I'm going to grab Andrew, and get in the cab, and you'll never see me again."

The bear was winning. Andrew, puzzled and frightened, was backing off.

"Richard!"

"Lisa, none of this is necessary . . ."

"Don't tell me what's necessary," she whispered furiously. "I'm not going back home and I'm not going back to Leo or to the Frolick. I busted my ass to save this stuff, and I'm not going to lose it just because you can't walk away from your old man!"

Richard couldn't explain. He felt tears well up in his eyes. Lisa's voice softened.

"I'll be there when you come out, Richard. I'm not going to steal the stuff. I really like you. I liked . . ." she paused, and he could see her face redden, "I liked what we did last night." She almost touched him. Her hand started to reach out but stopped midway. "But I'll leave you in a minute if you try to fuck me."

"Lisa, I would never . . ." he began, meaning it, and realizing he had done exactly that, last night, in every sense of the word.

"Then we have nothing to worry about." She looked at her watch. "It's nearly time. I'll show you where I'll be sitting."

He climbed the stairs to the second floor of the Planetarium. He walked past the set of scales that showed what his weight would be on other planets, past a collection of antique astronomical instruments, past photos of asteroids, planets, stars, and galaxies until he came to the Hall of the Sun—the thirty-foot, darkened tunnel with an olive-sized Earth at one end and an eight-foot sun at the other, a hundred yellow lights pulsing beneath its translucent surface making it glow like a living star.

He entered the tunnel. At the far end he saw the sharp profile of his father against the pulsing sun.

He walked past a three-dimensional map that showed our sun's position in the Milky Way, and the Milky Way in relation to the cluster of galaxies it travels with. He felt that he covered a distance as far as any bit of energy in the universe has ever traveled as he walked up to his father.

Steve held out his hand and smiled warmly. Richard nodded back. A guard drifted by. The choice of the Planetarium had been a good one. There were dozens of children around, and the guards were protection in case Steve caused trouble. And most important of all, against the backdrop of the universe his father seemed very, very small.

Steve continued the movement of his hand, raising it

and touching Richard's hair. Richard managed not to flinch. He studied his father's face as though it was a map, a hostile territory through which he had to chart a safe passage. Steve finished the caress by grasping his son's shoulder.

"You didn't bring the stuff," he said.

Richard remained silent.

"Is it with the girl?"

He didn't say a word. He didn't feel an inch of give in his face.

"I don't blame you for being angry, Richie. I'd feel the same way in your shoes."

"You put the cocaine in the jacket."

"Yes," his father answered.

"To smuggle it into the country."

Steve grasped his upper arm. He wanted to jerk away but didn't. He allowed the connection. A part of him cringed, but another small part melted.

"I didn't want to hurt you, Richie. You must believe me. It was a million-to-one chance it would be discovered. But even if the impossible happened, which it did, I knew your age and innocence would protect you . . ."

His father's words tumbled out, softly and urgently. His eyes were moist and imploring. Richard bathed in their passion.

"I thought about it, Richie. Even though I was convinced there was no way anything could go wrong. You were safe. You still are. I would never put you in a position where you could be hurt."

Richard's head throbbed with the pulsing sun. Steve was speaking from his heart, but still *he* was the one who had been shot at, *his* skull had nearly been cracked, *he* had been chased and threatened and lied to. *He* was the one betrayed.

"It's over now, Richie. No further harm can come to you, or to the girl, if you just give me the cocaine."

"Why?" Richard screamed in a whisper. "Why did you do it?" He felt his body shake with fury. With awkwardness and evident pain, Steve undid the buttons of his right shirt sleeve and rolled it over his arm. Pricks of white scar tissue made thin chalky tracks from wrist to elbow.

At first Richard didn't understand, and then the truth fell into place like the final piece of a jigsaw puzzle. His father was an addict. He touched the raised ridge of the scar with horror and fascination.

"You understand?" Steve asked. Richard nodded numbly. "That's why I sent you to Pierce. Did you think I didn't love you? Did you think I didn't want you with me?"

Yes! Richard screamed silently.

"I wanted to protect you, Richie. I didn't want you to find out about me."

He was grateful for the dark. It hid his tears and the growing lump in his throat. His father's position was so clear, so logical . . .

"And my mother?" The words just slipped out.

"What about her?" Steve said softly.

"Is that why she left?"

Steve nodded. He closed his eyes for a moment. He seemed to be in pain. "I was in bad shape after 'Nam. In and out of hospitals all the time. I guess she didn't want to spend the rest of her life with a cripple."

"And a junkie!"

Steve nodded again. His words came out dry, lifeless. "One day—you weren't even a year old—she just walked out. No warning . . ."

Not hard to understand, Richard thought. In fact easy to understand. What woman *would* live with Steve Knowles? It showed her character, to leave. Her strength. Her will to survive! Richard didn't hate her for it. He respected her for it, even loved her. But why—and the words twisted in his mind like a strangled cry—why hadn't she taken him with her? He was just a baby. *Her* baby. Why had she left him with a crippled junkie?

"So you see, Richie, it wasn't all my fault. She walked out on both of us. I did the best I could. If she had stayed . . ."

"No!" he whispered furiously. "You're not going to pin it on her! You're not going to get off that easily!"

Steve shrugged helplessly. He didn't try to defend himself. Richard found himself gasping. He couldn't fill his lungs with air. "Okay, what do you want now? Do you want me to forgive you? Is that what you want?"

"No, Richie. I just want you to understand."

"All right! I understand! I understand it all!"

The line was drawn. They could come no closer. Still, Richard saw a look of relief in his father's face. Then he realized that he felt a little better too. At least, for once, they had been honest with each other. He managed a deep breath.

"Let's get the stuff, huh?" Steve's hand was on his shoulder. "I've got a deal worked out with the police. I'm going to give it to them," he smiled. "Like they say in the movies, I'm going straight."

His hand moved to the base of Richard's neck and he squeezed to emphasize his words. "I'm going to kick this thing, Richie. I swear it! Now that I have you on my side I know I can do it! This whole stupid mistake is going to turn out to be a blessing for both of us, you wait and see."

A class of children passed, walking in two lines, holding hands. They couldn't have been more than six years old. Boy–girl . . . boy–girl . . . They looked so young and happy. Richard thought it would be nice to have a spaceship waiting outside just now. He could take them away from Earth. They could travel through the galaxy, just him and those kids, until they found a planet they could live on. Maybe Lisa could come too.

"It's gone," he said, and braced himself for the reaction. His father didn't seem to understand. "It was the only evidence the police had. I thought if I turned it over to them they would arrest you. So last night I flushed it down the toilet." He watched the comprehension dawn on Steve's face. "It was the only way to keep you out of jail."

Suddenly Steve Knowles was laughing. The sound filled the corridor and the double-line of children turned to watch him, red-faced, with tears at the corners of his eyes, gasping for breath. Then Richard could see some of them become frightened. It wasn't a normal laugh. One little boy started to cry.

Now he felt frightened too. He didn't understand his father's reaction and had no idea what Steve would do next. He didn't know whether to stay or run.

He shifted uneasily. "Hey, take it easy," he said to his father. A guard was walking over. And then, breaking through the line of children, Richard spotted a familiar, squat form. It was Mario, hurrying toward them! He ran to meet him halfway.

27

WHERE the hell was Wilhite? Where was O'Hare?

Leverton stood at the corner of the Planetarium park at Eighty-first Street and Central Park West. It was 12:35. A dozen yards away, Lisa was sitting on a bench, next to a derelict. The girl was plainly nervous. Richard was here somewhere, with his father. Where the hell was her team?

The news from the precinct was as puzzling as it was astonishing. Leverton had called in at eleven this morning, after Steve Knowles ditched her. The desk sergeant presented the case to her all tied up in a bow. Mario Federici had called the night before with the information that Richard was going to meet his father at half past noon at the Planetarium. But strangely, neither Wilhite nor O'Hare could be reached. And neither had called in, despite the messages that had been left for them.

Leverton couldn't understand it. They must have called in by now. They had to be here, somewhere. In the building, probably. Watching the boy and Knowles. She would cover the girl.

She walked casually toward the bench. There was a stuffed monkey in the girl's lap. She couldn't be more than fifteen, Leverton thought. Fifteen, and holding a stuffed animal, and turning tricks.

She paused for a moment, undecided about how to approach the child. Her breasts and shoulders still hurt from her battle with Knowles last night, and inside she was still furious over his behavior this morning. Not over his sulking and ignoring her—she had expected that. Not even over his ditching her at the hospital after handing her two one-hundred-dollar bills as payment for her services as a nurse. She had expected that too. After all, he was about to meet his son and pick up the cocaine. He didn't need her anymore.

No, what had angered her was that Knowles had managed his morning fix without her help. She could still see the sadistic pleasure in his face—satisfying his own need while intentionally ignoring hers.

And now, as a cold, wet wind beat against her, she knew exactly why she had been so hurt. She had felt deprived!

She had wanted her fix!

Where was O'Hare? goddamn it!

She walked over to the bench and sat down, startling the girl who turned her whole body and faced her.

"You remember me?" Leverton asked.

"Yeah, I remember you." The girl was scared. Her arms curled protectively around the stuffed chimp.

"May I sit here?"

"It's a free country." She slid closer to the drunk who was nuzzling at a bottle, not paying attention. "You come here with him?" Lisa wanted to know.

Leverton realized the girl was talking about Knowles. She nodded, not knowing quite what to do. Wilhite and O'Hare had to be inside. She played for time.

"Your name is Lisa, right?"

The girl didn't respond. The drunk closed his eyes and began to snore.

"Andrew!" Lisa shook him with one hand, trying to wake him up. Leverton caught a glimpse of two safety pins clasped over a slit at the monkey's throat. The cocaine! she said to herself, and took a deep breath. Of course. Richard wouldn't be carrying it with him when he went to see his father.

"My name is Anne. Anne Leverton," she said to the girl.

Lisa turned back and stared. Leverton felt a rush of feeling at the intensity in her eyes.

"Who are you?" Lisa demanded angrily.

The suddenness of the question was upsetting. "What do you mean?"

"In Leo's room you said you were a nurse." Lisa's slight body tensed; it looked for a moment as though she might run. "You a cop?"

Leverton blinked; this girl was too sharp.

She didn't want to lie—she wasn't sure she could get away with a lie. But if she told the truth now Lisa would run, and she would have to arrest her. And that thought was unbearable.

"Why? Do I look like a cop?" she joked.

Lisa squinted her eyes against a sudden gust of wind. "Everyone's a cop these days. Drug dealers. Johns on the street. I thought from the way you handled Leo . . ."

"I've been around," Leverton explained, attempting a tough, carefree attitude. "I've learned how to handle myself. You don't have to be a cop for that."

"Yeah," Lisa said, almost believing. But she still wanted an answer. "So what are you? A hooker or something?"

Leverton smiled at the question and mentally counted the score of men she had picked up and screwed in the past year—more? less? did it matter? She hadn't seen any of them twice—had never even known all their names. And although none of them had ever offered cash, she saw no point in quibbling over details, either with herself or with Lisa.

"Yeah," she said, "I'm a hooker or something," and for the first time saw the suspicion melt from the girl's face.

"It sucks," Lisa said.

"Yeah, it sucks."

She said the words and felt a suffocating vacuum in her chest. She couldn't breathe and instinctively pressed a hand against the base of her throat.

"You okay?" the girl asked, concerned.

She nodded. The vacuum yielded enough for her to breathe.

"Here."

Lisa was offering a tissue. She took it and wiped the sweat off her face. Lisa was watching with worry and confusion. Anne wanted to put out a hand and touch this child but feared that her skin, the boundary line between them, would dissolve.

One thing was clear to Leverton. There was no way she could arrest this girl. There was no way she could betray her. She had to figure out a way to tell Lisa the truth without frightening her. She had to find a way to begin to heal this child, and maybe, at the same time, begin healing herself.

"Lisa," she began, "I like you . . ."

The girl shrugged and looked down. She seemed embarrassed.

". . . and I want you to trust me."

The girl looked up, alert again, and wary.

"I won't hurt you," Leverton went on quickly. "I swear. But you have to trust me."

Lisa didn't say a word, but drew back slightly. Leverton took a breath.

"And yes, I am a police officer."

Lisa bolted to her feet. Her first thought was to run, but that wouldn't work. She couldn't run fast enough, not with the chimp in her hands. Besides, she had no idea what this

232

lady cop knew. She might not know the coke was in the chimp!

The woman had risen with her and was talking. Lisa interrupted her impatiently.

"What do you want with me?" she demanded.

"I want to help you, Lisa."

"I don't need your help!"

"I want to help both you and Richard."

Lisa turned and started to walk away. She didn't want to—she would be deserting Andrew, and Richard would think she had run out on him. But she had no choice. She had to get away from this cop. The woman followed.

"Quit bothering me, will you?" She picked up her pace.

"Lisa, please! I don't want to have to arrest you."

"For what?" she flared. "I didn't do anything!"

"I know. That's why I want you to trust me. You'll be all right, Lisa, I swear." The lady cop took hold of her arm to stop her, and then held out her hands. "Can I have the chimp?"

Lisa's world was dissolving again. She looked toward the Planetarium entrance, praying for Richard to come out. With him she had a chance. The two of them had handled cops before.

"Lisa, please?"

The lady cop had tears in her eyes and Lisa felt some hope. Maybe they could bargain with her. If Richard came out right now they could talk to this lady, or make up some story, or maybe just knock her down and take off. . . .

It was a miracle. At that moment, just as she was praying, he came through the revolving door. Lisa's heart jumped, and then fell. There was a man next to Richard— a stranger, short and fat—and they were talking. And behind them was Steve Knowles!

He had given in to his father! They were coming to

get the cocaine from her! She screamed, and then started to run.

"Goddamn!" Richard said under his breath, and took off after Lisa. How stupid could he be? He was supposed to come out alone!

"Lisa!" he called to her. "Stop! It's okay!" But she didn't. He passed Andrew, sitting on a bench, and managed to catch up with her about fifty feet later.

"It's all right," he said, grabbing her arm.

"Let go of me, you fuck!" She clawed and kicked. He caught her hand.

"Lisa, I didn't give the stuff to my father. There is no stuff! I flushed it down the toilet last night!" She was thrashing like a drowning cat. The toe of her shoe connected with his shin and he howled in pain. "Lisa, did you hear me? There is no more cocaine!"

She squeezed the bags of powder inside the chimp. "Liar!" she screamed. He could see Steve and Mario jogging toward them. Her struggle intensified.

"It's flour, Lisa. I made another switch. I couldn't tell you last night because I knew how much it meant to you. I'm sorry."

Her body sagged for a moment and he thought she understood. But her screams continued. "Liar!" The tears streamed down her cheeks. "Liar! Liar! Liar!" She broke free from his grasp and ran from him, holding the chimp with both hands. She kept screaming as she ran.

"Liar! Liar!"

And then the world exploded.

When he tried to re-create it afterward, Richard could only recall sounds and snapshots. Lisa running. Mario standing in frozen bewilderment. Steve watching, his body arched like a cat ready to spring. A woman running. A siren in the distance. Then a huge monster of a man catching Lisa in full stride and holding her up on his hip, high off the ground.

Then he was shoved from behind and was on the ground with a taste of blood in his mouth. He thought he heard shots. Dry twigs snapping. A hungry woodpecker working an apple tree. The squeal of car wheels next to his ear. Screams in the distance. Shrieks of birds in flight. And finally a dark dizziness that drew him in.

28

O'HARE hunched over the steering wheel, his concentration focused straight ahead on the northbound traffic of Central Park West. A bus blocked him and he slid dangerously into the southbound lane to pass it. He leaned on his horn to warn oncoming traffic, but couldn't hear the honk over the whine of the siren.

His head pounded but he hardly noticed that either. He was too intent on his driving, too furious at himself and at Wilhite to do anything but get to the Planetarium as quickly as possible.

Fuck-ups, both of them! he thought.

He knew his problem. He had come home from Rye last night sick to his stomach. To settle himself down, he had stopped at a liquor store and bought a fifth of Jack Daniels. This morning the bottle was empty. He figured he must have passed out before midnight, and he'd be sleeping still if Wilhite hadn't pounded on his door a few minutes ago.

That was his problem, but what was Wilhite's? Wilhite had fucked up beyond belief, too! Wilhite had gone upstate late last night to visit his brother. Coming back this morning he had had a flat, and didn't get into the City until twelve-twenty. Out of touch until twelve-twenty this afternoon! Unbelievable!

O'Hare's brain had throbbed with each pulse when Wilhite gave him the news. According to Federici, Richard had contacted his father last night and was meeting Knowles at the Planetarium at 12:30. It was already 12:40. O'Hare played back the messages on his phone tape as he frantically dressed. One call was from Federici. One was from Anne. And one was from the precinct. Everyone had the information but them!

The car clock now read 12:48.

The pain behind O'Hare's eyes obscured his vision, and he narrowly missed a bicyclist on the side of the road. Wilhite sat rigidly beside him.

He didn't want to deal with any of it anymore, he thought. Not his constant rage, not his grief over Pat, not his need for Anne, not his daily battle with the city scum. He wanted an island on the far side of the world with sand that would scorch his feet and a sun that would burn through the seventeen years of crust that covered him, and a horizon of green water. . . .

He eased up on the pedal and flicked off the siren as they approached the museum. Then he made a hard left into the Planetarium park. He drove slowly. The park was almost empty because of the day—gray and blowy with a threat of rain. Ahead, in the parking lot, he saw some movement.

Scurrying figures.

A body lying motionless on the ground!

Then he picked out Anne, gun drawn, in a running crouch, moving toward the action.

He wanted to check the body, but gunfire broke out as he pulled up. Three shots. Quick pops. Firecrackers, almost. Then he saw Casper's huge, white-haired bodyguard running and carrying a girl. He held her high on his hip as a shield against the bullets. Beyond him, by a white Lincoln, Casper was shooting across the lot at Steve Knowles, who was returning the fire with a handgun. Knowles squeezed off two shots, then broke and ran toward his BMW.

"Call it in, Ernie!" O'Hare shouted, and slid out of

the car, low, his weapon drawn, using the door as a shield. He looked up to see the bodyguard drop the girl. She hit the cobblestone hard and lay there, writhing.

"Police!" O'Hare shouted. "Throw down your weapons!"

The bodyguard looked quickly in O'Hare's direction and fired a nervous shot. Then he scooped something off the ground and ran toward the Continental.

"Casper, don't be stupid, you can't get away!" O'Hare yelled. The bodyguard shot again, twice, and O'Hare heard Wilhite return the fire.

"Ernie, no!" he screamed.

The girl had risen to one knee and Anne was running toward her, into the line of fire. She threw herself over the child and pressed them both to the ground. O'Hare felt a surge of nausea and fired two shots, high, but close enough to force Casper and the bodyguard to duck for cover. Then, from his left, came a staccato burst.

Steve Knowles stood by the open trunk of his car, an automatic rifle cradled comfortably in his arms. He used the weapon expertly—swinging it in a short arc through the target area so that some forty or fifty rounds would saturate a space ten yards wide. He fired a second spray. Bullets exploded—ricocheting off the cobblestones, over the mound of Anne and the girl, and ripping into the Continental. O'Hare took a two-handed stance and fired. Two rounds slammed into Steve Knowles's chest and his body thudded against the rear of his car. His finger squeezed the trigger one last time sending a wild burst toward the parking-lot entrance that nearly caught O'Hare. Then he slid slowly down. He was dead before he hit the ground.

There was no movement from Anne or the girl. Beyond them, a huge, white-headed body lay twisted in front of the Lincoln—one arm nearly shot off, the head turned at an impossible angle, its lifeless eyes staring at an equally lifeless chimpanzee. O'Hare looked quickly for Wilhite but the sergeant was nowhere in sight. Bystanders at the edge of the park were peering in. He listened intently but could hear no sirens. It must have been two or three minutes since Wilhite called in. Where were the cops?

With his eyes on the Lincoln, he ran in a low crouch over to Anne. She looked up and nodded her head. She was okay. He cautiously made his way to the front fender of the car. The bodyguard's corpse was at his feet. He was standing in a pool of blood.

"Come out, Casper," he screamed. "Toss the piece and come out."

"You dumb fucking cops!" Casper's voice rasped back. "We had a deal! No one had to get hurt!"

"I never had a deal with you!" O'Hare replied, and remembered the two thousand dollars in his jacket pocket. But it wasn't a deal! He hadn't agreed to anything!

From the corner of his eye he caught the shadow of a gliding figure, Wilhite, sliding behind parked cars to get behind Casper. Civilians were edging into the park. They had heard the shots. They smelled death. And still no goddamn backup!

"Michael," Casper called, his voice calmer but filled with urgency, "we'll be partners. Fifty-fifty. Take one bag and plant it on Knowles and give me the rest. No one has to know. It's worth two hundred grand to you, Michael."

Two hundred thousand dollars. A ticket to that white beach and green water. The monkey lay at his feet. Half the safety pins had been torn away; bags of white powder were clearly visible.

"Be smart, Michael," Casper urged. "You know what's going to happen otherwise? You'll arrest me and I'll walk. You can't connect me with the stuff. Not with Knowles dead. You'll get me for possession of a handgun and I'll get six months, suspended. And in two weeks the stuff will be back on the street. Someone is going to make money, Michael. Why not us?"

Why not? O'Hare thought. Why the hell shouldn't he make a deal with Casper, and in a few months retire on three-quarter pension and go look for that beach? In the distance, finally, he heard the wail of a siren.

"You got to do it now, Michael. You got to give me the stuff and let me get out of here right now!"

Wilhite, silent as a mist, emerged behind Casper and the issue was decided. No deal was possible now. They would have to arrest Casper. If he walked, he walked. If there was another round of "bureaucratic malfeasance" and the stuff disappeared from the property clerk's office, so be it. There was nothing O'Hare could do.

Casper stood up, facing him. His eyes were pleading.

"Sorry, Casper," O'Hare said. "Just put up your hands . . ."

Wilhite fired.

It was a clear shot from point-blank range, and a piece of Casper's skull flew off. For an instant O'Hare thought he had been shot. His face stung with pain; he couldn't see. His hands flew across his eyes and he wiped off gray and red-stained lumps. A sickening, warm tapioca. Brains. Blood. Splinters of bone. He bent down to vomit but there was nothing in his stomach. When the spasms passed he lifted his head and looked murderously into Wilhite's eyes.

"What the hell . . . !" he stammered. "Are you out of your mind? There was no need to . . . !"

And then, with no feeling of surprise at all, O'Hare understood. The stench of blood and torn tissue cloyed in his nose. He felt sick again. Bile rose up from his stomach.

Wilhite was the informer. That's how Casper knew O'Hare's personal habits, and about the Bo-Mond, and about the meeting here today. That's why Wilhite was deliberately late getting to O'Hare with the message. That's what Casper was talking about when he said they had a deal.

O'Hare swallowed down the bile. The sirens were louder and coming from different directions. Half a dozen police cars were converging. It had to be over five minutes since the first shots.

"You didn't even call for backup, did you, Ernie?" he said quietly. Wilhite's face was frozen. Of course he didn't. He had to be sure Casper would die.

O'Hare took a breath. His stomach was back under control, but something furious was happening inside of Wilhite. The sergeant's mouth was working but no sound was coming out. O'Hare thought of Wilhite's brother in a private institution, of the two kids Wilhite supported, of his widowed mother. . . .

Words emerged as twisted, agonized sounds. "I didn't think . . ." Wilhite began, his eyes fluttering at the carnage around him, ". . . I didn't think anyone would get hurt." Then he began to cry. He put a hand to his mouth to control a twitch that pulled at his lower lip. "I never gave them Anne," he sobbed. "I would never do that!"

Police cars squealed to a stop. Uniforms scrambled out, yelling at each other, pushing back the crowd. Two ambulances broke through, medics out and running even before the vehicles rolled to a halt.

O'Hare looked quickly around. Wilhite was sitting against a tire of the Lincoln, crying like a baby. Anne was attending to the girl. O'Hare casually picked up the stuffed chimp, walked the few feet to his own unmarked car, and tossed the animal on the floor in the back. Then he went to look for Richard.

He found the boy lying flat on the ground in front tothe parking lot. Federici, with blood streaming down his own face, was kneeling over him and calling for help. Two medics ran over. One led Mario away, the other began talking quietly to Richard, gently feeling for broken bones.

A uniform came over and O'Hare showed his badge. "Midtown," he said. "A case I was on. The shooting was in progress when I arrived."

The cop nodded and made a note on his pad, then looked at the lieutenant and winced. "What the hell happened to you, sir?"

O'Hare wiped his hair with his hands. They came away pink and covered with more of that pulpy goo. The officer swallowed hard and looked away. "We'll have a captain here in a couple of minutes, sir, to take your statement."

He went off and O'Hare surveyed the damage. The parking lot looked like a battle zone. Bodies on the pavement were being covered with coarse, gray blankets. He walked around the area to make a count. Knowles, Casper, the bodyguard, a male civilian . . . When he finished he sat on a bench near Richard. He bummed a cigarette from a passing cop and lit it with trembling hands.

He steadied himself as Anne came limping toward him, one hand pressed against her thigh.

"You okay?" she asked.

He nodded. Blood seeped between her fingers.

"Just a chip of cement or something," she explained. "Just a flesh wound."

Just a flesh wound. O'Hare wanted to rip open her pant leg and bandage it.

"How's Richard?"

O'Hare shrugged and they watched the ambulance attendant take the boy's pulse and check his eyes. "He looks okay. Maybe a slight concussion." O'Hare pictured a medic looking over Pat, feeling for vital signs. He was certain Anne was thinking the same thing.

He motioned to where two medics were working on the girl. "How is she?"

"Beat up a little. I don't think she's shot. A shoulder separation, maybe. A couple of broken bones."

"You were something, protecting her like that." He reached out a hand to touch her. She shied away imperceptibly. He took it back.

"You're cut too," she offered as an apology. Her fingers moved close to his face where a fragment of Casper's skull had scored his cheek. But she didn't touch him. They were both cut. They were both bleeding. They had both been bleeding for a year.

"You're not thinking of doing anything stupid, Michael," she said softly.

"Like what?"

She motioned in the direction of his car. "Like the monkey."

She had seen him take it! He felt a sudden shame. "Do you care?" he whispered hoarsely.

"Yes," she snapped back.

"Bullshit!"

"What are you going to do? Fly off to Colombia? Deal it yourself?"

"What difference does it make to you?"

"Michael, you can't . . ."

"I can do anything I damn well want! What I can't do is go on like this!"

He left the words hanging in the air between them, daring her to deny their truth, daring her to judge his decision. Praying that she would lean into his arms to be held.

"It's flour, Michael," she said with tears in her eyes. "Richard dumped the stuff last night. I heard him telling the girl. All this . . ." she looked around at the blanketed bodies and the blood already drying brick-red on the cobblestone, ". . . all this for a few pounds of flour."

Flour.

O'Hare felt lightheaded. The death and blood around him suddenly seemed unreal. "It's a joke," he said finally, unable to stop an idiotic smile from spreading across his face. "A dumb, fucking joke."

A few drops of rain began to fall. Anne didn't disagree. She just left him to go back to the girl, who had been put on a stretcher and was being carried to an ambulance.

Richard came to consciousness with a buzz in his ears. Static. Angry voices. A bad connection on a long-distance phone call. Many people talking at once, fading in, fading out.

Hands poked at his body. He tried to move but couldn't. He didn't know where he was or what had happened. A finger lifted one eye open and he saw a blurred face peering in. The face spoke.

"You're all right, son. Just don't try to move."

He opened both eyes and saw a second face, Mario's, smiling but with blood on his forehead. Then his memory came back. He was outside the Planetarium. He had just come out of the building with Mario and Steve. Lisa had seen him and had started running. He'd caught up with her and tried to explain. . . . He couldn't remember what had happened after that.

The man examining him looked like a doctor. "You're a lucky boy," the doctor was saying. "You're a little banged up, and you'll have a hell of a shiner tomorrow, but I don't think anything is broken."

Car radios crackled in his ears. He turned his head—the park was crawling with cops. Police cars were parked on the grass and on the pavement. An ambulance was nearby with doctors running back and forth. And across the park, by the sidewalk, hundreds of people stood watching, talking to each other, pointing.

"Lisa . . ." he murmured.

A few drops of rain fell on his face and he struggled to sit up. The doctor tried to stop him.

"We have to take you to a hospital, son. Just to check you out."

He saw her now. She was being carried on a stretcher. He scrambled to his feet but the doctor held his arm. "What happened?" he demanded.

"There was some shooting . . ."

He wrenched away and ran up to the stretcher. She was under a blanket, her face white and pained. She looked at him without expression.

"Lisa, I'm sorry," he began, but they had her in the ambulance before he could finish.

Now he looked around desperately. There was some shooting, the doctor had said. He looked for his father. He saw the blanket-covered bodies on the ground.

"No . . . no . . . !"

His chest heaved. The rain came down harder. Another ambulance drove into the parking lot and Lisa's ambulance left. Its siren sounded like an agonizing cry.

"No . . . !"

He ran up to the nearest blanketed body and, before anyone could stop him, uncovered the face. It was Andrew. He didn't look much different from this morning, when he was sleeping, except that now there was blood on his shirt.

"No . . . !"

He felt a hand on his shoulder and looked up. A large, square-faced man stood next to him.

"I'm Mike O'Hare," the big man said, and held out a blanket. Richard let him put it around his shoulders. "I'm the detective that spoke to you on the phone."

Richard remembered. "My father!" he strained. "Where's my father?"

The detective wiped the rain off his face, then combed

wet fingers through his hair. "He's dead, Richard," he said softly.

Richard heard the words but they were just that—words. Sounds that didn't matter. Certainly nothing that was true. The detective tried to put an arm around his shoulder but he jerked away.

"He was shot in the fight . . . I'm sorry."

"Where is he?" Richard realized he was screaming and quieted himself down. "I want to see him!"

The detective wiped his face again and looked around. Richard followed him through the parking lot to where two policemen were standing over a covered body next to a blue BMW. It looked like his father's car, except that the trunk and rear side were covered with bullet holes.

The detective nodded and one of the policemen drew back the blanket and exposed Steve's face. At least it looked like Steve's face. Richard examined it for a long moment and decided yes, that probably was his father. It was hard to tell. He had never seen Steve so still before.

The detective took his arm. It felt like a vise.

"I'm all right," Richard told him. "Leave me alone!"

The vise eased and he broke away. He ran and heard himself screaming. He ran blind, from the rain or from the tears in his eyes, he didn't know which. He choked, and wailed, and gasped for breath but he wouldn't stop running. He would never stop. He would run forever. He would run until he died.

29

O'HARE tugged at his dress uniform and sucked in his stomach, but it didn't help. The jacket was from a younger, slimmer decade. A roll of fat bulged through the midriff and he couldn't even close the top button of the pants. He hated dress uniform and hated ceremonies, but this morning they had to be endured. This morning he and Leverton and Wilhite were receiving medals.

The commissioner was at the podium. Smooth-worn phrases rolled off his tongue.

". . . but one example of our continuing crackdown against narcotics in this city . . . once and for all end this peddling of human misery by those with such callous disregard for human life and welfare . . ."

The ceremony was standard Department procedure. Every time a policeman fired a gun there was an investigation, and if a life was taken there was either punishment or reward. There was no twilight in this matter, and no forgiveness.

". . . serve final notice that this shameful exploitation of our youth will no longer be tolerated . . ."

He shifted uncomfortably in his dress shoes, which were too tight. The Knowles case had been judged a success. No police officer had been seriously hurt, and three drug dealers had died, one gratifyingly at the hands of another. And although an innocent bystander was slain, the autopsy showed that he hadn't been hit by police bullets. There would be no public outcry here. Medals were to be awarded to the three officers involved.

Bored photographers snapped pictures of the gesturing commissioner, and of the three heroes lined up behind him. Public interest had already waned. A month before the bloodstained cobblestones of the Planetarium parking lot had made the front page of the *New York Post*.

". . . and no clearer example of the dedication, the bravery, and the humanity of this police force than these three officers who risked their lives, beyond the call of duty, for two children . . ."

Wilhite stood on his left, tall and straight and handsome. It didn't matter, O'Hare thought, that no one knew why the sergeant's hands shook when he lit a cigarette, or why his eyes were so hooded, and always on the brink of tears. O'Hare didn't think he could have changed the outcome of the investigation even if he had wanted to tell the truth. Wilhite had killed a drug dealer who had been in a gun fight with the police. That was fact. The rest—that they were about to take Casper alive, and that Wilhite was in Casper's employ—was unprovable conjecture.

But the fact was, O'Hare didn't want to tell the truth. The fact was there was no truth to tell, only a tangled knot of part-truths, each too sad or damaging to reveal—Anne's shooting up, his desire to run off with the cocaine himself, the two thousand dollars he took from Casper and never vouchered. . . . A bigger piece of the truth was that Wilhite had more reason to sell out than he did. Wilhite really needed the money.

Ironically, in its own blind way the Department had hammered out a just result for Wilhite. It was obvious to all that the sergeant was having an emotional breakdown, and it was decided that he would take an indefinite leave. If he returned, they would put him at a desk. If not, he would receive medical benefits and, eventually, his pension. He would have to live with his conscience, but his family wouldn't suffer. O'Hare didn't even mind that he was getting a medal.

The ceremonies droned to a close. He drifted over to talk to Anne. Except for official business, they had hardly communicated at all since the shootout. If anything, Anne seemed to be avoiding him more than ever.

"How're you doing?" he asked her.

"All right," she said. "Saturday was tough."

He nodded. Saturday was the anniversary of Pat's death. He had called to ask if she wanted to go to the cemetery with him, but she had said no. They arranged it so that he went in the morning and she went in the afternoon.

"What's this business with you and the girl?" he blurted out, then silently cursed himself. He hadn't meant it to sound like an accusation.

"What do you mean?"

He spoke in his gentlest voice. "I hear you're going to take her in."

"I made the offer. She hasn't said yes."

He looked at her skeptically. He didn't want to sound judgmental, but damn it, he *didn't* think it was a good idea for Anne to get mixed up with this girl. What *was* a good idea, he couldn't say.

"She doesn't have a whole lot of choice, Michael. It's either me or some state school. Her mother doesn't want her back."

"She's a hooker, Anne, and probably a junkie."

"She's a fifteen-year-old kid, Michael!"

A photographer angled over and they stopped arguing to have their picture taken.

"I'm sorry," O'Hare said when the photographer had gone. He thought of Pat, and Richard, and the girl, and poor Ernie Wilhite. He thought of Steve Knowles, and Milton Casper, and that moronic bodyguard . . . even the unlucky derelict.

249

He fingered his medal. "It's really all screwed up, isn't it?"

She nodded sadly.

"I'm sorry for everything, Anne . . ."

"I'm sorry too, Michael."

Leverton had her own reasons to be sorry. The trauma at the Planetarium with all that bloodshed and death, and almost dying herself that day . . . the memory of the honeyed needle at Steve Knowles's house . . . discovering her overwhelming need for a fifteen-year-old girl . . . the anniversary of Pat's death. . . .

She was surprised at her reaction to that one. In truth, Saturday had turned out to be just another painful day. She wondered whether she had grieved Pat so fully during the year that there were no deeper levels of pain left. Or was it that these new events had changed her? Certainly a lot had happened.

O'Hare looked as though he wanted to say something, but he was having trouble finding the words.

"I didn't really want to kill Knowles. I had no choice."

She nodded. He was wrestling with a ghost.

"I feel so god-awful about it. At the beginning I wanted to destroy him for what he was doing to his boy. I thought that by doing that, if we could do that together, somehow it might help us with our own . . ."

He couldn't go on. She touched his arm. His hand covered hers. They hadn't touched in almost a year.

"Did you . . ." he began, stammering, trying for a nonchalant tone, ". . . did you sleep with him?"

Leverton almost smiled. What a curious question. What a typical question for a man to ask. How fragile they both were, and in such different ways.

"No," she said, and felt a flicker of care for this huge, thick-skulled, teary-eyed cop for the first time in a year. Another change?

He nodded, trying not to show his relief, then quickly changed the subject. "Good luck with the girl."

"Thanks."

"If you need any help, anything at all . . ."

She nodded, not trusting herself to speak.

She left him and and walked quickly away, accepting the congratulations of her fellow officers and exchanging the necessary pleasantries. Outside, safely alone, she began to cry quietly and deeply. It was different from the tears she had shed through the past year. There was no anger in her crying now, and no struggle. These were simply tears of grief. Pat was finally gone. It was unutterably sad.

30

WASHINGTON, Adams, Jefferson . . . Madison, Monroe, Adams again . . .

The clock on Richard's dresser showed 1:30. He still had an hour before he had to get dressed. He put down the list of presidents he had been memorizing and slid deeper into his bed. Fluffy cumulus clouds floated by the top of his window, and from below sounds from the playing field drifted up—cries and whistles—a soccer game in progress. So much energy, he thought. How did those kids do it? He had no energy at all. He had hardly been out of bed for three weeks. All he wanted to do was just lie here, and look out the window and take naps, and think about Lisa, and his father, and diverging realities . . .

And make lists. Lists had begun to intrigue him. In the last few days, just to pass the time, he'd made lists of things he knew and things he wanted to learn. He knew all the states, already, together with their capitals. He knew the Superbowl winners and losers and World Series contestants from 1960 on, and, in chronological order, every American astronaut who had gone into space. Now he was working on the presidents. After that he wanted to memorize the English kings, then the Nobel Prize winners in science, then some of that incredible stuff in the *Guinness Book of Records*. It was a lot of work, but somehow doing it seemed worthwhile. It made him feel better. He certainly could care less about his schoolwork, and he had no energy to run. He did feel bad about that, though. Since he quit track, the team hadn't won a meet. Well, in a few million other universes the team would be doing just fine.

Jackson, Van Buren, Harrison, Polk, Taylor. . . Jackson Van Buren Harrison poked Taylor . . .

He tried to think of what might be happening in those other universes, and after a few minutes gave up. The concept was too mindboggling.

The whole idea came to him that night they kept him in the hospital for observation. What if, he thought, his father had never met his mother? What if either of *their* parents had never met? Or *theirs*? Or *theirs*? The odds against his ever having been born at all were astronomical. And then, in the act of his conception, what if a different sperm had fertilized the egg from which he developed? Would it still be *him* lying in this hospital bed, wondering about all these what-ifs? Or would it be someone else? Someone who looked like him and acted like him, but had a different consciousness. And then, given the miracle of *his* birth, what if his mother hadn't left? What if his father hadn't gone to Vietnam, or suffered that accident, or become a junkie? What if the cocaine hadn't been discovered at Kennedy Airport . . . ?

The answer came in a sudden burst of inspiration. What if there was a different reality, a separate universe really, for every case? If that was true there would be billions of different universes, trillions, a googleplex of them. The gunfight at the Planetarium formed a juncture. A hundred different universes branched off at that moment and for some stupid reason, following his period of unconsciousness, he woke up in one in which his father was dead. He might just as easily have woken to a universe where Steve was fine, or only wounded in the shootout.

Mindboggling.

The only problem was, he couldn't test his theory. For days afterward he tried to jump the track to some other, better universe. He would lie in bed and shut his eyes and concentrate with all his might. Those other universes were still close by, he reasoned. If he had any chance at all it would be now, before they separated too much. He put his entire concentration into it, but it didn't work. Either he didn't have enough willpower, or the job was impossible. But he didn't doubt his new belief for a minute. Those other universes were out there. Somewhere.

Harrison, Polk, Tyler, Pierce, Buchanan . . . Harrison poked Tyler who pierced Buchanan . . .

He looked up. 2:30. The soccer game was over and baseball practice had begun. Richard could hear the crack of the bat against the ball—someone hitting fungos. He got out of bed and put on a clean shirt, then went to the floor bathroom and began brushing his teeth.

He looked at his face in the mirror. The resemblance to Steve was there; the nose and mouth were the same. His eyes were different, though. Probably his mother's. He wished he had a picture of her, so he could see.

He combed his hair and wondered if he really *missed* Steve. If Steve hadn't died at the Planetarium, he wouldn't have seen him anyway during the past three weeks. He might have gotten a postcard, but so what? His life here at Pierce wouldn't have been a whole lot different. It was the *idea* that Steve was dead that was so awful, the *idea* that he would never see his father again.

His shoes were pretty scuffy. He still had time to give them a decent shine.

The funeral had been weird. He probably wouldn't have gone if Mario hadn't strongly suggested that he should, and offered to drive him to Rye. Paul went too. They didn't know anyone at the chapel. Lexington Aeronautics had arranged the whole thing, and the few men who came wore gray suits and solemn expressions. They said nice things about Steve—that he was a good salesman and really knew his planes—but Richard could see they were just trying to be polite.

There was a surprise at the gravesite, though. The big detective showed up. It was almost comical, Richard thought. All three of them—he, Mario, and O'Hare—had bandages on their heads. Mario had scraped himself pretty badly ducking for cover during the shootout, and O'Hare said he had been hit by cement chips. They looked like war veterans as they stood there with Paul, while a minister who didn't even know Steve said a few stupid words about how difficult it was to find a straight path in the world today, and how Steven must have wrestled with his own private demons, and that it was not man's duty to judge, but God's. . . . Through the talk Richard watched airplanes circle in the south. He thought they must be in an approach pattern to Kennedy, across the Sound.

Afterward, O'Hare took him aside and pressed something into his hand. He looked down and saw a one-hundred-dollar bill, and a check for nineteen hundred more.

"We had to confiscate the money you and Lisa made selling the cocaine," O'Hare had explained. "I'm sorry, but this should help a little. The check's for college. The hundred is pocket money. Tapes, or books, or video games for a week—stuff like that."

Richard felt embarrassed about taking it. "It's too much . . ." he began, but his fist was closed around the gift by the detective's huge hand.

At the end, while Mario and Paul waited in the car, he watched two men shovel dirt on top of his father's coffin. He felt sad but he didn't cry.

He didn't go back to school that week. He stayed at the Federicis', returning to New York once to answer questions for the police. O'Hare took him to a delicatessen, and over the biggest pastrami sandwich Richard had ever seen he gave an account of everything that had happened following the discovery of the cocaine. O'Hare was terrific. He said there would be no legal problems for him or Lisa. Also, he wanted to keep in touch. Maybe come up to Pierce some weekend and watch Richard run in a race.

He picked out a nice tie and was tying the knot for a second time when there was a rap on his door and Paul Federici came in.

"Ready?" Paul grinned.

"I guess."

"Nervous?"

Richard smiled. "Yeah."

"Piece of cake," Paul replied. "The girl's crazy about you."

"Sure." Richard didn't try to hide his worry.

This one had been Jo's idea. They were sitting at the dinner table the other night and Jo had practically read his mind.

"Have you heard from Lisa?" she asked casually, passing the potatoes.

"No," Richard muttered. Not an hour had gone by that he hadn't thought of her, or of something they'd done together. He wondered how she was doing, but hadn't tried to call. And she would never call him. She had said as much. She would never talk to him again.

"Why don't you give it a try?" Jo had suggested. "She's still in the hospital. She had an operation on her shoulder, you know. Nothing serious, but it's probably painful. I'm sure she'd love to hear from you."

Richard had tried to explain how impossible it was to even think of seeing Lisa again, but the next day, with a hammering heart, he phoned.

"Oh, it's you," she answered. She definitely didn't sound thrilled to be hearing from him.

"I just thought I'd call, to see how you were doing."

"I'm okay." Nothing more. But, on the positive side, she didn't sound angry either.

"I heard you had a shoulder operation."

"Yeah. It's getting better."

She was quiet, speaking with hardly any feeling at all. Maybe she was just in pain.

"I thought, if you wanted, I'd come by sometime and say hello." She didn't answer. "Lisa . . . ?" he said.

"If you want," she finally replied. "It's a free country."

He climbed into the backseat of the car and hardly said a word as Mario drove them into the City. At the hospital Mario and Paul walked him into the gift shop, but they didn't go up to Lisa's room. Mario said he had shopping to do, and Paul wanted to look at some stereo equipment. They'd be back to pick him up at six, when visiting hours were over.

Lisa was in a private room with a large window. The sun was pouring in and yellow and pink flowers overflowed several vases. She was sitting in bed when he looked in, reading a magazine. He caught a glimpse of the cover. *Teen Romances*. "Teenage Sex—Too Much, Too Soon?" it said in big letters. Good old Lisa, he thought. She had passed from the old reality into the new one unchanged. His heart filled with warmth.

She looked up and stared at him. Through him, actually. It was as though a noise had attracted her attention, but no one was there.

"Hi," he said.

She didn't answer. Her arm and shoulder were bandaged, but her eyes were made up and a light gloss covered her lips. She looked beautiful. He had a box of candy in his hand, and put it on the bed. "Chocolate-covered cherries," he said.

"Thanks." Her tone was flat. She didn't look at him or the chocolates, but leafed through the magazine.

"You look great," he offered.

"I'll live."

He stood still, watching her read, looking for a soft spot in the armor. "You should have seen my face the other week. It looked like raw hamburger." She didn't laugh. She didn't even smile. He stepped closer, his vision blurring slightly. "Lisa, I'm sorry . . ."

"Oh, fuck you," she said softly, without anger but with a sad weariness. "I don't want to hear about your being sorry. I trusted you, Richard. I really did! We could have made it together."

"How?" he exploded, and then found himself pleading. "We were going to get killed! Either by Leo or Francie or Sprague or my father or a kid with a baseball bat. We couldn't keep going on like that!"

She didn't answer. She turned away from him and looked out the window.

"Don't you feel a little relieved?" he asked.

She turned back, angry. Her voice ticked off her miseries. "Richard, I have a broken shoulder. I am practically under arrest in this goddamn hospital. I have no money, and when I get out I have the choice of living with that policewoman or going to some reform school. No, Richard, I don't feel better at all!"

"She seemed like a nice lady," he said unhappily. "She likes you."

"Yeah, she likes me. She's paying for this room. She bought all these fucking flowers. She visits me every day like she was my goddamn mother!"

Richard didn't understand why Lisa was so upset. He watched her tear off the cellophane cover, open the box, and jam a chocolate cherry into her mouth.

"When I get out of here I'll stay with her a couple of weeks, maybe, and then split." Her words were garbled by the candy. "I'll go to New Orleans or maybe San Fransisco. I've never been out West. I can get a job dancing . . ."

Or selling your body, Richard thought, or dealing drugs. His voice sounded thin and hollow, matching his feeling inside. "What about school?"

"What about it?" She finished the cherry and snapped out the words. "I can get by just fine without school. You think everyone has to be like you? You think everyone has to be a scientist or something, and get a Ph.D.?"

There was no stopping her now. Her face was flushed and twisted with hurt. One finger pointed at him angrily.

"You're just like the rest! You think I'm a stupid little whore! Well, I may not be a brain like you, but I'm not stupid either. I can get by out there and I don't need you or Leo or my mother or school or any fucking policewoman to help me!"

"Lisa . . ." he tried.

"No one's helped me up to now. Certainly not you! You used me like everyone else. All you wanted was to keep from getting caught by the police, and to get laid. Well, I did both those things for you, Richard! And what did you do for me?"

The bitterness had run its course and all that was left was hurt. She turned her head so he couldn't see.

"It isn't true," he whispered. "I did care for you. I still do." But they were just words. Air. Nothing at all.

"Here!" he said loudly, and when her curiosity got the better of her she looked at his outstretched hand. "Take it!" Her eyes widened when she saw the one-hundred-dollar bill. "You can use it to buy your bus ticket to San Francisco, if that's what you want."

She reached for it hesitantly, then twisted it nervously between her fingers. "I don't know what I want to do," she finally murmured.

Richard felt a rush of feeling and sat in the chair next to the bed. She was close enough to touch, if he didn't mind risking a third world war. "If you stay around New York we can see each other once in a while. We can be friends."

"I don't know," she answered softly. She had twisted the bill into a green rope. "Maybe . . ."

He accepted her answer with a nod. He didn't dare ask for more. He had achieved a fragile peace, a thin possibility that maybe she would stay and live with the policewoman, maybe even go to school.

She held the crumpled bill out to him. "Will you hold this for me?"

He didn't understand.

"The nurses here are all kleptos. They'll steal it for sure. You could hold it and give it to me when I get out."

He took it back dumbly and basked in the warmth of her unspoken message. She trusted him again. They were friends. They fell silent but it was a shared silence now, not a hostile one.

"Why did Andrew have to die?" she finally asked.

"Why did my father?"

"Maybe God wanted them."

Richard thought of his divergent realities. Maybe they didn't exist. Maybe there was a God, as Lisa believed. Maybe there was absolutely nothing except this one planetary quirk that had somehow borne life. Maybe the world was just an enormous Ouija board with four billion hands on it, everyone's private little push lost in the massive board that seemed to move with a will of its own. Lisa rested against her pillow. A light film of sweat made her face shine. Through a gap in her nightgown he could see the curve of her breast. Maybe all his philosophical wonderings weren't worth spit next to his ache to climb into that bed with her and lose himself in her warm body.

"They called my mother," she said in a distant voice. "She didn't want me home."

"My father caused five men to die," Richard answered, balancing the scale.

"He also pushed you."

"Huh?"

"He pushed you down, away from the gunfire. He wanted you to be safe. I saw it."

Richard hadn't been sure who had pushed him at that moment, or why.

"Maybe he did care for you but just couldn't show it," she said.

The thought warmed him. He accepted it as a glowing coal, but knew that if he actually touched it it would burn. "Maybe your mother cares for you the same way," he offered back.

Lisa stared out the window. Richard touched the palm of her open hand and it closed around his finger. They stayed that way until a nurse looked in and announced visiting hours were over.

"I'll come again," he said. She nodded. "I'll bring more cherries."

At the elevator an elderly man approached holding a bottle of clear fluid in his hand. A plastic tube, attached to the bottle at one end, disappeared under his gown. Richard studied the setup and couldn't figure out whether the fluid was dripping from the bottle into the man, or from the man into the bottle.

The man clapped Richard on the shoulder, taking an obvious delight in the boy's sturdiness.

"Sonny, I'd give a million dollars to trade places with you right now," he said.

Richard felt a bittersweet flow inside. In three months he would be sixteen. The man's eyes were pink and rheumy, but the edges crinkled, and the corners of his mouth turned up as though the two of them were sharing a great joke.

"No deal," Richard said, and the old man laughed until the elevator came.